Praise for *Fierce*

"The best stories may be short, but never small; in fact, the ones that move us most deeply embody whole worlds. Such is true of the tough tales in Fierce . . . The sassy grit of her characters and their tenacious humour-wry, raw, even twisted-get them through. Now and then, naked emotion pierces through their stubborn wit, like a shard of glass."

The Montreal Gazette

"(*Fierce* is) as strong a first collection as we have any right to hope, and with flourishes and tones that speak of a long, interesting writing career. It would be a shame for readers to miss it . . . Boys, girls, men, women, young, aging: Holborn repeatedly demonstrates her skill in handling utterly disparate, and wholly unique, characters in surprising, and often surprisingly effective ways."

J. Wieresma, *The Edmonton Journal*

"Treat yourself to its unique mix of irreverence, compassion and horse laughs. And then pass it along to a loved one."

National Post

"Holborn's collection of stories is electric with wit and insight. Sassy, sexy, full of willful women, nasty business, a few freaks, some drunks, acts of adultery and abandonment, the voice of God and veins of gold. It's fierce."

Lisa Moore, author of *Alligator* and *Open*

"Holborn impresses with her eye for detail, the unusual and those living on the margins…her fiction resonates deeply."

Brett Josef Grubisic, *The Vancouver Sun*

"Holborn's double high-wire act leaps effortlessly between funny and tragic…(Her) visuals are cinematic."

The Globe and Mail

"…one-of-a-kind characters, in stories that run the gamut from unfortunately heartbreaking to unaccountably hopeful."

Canadian Living

"The stories in "Fierce" contain beautiful writing, offbeat characters, and strange scenarios . . . there is humanity and honesty in this collection that really makes it work."

Grande Prairie Ink

"…tragedy and violent drama crackling with comedic noir and irony that borders tenderly-spun farce."

North Shore Outlook

"Monty Python to Russian tragedy. Nothing is normal in Holborn's world."

Coast Reporter

FIERCE

Also by Hannah Holborn

All That Remains

Strange Lineup

Move-In Ready (spring 2019)

HANNAH
HOLBORN

FIERCE

STORIES AND

A NOVELLA

For Ian. Forever.

A Note from the Author on the 10th Anniversary of *Fierce*

You should know what you're getting into with this re-release of *Fierce*, my first published book. The nine stories and a novella are weird, absurd, and dark. No, not serial killer dark — yecch!. The scary events in Fierce involve things like man-made natural disasters, unusual birth defects, and daft life choices. There are scaredy-cat hitchhikers, fed up orphans, an ice-walking widower, and as the cover suggests, at least one seal.

If your tastes run to summer beach reads, there's good news! Although it's not beachy in the margarita and suntan lotion sense of the word, *Fierce* has an abundance of sand and surf. Heck, there's even a near drowning.

Still on the fence about *Fierce* despite my stellar sales pitch? To facilitate your decision-making process, I've provided two helpful questions for you to answer. Here goes: 1) Are you fine with sentences such as: "Mine is bigger than yours," and "There was still a trickle of water coming from the ceiling, so I rinsed"? And, 2) Are you unaccountably hopeful?

If you answered *Yes, that's me!* to either of the above, then CONGRATULATIONS! This book is for you! So, get reading and I'll meet you at the other end.

With love,

Hannah

There's a land where the mountains are nameless,

And the rivers all run God knows where.

"The Spell of the Yukon"

ROBERT W. SERVICE

CONTENTS

I HAD THIS DREAM. Well, a nightmare really. It was night. I flew over a suburb and thought, *Fine. You want me to fly, I'll fly. But I don't have to like it.* Then it started to rain.

In a yard below me there was a guy in a puffy chef's hat. He was basting and barbecuing a cat, fur on. Rain sizzled on the grill. I smelled hot sauce and roasted fat and my stomach grumbled. In another yard, a puppy played snap-the-raindrops by itself.

I wanted to eat the cat then and take the puppy home for later.

One puppy, a gourmand and me — those were the only signs of life. Every curtain in every house was opened, and all the houses had lights on even though there weren't any people in the rooms. It was like they'd all rushed out at once to witness the aftermath of an accident.

Suburbia eased off, becoming acre lots with mansions, and then stopped altogether at the outskirts of a public park. The sky grew darker, and thunder rumbled to the north. The weather creeped me out, but I flew on, unable to stop.

Something stung the shin of my right leg as lightning forked the sky. I twisted around for a look and saw a jet airliner the size of a sparrow. The cockpit lights were on, and I could see the tiny pilot behind the slip-slap of windshield-wiper blades. The way his eyes rolled as he picked up a radio mike and spoke into it made him looked half crazed. Seconds later a flock of jets swooped down on me. I recognized OccidentAir's Pacific fleet and knew they meant business. They flew above me in a V-formation and began to drop their firebombs.

I noticed a lighter clutched in my hand and thought, *Penny, girl, fight fire with fire.* From just one touch of the flame, the little jets ignited. Before long, orange balls filled the sky as OccidentAir's jet-liners plummeted, each trailing a cloud of black smoke.

I had won the battle, but flames engulfed my torso. As I lost altitude, I steered my body towards a horseshoe-shaped body of water in the center of a park. I whirled out of control faster and faster as the fire spread to my arms and legs. The smoke was thick, and I struggled to breathe. Glimpsing the shimmer of water, I aimed toward it.

I'd had this dream before, so I knew what was going to happen next. Sure enough, I overshot the mark.

Six a.m. It was another blue-sky morning, inside at least. I was going for a Jamaican look, so the walls were aqua and the bedding had a wave motif. There were shell-print cushions on the bed and a plastic palm tree in the corner that swayed in the breeze of a General Electric fan.

The palm belonged to the travel agency that sold my family their discounted tickets. I had borrowed the palm when an agent forgot to chain it down.

Outside it was still raining. I dressed for the weather: a padded bra on the outside of my Burning Airlines T-shirt, a teal angora sweater, and three skirts (one made of pink nylon, the second of black leather, and a third of green tulle) over black tights. Over it all, I added a lime-green rain slicker and galoshes. I skipped hair gel (it gobs in the rain) but still back-combed my hair into blue tumbleweed. Finally, I pocketed my bankbook and an envelope that had been gathering dust on my dresser.

When I left my apartment, my neighbor Rajpal was standing in the hall watching water blow in through a broken window. Tears streamed down his cheeks, and the chunk of granite that had broken the window was on the floor at his feet. That was weird, because we lived on the sixth floor of Victory Towers, but I suspected the mountain that backed onto our building. Our landlord swore it was as solid as a rock, but it looked to me like it might crumble any minute.

Rajpal was building a canoe on the roof of our nine-story apartment building, in case the town flooded. He had immigrated to Lanten from Bihar, India, after the great flood of 1987 because a stoned hippie had proclaimed our town the driest place in Canada. Rajpal had once offered me a seat in the canoe on the condition I help with its construction. "I don't know, Rajpal," I said to put him off. "Water is my element. All Dreadfuls are born to float. We just aren't born to fly."

"Penny Dreadful," he had replied, "if this fine city floods, you will be floating with rats." I promised to help him build, just to ease his mind.

Rajpal would die if he ever saw my apartment. It is full of water. Twenty-nine aquariums full. I raise two breeds of goldfish: comets, which are pure orange, and black moors, which are pure black. On the day of my OccidentAir dream, I had 321 fish, but the number was always rising. Three of the black Moors had busted swim bladders, so they looked dead. I had to scoop them up and make a chair with my hand to hold them when I fed them. Black moors can live that way for years.

"Rajpal," I cheered as I entered the lift, "think rainbow, not deluge!" As the lift creaked down to the lobby, I heard Rajpal keen.

Outside, the town was like a cornered wildcat. Disembodied shrieks and howls came from every direction. Our Victory Towers sign, which normally hung from hooks attached to a metal stand, was plastered against the wall of Luigi's Deli next door. Luigi's plate glass window had a masking-tape X, the hams were gone from their hooks, and the power was out. On the street and sidewalk, branches and garbage-can lids rode the wind as if riding a roller coaster. I had to gulp to breathe. A chicken carcass floated past in the gully of water between the road and the sidewalk, and I realized that Rajpal was right: we were all in for it now.

When I blew into the deli, the wind slammed the glass door shut. "You break it, you buy it," Luigi said. He looked older than usual in the natural light.

I was hooked on the deli because Luigi's eggs were almost as good as he was nice. Unlike most people, he appreciated young women with blue hair and understood our need to pierce.

Luigi's brow furrowed as he unscrewed the metal lid of a big glass jar that he kept on the counter near the cash register. He wiped a slotted spoon on his paisley-print apron, looked me over, and made his chest rumble with disapproval. "Skin and bones," he said. "You want an egg, I'll give you an egg, but what you need is a big plate of cannelloni Florentine: a little veal, a little white wine, spinach, some Parmesan, and a nice basil tomato sauce."

Luigi's cannelloni Florentine didn't come cheap, and my wages only allowed for food that could be bought on a poverty-line budget. When I didn't show enthusiasm for his suggestion, only smiled at the jar, Luigi fished out an egg with the slotted spoon and then offered it up for my inspection.

As I ate the egg, Luigi's broad face grew dreamy. He rubbed the black bristles on his jaw and said, "In this weak light you almost remind me of Mercedes." His daughter and I had been classmates at Holy Cross Senior High. Except for our nose rings and attitude, we looked nothing alike. She had run away from home a week before grad, on the night she met the drummer of the Crass Hallucinations when they played at Punky Ed's Discotheque on Main Street. Until that day she had maintained honor-roll status and been a member of the debating team. A year later she looked like Gwen Stefani, only a foot shorter and with a dark moustache. Sometimes Mercedes sent her father Polaroid snapshots just to prove that she was still alive despite his predictions. Luigi taped them to the counter beside the missing-person posters.

Luigi screwed the lid back on the pickled-egg jar and opened the till with his key. He dropped the fiver I handed him into the drawer and forgot to give me change.

I reached for the door, opened it, and admitted the gale. Water sprayed a shelf of the mixes used to make Italian Love Cake. The branch of a blossoming ornamental cherry scooted through the door and came to a rest at my feet. I picked up the peace offering nature had delivered to me, and backed outside. Water cascaded off the awning and drenched my back.

"Luigi?" He had forgotten I was there.

My grandma's neighborhood, one block over in the town center, was clinically depressed. Her building had bars on the windows, imposing columns and cornice gargoyles left over from the Greek and Gothic revivals, eras when the building was a single-family mansion. The mansion had become a mental health facility, and the neighborhood that used to outfit weddings and supply the dry goods to liven up parties now hosted new-medication trials for the mentally ill.

To the left of the asylum was Femme Elegance, the wedding shop where generations of Lantenites had purchased gowns and rented tuxedos. For the past four years the groom in the showcase sprawled naked at the feet of the newspaper-clad bride while she inspected the back side of an *Out of Business* sign. As far as marriages in Lanten went, theirs was about average, although the positions of the bride and groom were usually reversed. To the right of the asylum, handmade signs in the windows of Wayne's Fun-O-Ramma pleaded for customers. *Party Hardy!* read a pink poster board illustrated with noisemakers, bubbling champagne, and musical notes. Another claimed, *A Party a Day Keeps the Doctor Away.*

Broad steps led to the institution's columned porch. I stood under the shelter of the pediment and rang the bell until security came and let me in. In the reception room the day-shift nurse was asleep with her head on the desk beside an empty box of Dunkin' Donuts. The corners of her mouth were white with icing sugar. I dripped on the freshly waxed floor and watched the bank of monitors that the nurse should have been watching until one showed my grandma's room. She was perched on top of her laundry hamper, dressed for bed in Roadrunner pajamas.

As her last remaining relative, I had to put my grandma under psychiatric observation when she decided that she preferred to be a bird, and tried to fly off the roof of Victory Towers. "I can't always mind her," I told them as I signed their forms. "I have to work to support us." I only wanted home care, but her confessed attraction to power lines sealed her fate.

Most of the time, she didn't seem to care that she was committed. There were like-minded people for company, and the institution let patients wear whatever they wanted, so she got to fancy herself up like a starling on growth hormones, in feather-trimmed black silk dresses, jet bangles and a black wig. Sometimes I would sneak in a bag of birdseed to cheer her up.

"I won't have it!" My grandma stomped her tiny foot on the lid of the wicker hamper when she saw me. The lid threatened to cave in.

"Won't have what, Gran?" She touched both vein-riddled temples with shaky hands. "Zip, zip." She meant electroshock therapy. The bastards were at it again.

It took me more than an hour to get her off the hamper and back into her bed. She warbled the whole time.

Because of my grandma, I was late for my shift at Pesky's Fish and Amphibian World. "Strike three!" Mr. Waddles, my boss, gloated when I entered. He meant for that week. I wrenched off my galoshes and dumped the water out the door.

He hoisted a stack of job applications. "*These* people want your job," he said. "*These* people sit by their phones, waiting for *my* call." He lifted the phone's receiver.

"Go ahead," I bluffed. "Call them." I draped my slicker over an aquarium to dry, and then navigated my way through the scattered sacks of colored rocks. A trail of footprints marked my progress across the floor. "No one will answer. They've all moved to Vancouver." No matter how much I badgered him, Mr. Waddles couldn't fire me. I got the job at Pesky's because the owner had been my father's best friend.

Mr. Waddles dropped the receiver onto its cradle, rifled through the applications, and then flopped onto his lemon-yellow swivel chair. "You'll be the death of me, Dryden," he said. "Is that what you want? Is it?"

I stopped short. "There are no Drydens."

"Yeah, well, my records say that Art Pesky hired one Penelope Dryden."

I shrank away from Mr. Waddles, away from the aquariums full of sick and dying fish, away from the sun-bleached posters of exotic animals that had been tacked to the walls of Pesky's since before my birth, away from the cash register where my dad had paid for my first black goldfish and a rose-shaped bowl, which had broken before we got it home.

"Enjoy it, Dryden," Mr. Waddles said. "This breakdown's the last one you get for free."

It took me twenty minutes to reach Jersey Park three blocks away, and by then every part of me not protected by my slicker was soaked to the bone. For the first time I could remember, I had my choice of any swing, not that it mattered with the way that they were tangled.

A duck snapped at submerged insects at the base of the monkey bars. "Hey," I said, "nice weather." The bird quacked and hobbled off. One of its neon orange legs trailed a green plastic man with a tangled parachute.

A water-filled trench encircled the merry-go-round. It was deep and wide, so I had to jump over. The platform revolved when I landed, throwing me against the safety bars. I removed the envelope from my skirt pocket and shook out its contents. Rain darkened the paper in splotches. The insurance company wanted to transfer the money electronically, but I made OccidentAir write me a personal check. It made them cranky to acknowledge my new legal name: "Pay to the order of Penelope Sydney Dreadful." Their checks were blue and had their logo: a jet with its nose up, breaking through a cumulous cloud. There was a bit of chicken scratch at the bottom to make it look official.

If the airline officials had raked their skin raw or torn out their hair in a show of grief, I might have accepted their apology for killing my family. I might even have cashed their check instead of stowing it away for two years. But they had been too busy hiring lawyers. I looked at the check in my hand. It was a flimsy piece of paper made for hushing me up. It was candy for the crying baby. I folded the check into a paper raft and thought about my little brother, Morty. OccidentAir's insurance adjustors had valued his life at nothing. They had refused to count his hugs and silly laughter, even though I described them in a letter and offered to go to demonstrate. They had refused to count his pet rat, which died of starvation in the aftermath. They even refused to count the new adult tooth Morty only got one month to use.

I placed the paper raft on a ripple of water. In seconds it sagged under the weight of the rain. One of its sides collapsed and water rushed in. The wind picked up and gave the merry-go-round a spin. I slipped around slick bars to stay with the raft. It was sucked under the platform. I waited for ages, but it didn't pop back up.

I wanted more than anything to hear Morty snigger at my effort. I wanted to tickle his hard swimmer's belly and stick my nose deep into the crease of his neck. I wanted to touch his hair as pale and delicate as the roots of plants. But I couldn't.

I was exhausted. It was how I had felt right after the accident, too tired to twitch a muscle. So I lay down and curled up on the merry-go-round. One galosh trailed in the puddle. I watched the wake it made until the rain blurred my vision. Water was everywhere — above me, under me, welling up inside.

"Morton," I whispered. But the sound of splattering raindrops blotted out my little brother's name.

I felt a lot better the next day, so I called in sick to work. "We can only hope," Mr. Waddles said when I told him what I had might be lethal.

After my breakfast of pickled egg, I slogged over to the pool wearing a slicker over my polka-dotted bathing suit with the white frilled skirt and my favorite fanny pack. Only one person was swimming when I arrived, the deaf guy everyone called Frogman. His eyes were big and green, and when he swam all of the action took place underwater. On busy days, kids splashed past, kicked the water into froth, and pretended to drown. Still he kicked, pulled, and blinked. He did this for hours, back and forth across the pool. We were about the same age, so I guessed that he was depressed. Most young adults in Lanten were.

Anyway, that's what Frogman was doing when I dove into the cold water. The shock of the low temperature sent me to the wall, where I clung like a limpet. "Hey!" I shouted to the lone lifeguard. Instead of a Speedo, he wore a wetsuit and sneakers. "Don't you guys heat the pool anymore?"

The lifeguard shrugged.

Between swimming laps to forestall hypothermia, I passed the time playing a pool game called Find the Penny. I threw a handful of pennies into the water, and then saw how many I could retrieve in one breath. My childhood record was forty-nine, but that time I almost died. I had reached twelve when Frogman dove beneath the surface. He grabbed a penny from the bottom and glided over, holding it behind his back. His grin said, *Ha. Try to get it!* Bubbles escaped from his mouth.

I used to have brothers, so I knew this part of the game. I grabbed him around the middle. He sucked in water when he tried to shove me off.

We scooted together to the surface. Frogman's face was crayfish-red.

"Sorry," I said. "I didn't mean to surprise you." Then I remembered that Frogman was deaf. "I'm Penny." I tapped my chest and displayed a coin. "Penny-penny!"

"I know." He drew out his syllables to get them right, but otherwise sounded fine. The sad look on his face made me want to hug him. I think he guessed my intention, because he lowered his chin into the water and kicked. Kick, blink and pull. His timing was way off.

"Frogman!" I called, but he didn't hear his name.

When he reached the far end, he got out of the pool and then climbed the steps to the high board. He performed a beautiful dive, entering the water like a knife without making a ripple. His effort scored a perfect ten. When he popped above the surface, I applauded. He took a bow, treading water, and then shouted my older brother's name. He held up ten fingers before pointing to the electronic scoreboard.

"Freddy was the best," I agreed. "Better than the best."

Frogman nodded his head. "Too bad." His fingers sliced through the air like a jet.

"No!" I cried, but it was too late. His jet exploded mid-air. It twisted and turned, then crashed into water, but he was wrong: There wasn't any water. There was only land and fire.

Frogman seemed startled by what he had done. He turned and swam away.

I fled to the family change room.

When we were young, my mom used to have all four of us children change in there together instead of in the Boys and Girls. It was the only way she could keep her eye on us. We were a wild bunch, but Freddy, as the eldest, was the worst. As soon as a few of us were dressed, he would dart into the shower stall, heave back the curtain and spray. Mom put plastic on the station wagon seats and pretended not to notice. She said she hadn't had children to get mad at them. She said she'd married our father for that.

I sat on the wooden bench. Someone had left a Canucks towel on a hook. My teeth chattered, so I tugged it down, and then wrapped it around my shoulders. Hair in a palette of earth tones mingled on the petri-dish shower stall drain. All I could smell was chlorine. I concentrated on feeling for emanations from the walls and ceiling, where something of my mother and siblings might remain, but didn't get a thing.

When my family left for Jamaica, leaving me behind because I had failed algebra and had to go to summer school, they had taken every molecule of themselves along for the ride. All they left behind was an imperfect Dryden specimen — one with plucked-chicken skin, hairy armpits, short black fingernails and an outsie belly button with a death's head ring.

Not much to support the growth of a family tree.

Someone tall rapped on the change room door. I opened it a crack and saw a bald man with a Down syndrome kid at his side. The man's blue irises clashed with the green bags beneath his eyes. Both man and boy were dressed in blue jeans and peach golf shirts, but the boy's shirt had a smear of ketchup down the front.

"That's our towel." The man placed a proprietary hand on the boy's ultra-fine hair. "I'd just leave it but, hey, my son gets attached to certain things, you know."

"Yes," I said, "I do." I was finished with it anyway, so I handed the boy his soggy towel.

"Well . . . thanks! That's great!"

If we had been in an Ethical Addictions coffee shop, instead of a pool's family changing room, the man would have taken the seat beside me. While he sipped his tall decaf, he would have casually mentioned the amniocentesis test that had dashed his hopes for father/son basketball games, would have hinted that his wife's frigidity began after childbirth. He might have left a sweaty handprint on my jeans.

Instead, he took his son by the hand and together they silently trudged away.

When I returned to the pool deck, I couldn't see Frogman. I scanned the beneath the water's surface and checked the wheel-chair ramp. Then I spied him stretched out on the diving board. He had combed his hair and changed into an expensive pair of swim trunks that I suspected he bought at the swim shop to impress me.

When I waved, he pointed at my hair, made the rolling gesture for lunatic and grinned like he approved of blue hair.

I jumped in the water and came up coughing.

"You okay?" he signed.

I shrugged. It had only been two years. Too soon to tell.

I swam to the center, and then tread water by myself. As I contemplated the merits of slipping under the surface forever, Frogman snuck up behind me. He touched my shoulder. I twirled around and there we were, face to face in the deep end. For the first time, I noticed his cute cowlick.

"I'm Calvin," he said. "Cal-vin."

The hairs on his arms were sun-bleached blond, but those on his chest were dark brown. I liked his two-tone look.

The lifeguard sipped something hot from a ceramic mug with his eyes closed. If we drowned, he would miss it.

I scooped up a handful of pennies from my fanny pack, enough for two. I showered the pennies into the air. There were so many that it looked like hail when they landed. "Find the penny," I said. Frogman looked deep into my eyes, held his breath, and then dove.

He came back up with a handful. "I like you," he said. I could see that he was scared to say this. I wondered if he knew how scared I was to hear it. "Friends?" he said.

The floodwaters, which the local media should have done more than hint might come, chose that moment to crest the river's banks and infiltrate the recreation center. "Friends," I agreed as we swam for our lives.

On the Monday after Lanten's worst flood in half a century had ebbed, leaving behind a swampy mess, I went back to work. As I cleaned mud from the outside of the piranha tank at Pesky's, suspecting nothing, Mr. Waddles came over. He dipped his fingers in the water to stir the fish into a frenzy. "Um, Penny," he said, "with the town's reduced customer base, Art Pesky has no choice but to let you go."

"Go where?" I asked.

"Anywhere you won't be seen by our few remaining customers. You're fired." I was speechless, but he put a finger over my lips anyway. "Hush," he said. "Shush." Which is what he said the time he tried to touch my tits in the broom closet.

"Mr. Waddles," I pled, "Don't fire me. I love this job. I love fish and amphibians. I love you."

But he knew that last part was bull, because that time in the broom closet I kicked him in the balls. So he said, "Penny, I'll be honest with you. Despite their loyalty to your parents, Art wants you fired because you smell bad and look worse. Blue hair just doesn't cut it in the workplace. This shop has a reputation to protect."

I fell to the floor despite the thick layer of sediment, grabbed his bare leg below his shorts, and then kissed him right on the freckled skin of his knee. "It's not me that stinks, Mr. Waddles," I said. "It's my clothes. I buy them secondhand. I'll get the jackets dry-cleaned. Better yet, I'll change. I'm not committed to punk. I don't even listen to the music." I was still hanging onto his leg, so he dragged the leg and me across the room to the front door.

"I have…to…open," he grunted.

"How will I feed my three hundred and twenty-one goldfish without my employee's discount? How will I eat? Who will pay the rent?"

"OccidentAir will pay for everything," the bastard said. "Just as soon as you settle."

Mr. Waddles unlocked the door to let a customer in. He sweated as he directed her to the cricket tank and fish pellet aisles. Because of the flood, the woman didn't want the sunken treasure figurines for 75 per cent off. He tried to shake me off his leg, but I was too strong.

"Penny," he said. "You're bloody freaking nuts."

"That's it," I said. "I'm leaving."

When my grandma saw my fragile state, she cooed. I didn't mean to tell her about Mr. Waddles. The flood and being crazy were burdens enough, but I couldn't stop myself. I even confessed to kissing his knee. "I'm traumatized," I said.

"Stop looming large, dear. Rest." She pointed to the floor, and then tossed me a cushion embroidered with the words *There's No Place Like Home*. I reclined on the floor and made my head fill the cushion's cross-stitched nest.

My grandma took a seat on the bed. She propped my feet on her lap, removed my sandals, and then grasped my big toes. Her hands felt like those chicken feet they put in Chinese soup — rubbery. "Mr. Widdles," she said as she massaged, "must live in damp storage or a leaking attic. He reeks of mothballs and mouse droppings and fungus." Just for a moment my grandma looked like something from Hitchcock's *The Birds,* and I don't mean the actors. This look was part of why they locked her up.

"Mouse droppings?" My grandma's neighbor, Doris, peeped in at the open door. She was six feet tall and dressed in a black feathered dress and jet beads. I suspected an institution fashion trend started by my grandmother.

"Go change, Doris," I said. "Find your own sense of style."

A heart-shaped stain spread on the ceiling tiles above me. As I extricated my toes from my grandmother's claws, a tile gave way and down dumped a gallon of sudsy water.

"Oh!" my grandma said. She shook off water and fluffed imaginary feathers. She took one look at me, drenched, then she dug up a rose-shaped soap from a dresser drawer. I recognized the soap. It was my mother's brand. "Penelope," she declared. "It's time for you to cleanse."

I knew she was right. I rubbed the soap until my mother bloomed on my hands. Then I stripped off my favorite T-shirt, the one that promoted Burning Airline's *Come Fly the Flaming Skies* CD. I used it to scrub the makeup from my face. There was still a trickle of water coming from the ceiling, so I rinsed. I removed my eyebrow ring, nose ring, and lip stud, then scrubbed away fake tattoos and fake punk band autographs.

As I turned clean and real, my grandma rummaged through her closet. She came up with a muumuu decorated with fish. After I put the muumuu on, my grandma twirled me around for a look. She pecked me on the cheek. "My daughter was your mother, Penelope." She told this like a secret.

"I know. It made Mom so proud that you hatched her."

A nurse stormed into the room. Her eyes bulged towards the flooded carpet and then bulged towards me. "Leave," she ordered, as though the flood was my fault and not one of God's random acts of kindness. "Lunch," she hollered at my grandma, who wasn't deaf.

"Take a pill," I suggested.

The nurse called security.

"Grandma," I said as security hustled me away, "don't let the buggers get you down."

"Don't worry, Penelope." Her voice was small and getting small-er. "I'll stick to the air."

Out on the sidewalk, I was sunk. No shoes, no keys, no money for a cab. My only company was one of the official-looking soldiers sent to Lanten to oversee the cleanup. She had a leather briefcase, tight Afro, and spit-polished shoes. She also had a cockeyed smile meant for me.

Had I ever seen the ocean in Jamaica? she asked. She stared at my muumuu and pointed to a color on the sleeve. "It's the same aqua. That gorgeous." Behind her, Lanten's antique steam clock puffed out vapor that made a halo around her head. I thought, May-be this person is special. Maybe she's God's messenger. Maybe she's here to deliver an apology.

I chanced it. I told her what I thought of Jamaica. I told her how I had been furious at my family for leaving me behind, how I hoped their plane would crash. How it did. I told her that they burnt to their deaths while surrounded on three sides by water. I told her that I destroyed the airline's check to damn its soul.

Her smile lost ground to a tremor.

"OccidentAir, flight 309," she said. "Your photo appeared in the paper next to mine. We were scenes of grief."

Her face crumbled into one of those scenes. I touched her hand. It felt hot and firm like a rock on the beach. She smelled of seaweed and I realized that if she was the beach, then I must be the sea.

"I'm so sorry." We said it together, waves lapping shore.

Maybe it was wrong, but we laughed at the coincidence. We laughed like maniacs. Me with my blue hair, bare feet, and fish muu-muu. Her with her black skin, officer's uniform, and briefcase. Peo-ple stared, but we let them. We laughed and laughed and laughed until our laughter snagged the past.

Then we merged and wept.

DULCEY CHISHOLM STAYED PUT, ignoring the urge to pee. Nothing had changed while she'd slept off her bender. Not the jumbled blocks of shadow and light on the surface of her canvas tent, not the impersonal Yukon wilderness, nor the uneasy feeling that had followed her around like a stealthy beast all August.

Nothing had changed that is, until she paid attention to her ears. Then she heard the unexpected — the sound of someone whistling. Her mind supplied the familiar tune of "Buffalo Gals" with lyrics. But she wasn't a Buffalo Gal, and she didn't like to dance by any kind of light, let alone the light of the moon. Worse, she felt confounded by the unaccustomed humanity of the sound, as much as by the whistler's absurd choice of song.

It had to be a joke. If so, the culprit was either Iona or Patrick, since either sibling could whistle like stink. When they won a talent contest with their rendition of "Riel's Farewell," they came home from the fair with a first-place ribbon and one of Mrs. Olive Kemmett's famous apple cobblers. Who it wasn't, for sure, was Treeny, the youngest and most irritating member of the family. The child's mouth lacked dexterity for anything more difficult than mindless chatter.

Through the mosquito netting, Dulcey watched a ground squirrel scurry up a tree. Its alarm prodded Dulcey into action. "Patrick?" Her heart palpitated as she struggled to move the rusted zipper of the canvas-and-net door. "Iona?" No one answered. "Treeny?"

The squirrel hung upside down clinging to the trunk of the tree with its sides heaving. Dulcey called out. The silence that wasn't silence returned. No Patrick. No Iona. Not even a Treeny to disturb her day.

Old fool! She resisted the urge to smack sense into her head. Her imagination was acting up again, thanks, she supposed, to the Crown Royal she'd polished off a few hours before. She was in the twenty-first century, not the nineteen thirties, an ugly fact she had to accept despite the lack of a calendar. Iona, her favorite sister, would be well into her eighties by now, and she'd never been exactly vital. When Iona's Christmas cards stopped coming in 1987, Dulcey had not allowed herself to find out why.

And Treeny wasn't a child anymore. She was now Mrs. Trina Mendelos, retired ballroom dance instructor. Dulcey forced herself to imagine her youngest sister a mature sixty-nine, sitting at a kitchen table nursing a black coffee and complaining about sagging breasts, the agony of bunions or, worse, a dry vagina. These days, society held no subject taboo as Dulcey knew all too well from the daytime television she was forced to watch on her infrequent trips to Jo-Jo's Bar & Grill in Everlasting.

Needing purposeful activity, she put on a long-sleeved shirt, a pair of mud-stiffened Levi's, a gold nugget belt, which she left undone for the time being, and steel-toed boots. The act of dressing in dirty clothes brought to mind Gummy McTavish, a fellow prospector who'd worn his long johns like a second skin for so long he'd perished on the operating table as they struggled to flail them off him to get at his swollen appendix.

Dulcey made a dash for the makeshift latrine, then sunk into a squat over the smelly hole, ignoring the complaint of her knees.

She tried to let loose, but only managed a disappointing trickle that made a run along her thigh.

There were, at least, a flock of butterflies to take her mind off things. Nearby, hundreds of painted ladies shuffled around the ground in a warm patch of sunshine. A few dozen munched on the leaves of a nearby milkweed plant. A pretty show ruined when Treeny, of all people, pranced into the midst of the insects. The child wore a blue and white bathing suit with droopy bum fabric. Her welt-covered legs were starving saplings planted in her mud-caked feet.

"Don't stare," Treeny said. "It's not polite."

Dulcey hitched up her jeans to hide her privates. No time for wiping, not that it mattered with the way her bladder leaked. These days, a whiff of urine was a constant companion.

"You called for me?" the child said.

"I only said your name by accident, so scram." Dulcey threw a stone at her sister, aiming low to scare, not maim. A mass of butter-flies flew off. In the same instant Treeny vanished.

It irked Dulcey when she recognized her mistake. Despite the evidence of her eyes and ears, there was no child, no whistling trick-ster, no nothing. Just bush, bush, and more bush. Much as she de-tested the thought, she would need to dose herself with human contact, and soon. Civilization was the only known cure for what ailed her.

"That's right, honey," the now-adult Treeny piped up. "You're bushwhacked. But don't blame yourself. Twenty-two straight months alone in the woods will do that to the hardiest of fellows."

"Shoo," Dulcey said.

Treeny left slowly this time, from the feet up.

To counteract the Crown Royal effect and stave off recurring hallucinations, Dulcey needed food. She set to work, heating water on her one-burner propane stove and lowering her food bin from a tree limb. When the water came to a boil, she stirred in the last of the Red River cereal. While she ate, a white-winged crossbill landed on a beachy bit of the nearby river's shoreline.

"See that jack-ass bird?" she said to the invisible Treeny. "It's just like you. Not a speck of common sense in its entire body." The species, Dulcey knew, travelled long distances in search of conifer cones and sometimes reared chicks in the dead of winter. Likewise, Treeny had deserted the family at age fifteen to breed with a knock-kneed Mexican in faraway Montana Springs.

"At least Emanuel's good in bed," Treeny said. She passed through Dulcey from behind. "If you weren't a virgin, we could compare experiences."

In her rush to put some space between herself and her odious sister, Dulcey tripped over the camp stove. Red River cereal flowed along the ground, steaming as it went. "Now look what you've done," she scolded. "Budging in where you're not wanted. If you have to be someone, why can't you be Iona?"

Treeny dipped a finger in the spilled porridge. "I can't be Iona because she's dead."

With great effort, Dulcey made Treeny disappear again. She had better things to do than make chit-chat with a liar. Iona might be unwell, but she wasn't dead, that much she was sure of; someone would have made the effort to fetch Dulcey for the funeral. It still saddened her that she could no longer count on her eldest sister to show up and spare her a trip downriver. Until a conflict over the family sauceboat and snuff mull had divided them, the widowed Iona had made an annual pilgrimage from Terrace, B.C., to the Yukon. She'd even come on a number of field trips, although she was more of a burden than a help, what with her arthritic back and hands.

Dulcey felt bad about the loss of Iona's company, but war was war, and the treasures belonged to her, no matter if she had never used them and never intended to. No matter either if, unlike Iona, she didn't have greedy offspring to pass possessions down to. Their father had willed the loot her way and, as she liked to brag, Dulcey wasn't born the daughter of a savage Celt for nothing — she knew how to protect what was hers. Besides, the two pieces of worthless crap were the full extent of what their father had ever given Dulcey. Everything good had gone to the others.

"Feros ferio," Dulcey said aloud to prove her point. *I am fierce with the fierce*, the Chisholm motto. The family name derived from the Norman phrase "to choose." When her parents divorced in Ducley's thirty-fourth year, the line was drawn, and she knew which side to land on. Unlike Treeny and the others, it wasn't with her sickly sweet-spoken English mother.

In preparation for her trip downriver, Dulcey moved each limb, checking for range of movement and injury. She had to pee again, so her unreliable bladder, tennis elbow, and a badly swollen knee made up the tally of painful areas. The elbow was chronic, but mild. The knee injury that had necessitated the whiskey, however, was from yesterday's slip down a crumbly bit of overhang.

"You ought to be more careful," Treeny said. She was a teenager now, dressed in one of Dulcey's hand-me-down dresses and perched in a sluttish manner on a wood-chopping block. Her lips were a waxy cherry red. "If you get hurt, you know, there's no one out here to help you."

"Prospecting's a healthy lifestyle. Read the literature."

"Maybe for young bucks like your beau Lawrence Phillips. Now there's a man I'd like to encounter in the bush."

"I was done with Lawrence decades ago, and I'm done with this conversation. You aren't even real."

"I'm real enough to know you aren't up to gold digging anymore."

She'd rather die than admit it to Treeny, but prospecting's dangers and demands were hell on older bodies, even tough ones like hers. Not that eighty-two was old. She derived, after all, from a line of long-lived Chisholms. Their father, named after the Hugh Chisholm who'd conveyed the Bonnie Prince Charlie safe to the coast of Arisaig, had lived to ninety-eight. If Dulcey had her way, she'd live well past a hundred and expire on the shelf, a loaf of bread gone past its freshness date but not devoured.

Where she wouldn't die was in an overheated hospital where they force-fed poor buggers tasteless pap and tied them to plastic toilets on wheels.

"Mother died with grace," Treeny said. "If you'd been there, you'd know."

"I can think of more interesting topics."

"Like what?"

"Striking it rich, for one."

Dulcey had done just that the day before. Despite the naysayers' warnings, she'd added her present holding to her portfolio even though it had been fine-tooth-combed over by a grand total of seven predecessors. But a month of rock and soil sampling, hand trenching, and the start of a geophysical survey had turned up an immodest deposit of the yellow stuff.

Maybe she wasn't a mining engineer and geologist like Kim Dodge, the lucky bastard recipient of Yukon Prospectors Association's Prospector of the Year Award, but she did have stick-to-it-iveness. She didn't need the approval of Kim and his ilk, men with supportive wives to keep the home fires burning, men with education, men with access to the deep pockets of big mining outfits. She didn't need a Prospector of the bloody Year Award, no matter how much she deserved one. Primroses like her mother went in for the kind of glad-handing that won kudos. True Scotsmen like her father just got the job done.

Forgoing breakfast, she scrubbed the pot out with sand, then filled an ancient duffel with the items she'd need for a day and a night in town — windbreaker, moose jerky, hard biscuits, boiled water, and a vial of gold dust to settle outstanding accounts. She shuttled the bag and a few other items from the lean-to over to the back eddy, where her canvas canoe waited.

"Oh goody," Treeny said, "we're going on an adventure." Now middle-aged, she positioned her ample bottom on the canoe's forward seat. She wore a ball cap with the sequined words *Shopping Bag*, and a life preserver.

Dulcey focused on the classic lines of the vessel she'd built with the help an Indian, Sam Lightfeather — or was it Lightfinger? The canoe displayed good workmanship, from the solid molded hull to the white cedar ribs and hardwood stems. And the canvas, with its layers of paint and varnish, had kept its shape through years of hard use. Like so many things from the last century, the canoe had outlived its maker.

She tossed her ancient, faded red life jacket into the canoe. It acted as protection for hemorrhoids, an embarrassing complaint that had developed after years of squatting over scrub to do her business.

"Let's swap secrets," Treeny suggested after they cast off. "You first."

"Here's one," Dulcey said. "You aren't here." She knew better than to let down her guard. She had once, during their final long-distance conversation. She'd admitted to having a nether-region itch. Instead of practical advice on how to cure it without consulting a doctor, her sister had jumped all over the opportunity. She'd asked the unthinkable — whether or not Dulcey had really been born with a penis.

"A what?" Dulcey feigned ignorance, but felt sick.

"It's okay, if you were, honey. God doesn't make junk."

"That's because He foists the task off on the Taiwanese," Dulcey had shot back before hanging up forever.

The canoe curved around the jumbled mess of a beaver dam. Treeny laughed, seemingly delighted when a fat rodent slapped a threat with its tail before disappearing beneath the surface. She was a shallow person, Dulcey decided, far too easily entertained.

How Treeny'd caught wind of the secret was a mystery Dulcey would rather not solve. Who else among her family members, besides their mother, had known? And to be fair, the thing wasn't really a penis, it just looked like one. At twenty-seven she'd screwed up enough courage to consult a doctor in Whitehorse, one R. P. Pigeon. The good doctor's right eye had ticked with the precision of a metronome as he consulted his notes, post-gynecological exam. "Well, young lady," he'd said. Dulcey subdued an urge to still the ticking eye forever. "Everything seems to be in order here."

Back then Dulcey wore tailored dress suits. She'd smoothed the fabric of her shirt. "I've seen naked women," she confessed.

Boy oh boy, had she ever. Years before, when her brother Patrick had gone off to war, she'd lifted his mattress to air it. Underneath she found copies of *Nude Sunbathing for Health, Black Nylons, Male Life* and other girlie magazines. Beyond the spread legs, she'd seen tidy, tiny and not nearly as hairy private parts. Perusing all twenty-six periodicals nearly killed her.

The acrid smell of fear had wafted out from under Dr. R. P. Pigeon's arms. "While the size of your, hmm, female apparatus does fall in the outer limits of normal, I have no reason to believe that it will interfere with your ability to bear children should you marry."

Dulcey risked a suggestion: Could he cut the damned thing off?

Dr. Pigeon scrawled information on a notepad. "The best I can do, Miss Chisholm, is to refer you to a priest."

But Dulcey was too sick for spiritual counselling on the day of her appointment, and never did recover from the bad case of gold fever she had caught that spring.

The canoe nosed past Dulcey's homestead. The cabin and an outhouse were partially hidden by a stand of trees, just the way she liked it. Whether she was home or not, she didn't want busybody tourists infringing upon her privacy.

"I've never seen your home," Treeny said. "Let's stop. You can give me the grand tour and feed me lunch. I'm famished."

"I didn't pack extra."

"No problem. Figments don't eat real food."

Dulcey paddled to shore, driven by a sudden hankering for home.

"I hadn't expected feminine touches," Treeny said as the sisters tramped past a garden of roses, bluebells, and yellow mustard to reach Dulcey's cabin. They passed under a hornet's nest growing from a pair of moose antlers hung from the portal of the door. The door was wide open.

During the long, dark season of cabin fever, Dulcey'd often wanted to trash the place, but now someone else had done the honors. Her worldly possessions — snowshoes, camp bed, oil lamp, and tree-stump chair — were hacked to bits, and the buggers had scrawled *Gone to the Dawgs* on a ceiling beam. Worse, the Georgian sauceboat crafted by Lothian & Robertson of Edinburgh, and the snuff mull with its polished body of horn and intricate thistle-patterned silver top inscribed *Fearghus Chisholm Servant to Mrs Toirdhealbhach Mac an Fhleisteir 1796* were both smashed to smithereens.

"Well, now," Treeny said as she looked down at the artefacts. "I'd call that ironic justice."

Dulcey picked up a torn bit of photograph. It showed Treeny's torso, with nipples and pubic hair scrawled in over the purple jumpsuit she wore. She slipped the offensive snippet into a pocket to dispose of in private later.

Other images had also suffered debasement, she soon discovered. Dulcey had had suitors in her time, and once, upon his insistence, she'd posed for a photograph with a certain Hans Crudup, a hunting and fishing guide with a bear's furry body and yellow canine teeth. She'd used a curmudgeon façade to drive him away, but now felt outraged that some bastard had sketched in a set of king-sized reproductive organs over the front of his pants. Beside him, a much younger, and prettier, Dulcey sported a matching set, as well as a chest-length beard.

"Seen enough?" she whipped around to confront her sister's ridicule, but Treeny had left the cabin when Dulcey wasn't looking.

Treeny reappeared three hours later, just as Dulcey and her canoe neared the village of Everlasting. She was older now, at least sixty. "Miss me?" she asked.

Dulcey refused to answer. She felt greedy for the first drift of man-made sound, almost as greedy as she felt for the glass of whiskey waiting for her at the pub. Instead of sound, however, the familiar hush of nature continued. *Going, going, gone*, storefront graffiti warned.

"Looks like everyone vamoosed," Treeny commented. "They must have seen you coming."

"Shut up," Dulcey said and Treeny grew dim.

As the canoe nudged into a back eddy, three skin-and-bones husky pups waded into the water to greet them. They wagged their tails and whined. None had collars and all had festering sores. When Treeny insisted on tossing moose jerky onto the shore for them, the dogs fought over the scraps.

Ignoring the dogs, Dulcey climbed out of the canoe, secured the line to a bush, then made her way up the bank to the road. Dust swirled like phantom smoke as Dulcey headed down Front Street. As she passed their homes and places of business, she called out the names of friends and acquaintances. It astonished her that no one replied. How could so many people have either moved or passed away when they'd demonstrated good health and community spirit less than two years before?

She felt light-headed and thirsty. A shop window advertised a *Going out of Business Sale.* At Jo-Jo's Bar & Grill, her longed-for destination, the front door hung crooked on rusted hinges. Along with some creeping charlie, she made cautious inroads into the cool, musty interior.

An empty whisky bottle was imbedded in the television screen and the bar showed signs of fire.

"Nice ambiance," Treeny said. "Do you think they serve flame-broiled steak?"

Dulcey took a seat on a torn bar stool. She rubbed at a burning pain in her jaw.

"What about you?" she asked Treeny. "Are you gone too?" She couldn't voice the word *deceased.*

"I'm whatever you want me to be," Treeny said.

Despite her annoying qualities, if Treeny was gone, it didn't bear thinking about. In another time and place, when Dulcey was a girl with long braided hair, a sweet disposition, and high hopes, the youngest Chisholm had been a newborn baby with peach-soft skin. No matter what happened between them afterwards, Treeny was hers, the sibling she'd been paired with to help their overburdened mother.

Dulcey's heart did a nasty cartwheel in her chest. "Damnation," she said as she slid from the stool and, unable to stand, landed prone on the floor. The pups arrived to slobber over her face and hands. They nudged their dry noses into her pockets. The smallest pup licked at the blood of her wounded knee through the tear in her jeans.

"Sorry to say it," Treeny said, "but this looks bad. I don't hold out much hope for an open-casket funeral when those rascals are done with you."

The smallest pup nipped at Dulcey's fingers. The largest growled. Dulcey drew her knees close to her chest. She cupped a hand over her crotch.

"That a girl," Treeny urged. "Protect the family jewels."

The dogs howled.

"You never loved me," Dulcey said.

"Oh, honey, I sure did, but you made it so hard."

"You shouldn't have sent me that bloody plaque."

The plaque had belonged to their father, but Treeny had sent it to Dulcey after the ill-fated phone call. She sent it despite knowing what she knew. It read: *When God made Scots, he made them a wee bit better.*

Dulcey felt the warmth of a human hand stroking her forehead. Old muscles trembled beneath the butter-soft skin of the fingers. "You were the only Chisholm it was true for," Treeny said. "I just wanted you to believe."

Then someone somewhere whistled Dixie.

SURE, IN AN IDEAL WORLD, I might be unbiased, but the sad truth is that some human beings are more endearing than others. Take the members of the Wilsie family for instance: they are simple people without being stupid, though the youngest child may be an exception (only time will tell). They roll with the blows and express gratitude, however lamely, when their fortunes rise. Best of all, they work out their troubles with a minimum of fuss. Some people rage at me or try to barter off their first-born when they screw up their lives. Then it's, "Yo, big guy. How about offing my witnesses so that I can walk?" or "Oh, Goddess Mother, please reverse those numbers on pork belly futures." It gets old.

But enough about me, we were talking about the Wilsies. Last summer was a case in point. Harold Wilsie, the family's figurehead patriarch (as is common, the eldest daughter holds the real power), had messed up big time. Despite a previously decent life, he'd suddenly run away with a wily secretary who offered him a round-trip ticket to Hawaii. This spur-of-the-moment holiday devastated his wife and hit the kids hard.

About a month after Harold left, I dropped in on the remaining Wilsies to see how they were managing. The kids were down at the beach and I arrived on time to see ten-year-old Carmen-Louise emerge from the ocean. Her shoulders were draped with surfgrass and a clam crowned her head. I suppose because of the shell, she reminded me of Aphrodite. However, unlike Aphrodite who was dignified from birth, Carmen-Louise opened her mouth and proclaimed, "I have beautiful boobies!" Three crows stopped their mutilation of mussels to look her way.

Leein, her sister, rolled over on her beach towel and shaded her eyes with a *True Confessions* magazine. "You are an idiotic child," she said as she adjusted the edge of her white bikini pants.

Carmen-Louise, you see, had stuffed her bathing suit top with two mounds of sea lettuce. "I'm going to keep them until bedtime," she declared of the seaweed falsies. The three crows cawed derision.

"Fine. You do just that." Leein's face took on a look that said now-bugger-off-I-was-deserted-by-my-father-on-my-sixteenth-birthday-and-have-been-in-a-bitch-of-a-mood-ever-since.

Instead of leaving, Carmen-Louise yanked Leein up off the blanket. She careened across the sand, pulling Leein along behind her, towards a divinity student on vacation whose towel sported a lurid map of the Hawaiian Islands. His baggy swim trunks were festooned with what looked like mud sharks.

"Let me go, Cramps, you ass!" Leein said. "Or I'll kill you."

"You're no fun anymore." Carmen-Louise's chest squelched against her sister's coconut-oiled skin. "All you care about are boys and clothes."

"That's someone else's sister, you dimwit!" Leein's thin body writhed like a cornered eel as her heftier sister pinned her to the ground at the student's feet. "Get off me, Cramps, and go home. Now!"

I was too busy chuckling to intervene when Carmen-Louise reached for the bow that held up Leein's bikini top. "I'll go home," she said as she untied it. "But only 'cause it's suppertime, not 'cause you said." She released Leein and trotted off across the hot sand.

"And I'm telling Mom you swore." Her voice faded as she entered a passageway that lead through the wild rose hedge to the Sea Spray Mobile Home Park and the Wilsie's 1973 trailer. "You're gonna catch shit."

"I'm M-M-Merlyn," the divinity student stammered. "Merlyn Shipperbottom. You know, like Merlyn the m-magician." He offered his hand.

"Now you see them. Now you don't," Leein said as she retied her top. "It's magic." Merlyn Shipperbottom, good boy though he was, had introduced himself to her breasts.

In the Wilsie trailer home kitchen, Malva nibbled a lighthouse-shaped cookie while she considered the mystery of sex. To her mind, the intimate act was a simple thing — yet, of late, so very confusing. Her estranged husband had considered laughter, bottles of red wine, and ample breasts, even if they drooped, sexy. With Harold, sex had been good, clean fun.

I watched as her cheeks flushed in memory of the previous night's blind date, which had ended long before the proposed all-you-can-eat seafood buffet at Wo Fat Chinese Restaurant. Poor woman — how could she have known what to expect from men? Her first and only love had been Harold. Harold, that peach of a gentleman, hadn't gone for the gusto on their first date. It had been a slow buildup over months. By the time they went all the way on their wedding night, she had already discovered the climax. Malva had not expected a kiss from her blind date, let alone the need to fend off heated front-seat fumbling when he insisted on taking a detour to Lovers' Lookout before dinner. Had she expected it, she would not have padded her bra with toilet paper, even though it sagged because of her recent weight loss.

Smoothing cookie crumbs off her blouse, she flicked on the black-and-white television set. Harold had taken the new Panasonic with Dolby sound, not that she minded. He had left them every-thing else, except himself.

"Temperatures are expected to continue to rise until the end of the week," a svelte blonde news anchor on the Weather Channel informed us. "When you hit those beaches, remember to slather on the sunscreen." I found it mildly irritating that the woman's smug look suggested she had personally arranged for good weather.

"I could go on the television and tell the world a thing or two about rising temperatures," Malva said. The weather woman reminded her of the wily secretary.

A timer jangled. Malva donned oven mitts to remove three Stouffer's Lean Cuisine dinners from the oven. She set them on the table and then peeled off the lids. I got close enough to sniff the clouds of fragrant steam.

"Make her lose those, Mom," Leein demanded as she pushed Carmen-Louise through the open door. "They nauseate me."

Malva removed the plastic film from a TV dinner. "Honey, do you mind? Seaweed doesn't belong at the supper table."

"In Japan people eat it," Carmen-Louise said as she took her seat at the table. "They even farm it."

Leein slumped into a chair and sniffed at her lemon pepper fish filet. I almost slapped her hand when she pushed the tray away and who would have blamed me? Jenny Craig perhaps, but certainly not the starving Sudanese. Of course, she might not have survived my touch, most Westerners don't. "Cramps thinks she's sexy," she said.

"Mom stuffs her bra to be sexy," Carmen-Louise said.

"Not to be sexy, dear, only because I can't afford new clothes. And, believe you me, I'll never try that trick again, no matter how poorly something fits." Malva rubbed the pale skin on her bare ring finger. She longed to tell Harold about her date. He would split a gut laughing. What she missed most about her husband was his laughter, that and all those nights of good, clean fun.

Harold, the poor sod. I had planned to let him stew for a year or two over his decision, but he already regretted it. In Hawaii, where he'd initially gone with Rosa Quarell, he'd bought seashells and coral for something to do besides mope. Jet lag made sex out of the question, or so Rosa had insisted. When they returned home to Rosa's frilly pink apartment he had piled his purchases on top of his Panasonic TV. A stag coral had scratched the imitation wood finish. Because the TV was the only thing besides his clothing and personal effects that Harold had taken from home, the scratch bothered him more than it ought to have.

Harold kept the TV in the bedroom. If his daughters ever came to visit, he didn't want Leein to see it. Leein's rage was fierce over the loss of the new set. "Why can't you just die like other fathers do?" she had said. Her fists had pummeled Harold's back as he made for Rosa's silver Acadian. He dumped the TV in the open back and then bungee-corded down the hatch. "It's not too late. You could jump off a bridge or drink poison."

Harold made a run for the passenger side and locked himself in as Leein circled around to the front of the car.

"Drive!" he begged Rosa.

"A television set? That's all you got?"

"Just drive, please!" Leein grabbed a rock from Carmen-Louise's beach bucket and wound up. "For goodness sake, Rosa! She means business."

"All right, already." As Rosa shifted into reverse, the rock smacked the glass in front of Harold's backward-fleeing face. It created a spider web of cracks.

"Little bitch!" Rosa rolled down her window to shout. "I'll bet you take after the cow."

I hinted at a happy ending, and we're getting to that now. That night Harold slipped from Rosa's bed. He tiptoed down the stairs to the kitchen and picked up the phone. I could hear his heart pound as he dialed. He prayed that Carmen-Louise would answer, because she would be easiest; I sent Leein in her place.

Harold almost hung up. "Hi, sugar," he said instead. "It's me. Your daddy."

"Oh, really?"

"What's new?"

"Hmm. Let me think." Leein paused for effect. "Recently my father deserted us for a shrew named Rosa. That was a high point. Then, just this evening, Carmen-Louise sprouted green breasts and my bathing suit top fell off at the beach in front of a strange man who looked like a pervert and who knows where we live. In fact, I think I hear his scratch at the window as we speak. No, sorry. False alarm. This time it's only a branch in the wind. Then there's my mother. Last night she dated a divorced logger with really bad body odor. But I don't think they had sex. In fact, I don't think they even had dinner, the date was so short. Other than that, things have been quiet."

"Oh," Harold said.

"That's right, Harry. Oh."

After her father's call, Leein remained in the kitchen. She listened to the refrigerator run through its cooling cycle and the surf pound the shore beyond the wild rose hedge. An hour passed, and it would have been easy for her to pretend that everything was still the same: within easy reach were four chairs at the tiny kitchen table, the white refrigerator with its collection of fish magnets and family photographs, and Harold's fishing vest, left behind on the hook by the door. It would have been easy — just not easy enough.

Leein drifted down the hallway and entered her parents' bedroom. Malva lay asleep on her side, clutching Harold's undershirt. Wadded tissues glowed like jellyfish on the floor. Leein slid under the covers and pressed her face into the pillow, where Harold's spicy Nautica cologne still lingered.

If I could have, I would have kissed them both.

Instead, I woke Harold with the light from my moon. Beside him, Rosa lay on her back, uncovered. Her mouth was slack. If he'd wanted to, Harold could have counted the teeth in her mouth, but he didn't want to know Rosa that well.

Harold trained his eyes on Rosa's face to avoid the sight of her breasts. There was something about the tiny mounds and bland nipples that he simply could not face. Who would have thought? He wondered. No energy, that's how Rosa explained it, but he'd noticed that she had energy enough to shop with what remained of his money.

I nudged Harold's thoughts towards Malva. Before long he

remembered what a warm and welcoming, if large, body she had. She was a woman who knew how to devour a man. His member stiffened at the thought.

As Harold reached under the bed for his jar of petroleum jelly, Rosa mumbled something in her sleep and rolled towards him. One of her nipples nudged his back. Harold jumped as though he'd been touched by the mouth of a shiner perch. Then he laughed until his laughter shook the bed. As I left him for the night, he was making plans.

We could hardly wait; Harold Wilsie was going home.

LIAM DREADED FIRST DAYS, hated the blur of them, the indistinct structure, the unidentifiable smells, and the generalized blackness similar to the "fugue states" his mother claimed to suffer from. Hated them, but somehow survived them. He had done so again today, his first day, three-quarters of the way into the school year, at Fenny Junior High.

After the bell, invisible to all, he'd slunk safely past groups of less lonely kids to retrieve his bike, only to find a girl had beaten him to it.

Liam appraised her featherweight body, fluffy hair, dark blue eyes, and the braided leather choker around her neck, even as she trashed his bike. Life had numbed his instincts for flight and fight, so he simply stood there while she slashed the banana seat with a pocket knife, punctured both tires and kicked in the rims. Next she scratched an invitation on a handlebar for him to kiss her ass before pushing the bike his way.

She hooked her thumbs over her hip bones and glared. "Aren't you going to turn me into roadkill?"

Liam righted the toppled bike. "Not today."

"You're kidding. Right?"

"Wrong."

"Wow! I can't believe it. Someone actually passed my friendship test. Now for the clincher: All males are effing pricks. Is this statement true or false?"

For the most part, Liam thought they were. All of his mother's boyfriends, a few of his teachers, and even his father qualified. But then, he hadn't punched the girl in the mouth like he wanted to, so what did that make him? Instead of answering her stupid question, he trudged towards his apartment with his mutilated bike.

"Wait!" The girl jumped on her BMX to follow. Liam ignored her. He would go home, check on Rae, and watch his favorite reruns. He would forget the day ever happened.

Three blocks later, as he neared a duplex with a weedy lawn, the girl was still with him. She zipped around him and skidded to a stop. "Guess you're in luck." She nodded at the duplex. "This dive is where I get off."

Bricks secured a tarp to a section of mossy roof. An unpainted shutter hung loose. "It's not so bad," said Liam, who had lived in a Pontiac and a homeless shelter.

"Bullshit. It's an effing dump." The girl rode onto the lawn, and then wheelied over a prone sign that advertised *Bike Repairs*. "I wouldn't have slaughtered your ride, you know," she said. "Not if I'd known you were cool."

The sign gave Liam an idea. "Who fixes the bikes?" he asked.

"My dad did. Before he skipped town."

"Where'd he go?"

"Nova Scotia."

Liam rested on his bike's handlebars. "What's there?"

"My mom says nothing but a bunch of fiddle-playing alcoholics. She says, except for the music part, my dad fits right in."

"My mom never stays in one place very long. At Christmas she went all the way to Wawa in Ontario because she said she needed peace and quiet, but all they had was heaps of snow. My dad used to take off sometimes too. He can't anymore, though. He's stuck in a prison."

"What for?"

"He crippled our neighbor. We had to move. My mom said she wasn't going to let a cocktease who deserved what she got make her feel guilty every single day of her life."

The girl picked a spent dandelion and flicked it. She blew the drifting seeds towards Liam's face. "My name's Caitlin. It means pure which I'm definitely not, so I make everybody call me Cally."

"Like the goddess of destruction," Liam said. Among other things, his mother was a semi-practicing Hindu.

"Sure, that's me. Come on."

"Where?"

"To fix your bike. When dickhead left he didn't take his tools."

When Liam arrived home, he found his mother, Rae, sprawled half-dressed on her bed in a heap of blankets. A silk-screened Shiva meditated on a cloth draped over an open closet door, and a rattan hanging chair lay sideways on the floor, just as they had before he left for school that morning. Rae's eyes were half closed, making it hard for him to judge her mood. He waited for her to speak first.

"How'd school go?" she said. Her voice sounded more sleepy than drugged.

"Good."

"D'you like your new teacher?"

"She's okay." Liam wandered into the room. When Rae showed an interest in his school day, their evening usually went well. Sometimes they even played cards or watched his shows together. He picked up a burning incense stick to wave it. The heady scent, indistinguishable from home, made him dizzy.

Rae dragged herself into a sitting position on the bed. She gazed at her face in the dresser mirror, ran her fingers through her hair. Liam wondered if she loved or hated what she saw today. He wasn't sure how he felt about her himself.

"Did you make any friends?" she asked.

"One. Sort of. A girl."

Rae's eyes shifted to Liam as she slid to her feet. "Oh, god. Chasing skirts already. You're becoming just like your father." She began dumping cotton peasant blouses from a dresser drawer into an empty gin box. Liam counted six, enough to last his mom a week, longer if she didn't change her clothes every day.

He felt a pang in his stomach. It was hunger — he'd felt too nervous to eat the ginger tofu Rae had provided for lunch — but something else too. On Friday, when they'd moved into the new apartment, Rae had said she liked the town of Fenny. She'd promised he could join a baseball team. She'd patted his head and said, "Welcome home, babe." He had wanted to believe her.

"Why are you packing?" he said.

All of the kindness left Rae's eyes. "Don't make this hard on me, baby. My head's killing me. You know I can't cope when you make things hard."

"Should I pack too?"

When his mother didn't answer, Liam left the room. In the kitchen, he found a jar of tahini in the refrigerator. He decided to eat the sesame seed butter straight from the jar with a spoon in front of the TV, and watch his favorite DVD.

Rae entered the living room carrying a leather boot and a slim joint. Narrowing her eyes at the television, she released a cloud of smoke. "How can you watch that crap?"

When Ginger vamped through a song and dance number for the sake of the Professor and Thurston Howell, Liam laughed despite himself.

"God," Rae said, "you're hopeless." She switched off the set.

Liam's fingers found comfort in the burn holes that marred the cushions of the sofa that his father had bought for ten dollars from a thrift store. Alone among the man's possessions, the sofa had survived the family's repeated moves. "You said you liked it here," he said. "You said we could stay awhile."

A horn honked. "Plans change," Rae said. She hobbled back into the bedroom. "That's Forest. I've got to go."

"I want to come with you."

"Forest has a thing about kids. They make him anxious." Her

voice was muffled.

"When will you be back?"

"Years before your good-for-nothing father will be." Rae emerged from the bedroom wearing both boots, an afghan shawl over a cotton dress, and carrying the gin box. She shifted the box to one arm, adjusted an embroidered carpet bag over her shoulder. When she tried to tousle Liam's hair, he moved away. "Be good. Okay?"

Liam switched the television set back on.

After Rae left, Liam returned the tahini to the refrigerator, washed the spoon, and set it on the counter. Then he gathered candles. He played with the flames to the music of the Grateful Dead while he waited for the social worker who might or might not come. Sometimes his mother forgot to place the call. When that happened, Liam stayed on his own until either loneliness or hunger overwhelmed him. Once, at eleven, he'd lasted eight days before informing the authorities of his parentless status.

When the afternoon faded into evening, he rifled through Rae's belongings. He found a deck of Aquarian tarot cards left behind by one of her boyfriends. The man had conned Rae by predicting wealth, health, and love for her. After fanning out the cards on the table, Liam burnt them one at a time until only the Death card remained.

Just after midnight, a knock sounded on the apartment door. If Forest was like the last man Rae ran off with, he'd find his mother black-eyed and bleeding. She'd have an excuse for Forest's violence and expect Liam to bandage her up. But when Liam opened the door, Cally stood there instead. She clutched a fuzzy pink pillow and her eyes looked owly in the sudden light.

"Don't look so freaking shocked," she said. "I know where you live because I followed you home today." She craned her neck to peer into the apartment. "Where's your mother? I need to stay the night. My old man came home for his tools and now he says he's teaching my mom and the guy she was screwing a lesson that they won't soon forget. I can't believe his effing nerve."

Liam pocketed the tarot card. "Rae's dead," he said.

*

"This time you've got to behave," Liam's frazzled-looking social worker said as he knocked on the door of the house belonging to Liam's new foster parents. "Please."

Liam considered the yard's close-shaven grass and three miniature windmills lined up in a row. He'd had Dutch foster parents before. Nice people with two little kids and a friendly spaniel who said they would have kept him forever if Rae hadn't turned up to claim him back.

"I'll try," he said.

The foster mother who answered the door looked more like a grandmother. "These kids think death's a joke," she said to express dissatisfaction of the skull designs on Liam's skate shoes and clothing while escorting the pair down a cluttered hallway to the back half of the house. "He'll use my husband's hobby room," she said, speaking of Liam as though he wasn't there. The small space contained a leather chair, a queen-sized bed and dense green curtains. A sequined dress and a full-length fur coat skulked in the gloom of the open closet.

"I forgot to warn you," the social worker said as the woman draped pairs of blue jeans over hangers. "Liam's a vegan. He refuses to eat meat."

"And dairy." Liam shifted a curtain. The backyard, though well-groomed and full of windmill paraphernalia, looked as unused as the front.

"I cannot cook without meat and cheese," the foster mother claimed.

"He eats bean curd," the social worker said.

"You'll like it," Liam added. "It's cheap."

The following weekend, while the woman grocery shopped and her husband did yard work, Cally came to visit. She put on the fur coat, raided the kitchen for cookies, and then made Liam lead her on an exploration of the house. In time they reached an unfinished basement cluttered with a wilderness of power and hand tools. Jars full of nails and screws hung like squat stalactites from lids nailed into the low ceiling. The cool air smelled of mushrooms, oil, and lubricants. Liam picked up a *Field & Stream*, exposing *The Swing Set*, a magazine with three half-naked people on the cover.

Cally grabbed the magazine. She sat on an overturned crate and flipped through the pages. "What kind of pervs are you living with?"

Liam shrugged. He eased a handful of cookies from the bag Cally held, then positioned a folding chair near the basement's only window for the light. "They don't bug me."

"Yet," Cally joked.

Ten minutes later, engrossed by cookies and photographs of fly-fishing and group sex, they missed hearing the sound of footsteps on the stairs.

"Oh crap," Cally said at the foster father's appearance. She tossed *The Swing Set* back on the pile of magazines. It landed open revealing a scene of cunnilingus.

"You like my coat?" the old man said.

"What can I say?" Cally nuzzled the coat's collar with her face. "It's soft."

"You like this too?" As the man walked towards her, he lowered the fly of his work pants. White briefs with a yellow stain bulged out.

"Freak," Liam said.

With his free hand the man held out two fifty-dollar bills towards the teens.

Cally laughed. "Double mine," she said, "and I'll pretend your dirty underwear belongs to Ashton Kutcher."

Liam crossed the room to Cally. He took her hand. "We're going upstairs."

As they passed him by, the man grabbed Cally by the arms. He backed her into a garbage can filled with scrap wood and sawdust, knocking it over. "Go on," he said. "Show me."

"She was joking. Let her go."

"Yeah, man. Can't you tell a joke when you hear one?" Cally laughed as she twisted to evade him. Her head smacked a piece of machinery bolted to the wall. Her eyes widened with disbelief as she looked at Liam. She wet her fingers in blood that trickled down her head and neck. Then she collapsed.

Liam didn't think before he charged the much larger man. Despite his lack of size and strength, he landed a punch, splitting the man's lip and his own knuckles. The man pushed him to the ground.

"Sicko," the man said as he looked down at Liam. "You hurt that poor little girl."

"There must be something about you that brings out the worst in people," Liam's social worker said. They were parked outside a 7-Eleven convenience store one block from Fenny General Hospital after Liam's release from the emergency ward. Inside the hospital, Cally waited for a CAT scan. Skateboarders dressed in low-slung pants and oversized hoodies hung around near the car. "Do you know how hard it is to recruit foster families? Do you know how many homes your allegations have closed to date?"

"Three." Liam set his untouched Big Gulp in the car's cup holder. He adjusted his hat to shield his eyes, and sunk lower in his seat.

The social worker guzzled his pop. He forced eye contact on Liam. "All I'm saying is you'd better be damned sure you aren't lying."

"I'm not. Cally's not either."

"Now there's a trustworthy victim."

They both watched a skateboarder land a kickflip in front of the car.

"The point is, I'm running out of options for you," the social worker said. "I had to scrape the bottom of the barrel for your next placement. They aren't even white."

"You ever try Indian ice cream?" asked Starlene John, Liam's First Nations foster mother who, he had learned, attended Fenny University's Indigenous Corporate Relations program. She dumped bright red berries into a bowl of water and then whipped them into froth. Liam accepted a spoonful of the mixture. "It's made with soapberries," Starlene said.

Liam tried the concoction. It tasted bitter, but good.

"Where do you get them?"

"Around. Sometimes they hide near lodgepole pine."

The next day Liam spied a book on Aboriginal food plants on the family room bookshelf. The index listed soapberries under "Canadian buffalo-berry or soopolallie." He spent the afternoon searching for the plant in a nearby park. He found bags of reeking garbage, a shattered Panasonic television and plants with brown scabbed branches and green oval leaves. None of the plants sported soapy berries.

"Buffalo-berries don't like crowds," Liam's foster father, Benjamin, said that night during a supper of Kentucky Fried chicken, sun-dried salmon and canned peas.

The elder of the family's two daughters, a fourteen-year-old named Franky, peered at Liam from beneath the sleek bangs that fell over her eyes. Liam fell in love when she nudged his leg under the table with her foot. "Don't listen to my old man," she said. "He just likes to sound mysterious. It's the Indian act."

In August, when Liam had lived with the John family for four and a half months, they drove their wood-paneled station wagon to a powwow in Vernon. They pitched a teepee near an oak growing in a field that doubled as a parking lot. A piece of indoor-outdoor carpet, lawn chairs, a cooler filled with canned pop, and a TV dinner table created an impromptu living room beside the teepee.

While the family went their separate ways to search out friends, Liam took shelter in the teepee and closed the flap to seal himself in. Franky and her sister Darrell had dumped their fancy dance costumes in a pile and their buckskin dresses smelled wildly sweet. Liam lay close enough to breathe in the scent. He ran his hand over the rabbit-fur hair pieces and the father's cool bone hairpipe beads that lay nearby. Through the shelter's open top, he glimpsed the shimmer of leaves and a patch of clear sky that seemed to buzz with heat.

The sounds of muffled conversations, bursts of laughter, drumming, car horns, and competing boom boxes gave Liam a full, satisfied feeling. He closed his eyes and slowed his breathing to match the thump of the drums. In his mind's eye, his body began a longed-for metamorphosis: his dirty-blond hair darkened, his round gray eyes became almond-shaped, and his thin lips took on a firmer set.

Next his nose broadened, his skin lost its anemic pallor, and his concave chest developed tone. Self-loathing slipped like a coat from his shoulders. He became someone who belonged with the family — not a scrawny white boy who, when he was with the Johns, drew hard stares from both First Nations people and other whites.

The tent flap opened, dispelling the fantasy. Franky poked her head in. Two teens stood behind her. The boy, short and pock-marked, palmed a cigarette. He ran his free hand through bleached-blond hair with black roots. The girl, skinny with a pierced nose, crossed her arms over her flat chest. She wore sunglasses and seemed to stare with boredom somewhere beyond Liam. "These are my cousins, Martha John and…" Franky made a guttural sound. "His name means 'dog-salmon.' It sounds better in Wakashan, so we just call him Dog. Come on. We're going to show you around."

Neither cousin shared her enthusiasm.

Liam stumbled to his feet, blinking as his eyes grew accustomed to the bright sunlight. Dog opened the family's cooler. He offered an iced Coke to each of the girls and then made a point of slamming the lid shut.

Franky popped the tab of her can, took a sip, and then passed it to Liam. She grasped his arm and steered him through the parking lot towards a group of tables. Aboriginal arts and crafts interspersed with gaudy clothing and hot dog stands.

"Got any money?" Franky asked.

"Some." Liam glanced back at her cousins.

"No one's asking you to share." Franky tugged on his faded Def Leppard T-shirt. "But if you're going to hang with me here, you're going to need some new threads."

Evening had brought its welcome cool when Liam settled on a lawn chair beside Franky's parents to watch the women's traditional dance. He felt bolder in his new turquoise headband, cowboy shirt, and the aviator-style sunglasses Franky had chosen for him. He sat straight-backed, feeling like someone who belonged.

The drumming began and a line of female dancers shuffled into the Dance Circle, their feet never breaking contact with the earth.

Franky, with one feather in her hair, which she'd told Liam signaled her unmarried status, chanced a grin for her family when she entered. Her father lifted his camera to take a picture. She danced on, mirroring the other women who made the fringe of their shawls rock like cradles. Her gaze turned inward, tuning her family out. She executed perfect, fluid movements. To Liam's mind, she seemed like a graceful, cautious deer moving through a forest. Then she twirled and became a waterfall. When she slowed she was moss on rock.

Liam longed to be the rock.

On a Saturday in December, despite Liam's effort to keep Cally and the Johns apart, Cally showed up in their driveway. The family was crowded into the station wagon, about to leave for an evening of dancing at the Friendship Center. Leaning through the open car window, Cally grinned at Starlene, Benjamin, and Darrell.

"Hi all," she said. "I'm Cally, Liam's best friend." She peered into the back seat. "Hi, Franky." Then, to the others, she added. "We know each other from school."

"Unfortunately," Franky whispered.

"We're supposed to be in the same grade, but I had a brain contusion," Cally continued. "I forget so much stuff the principal dropped me back a grade. Not that I was a genius before my accident. Right, Liam?"

Liam crossed his arms over his chest and stared at the dome light. He didn't want to see the family's reaction to Cally's low-cut top, short skirt, and thick makeup. "I don't know."

"So," Cally said as she opened the rear passenger door. "Are we going somewhere special?"

"*We* are," Franky murmured.

"To a dance," Darrell said.

Cally climbed over Franky to secure a place for herself in the back seat beside Liam. "So, let's rock and roll."

No one said anything. After a moment, Benjamin started the car.

When they'd gone three blocks, Cally took a compact from her purse, then applied shadow to her already colorful lids. She tapped Franky's father on the shoulder with her makeup brush. "So, were you guys raised in residential schools, or what?"

"My wife's parents were." Benjamin took a cautious left-hand turn.

"Cally, hush up," Liam said.

"Why should I? It's not like that crap's classified information or something."

Franky interrupted. "Caucasians call what they did to us assimilation. What do you think, Cally? Were they successful? Are we the same as you now?"

"I haven't got a clue."

"Well, I think that you people still have a long way to go before you catch up."

Cally wriggled to claim more room on the seat. "If you hate white people so much, then why do you have a crush on Liam?"

Franky's sister giggled.

"Quiet, okay?" Starlene said. She turned on a Mary Youngblood CD. When Cally tried to speak again, she turned up the volume.

At the community center, Franky's parents skirted puddles as they crossed the potholed parking lot following Darrell. Cally climbed out of the car after Liam.

When Franky remained seated inside, Liam slid back in and locked the door. Franky picked up a raven's feather lying on the seat. "Is Cally really your best friend?"

"No."

"Who is?"

"You know you are. And more."

Cally rapped her knuckles on the glass. "Hey, assholes. I'm freezing my buns off out here. Hurry it up."

Liam and Franky watched as Cally stuck out her tongue, then pressed it against the window.

Franky turned her gaze on Liam. "You should tell her to take a hike."

"I can't."

"Why not?"

"She's had a tough life."

"Yeah, well she's going to make *our* lives tough if she doesn't keep her mouth shut. My parents don't want to know how we feel about each other," Franky said. "If it becomes too obvious, they'll have to kick you out of our house."

"Because I'm white?"

"No, stupid. My parents aren't racists. Because you're damaged goods."

"Do you like surprises?" Cally called to ask Liam the day before his sixteenth birthday.

"Not really. Why?" Liam pressed the receiver to his ear with a shoulder. He was searching through drawers in the family's craft room for supplies. He wanted to make a new skull-and-crossbones headband he planned to wear at his birthday party — red jasper and black hematite beads, a needle, and a spool of fishing wire.

"The Johns are planning a big one for tomorrow."

"I know about my party."

"That's not it. They're going to offer to adopt you. They said the last two years went so well, they want to make it permanent. I saw Mrs. John at the mall and she asked me if I thought you'd say yes."

The material on Liam's lap blurred. If it was true, he wanted to accept, but couldn't. Adoption would make him Franky's brother, and he still had a mother, even if he didn't know where Rae was. But how could he say no? No one had ever offered to adopt him before.

"What did you say?"

"Not a chance in hell, assholes," Cally said. After a pause, she added, "I'm just joking, Liam."

"About which part?"

Franky flounced into the room and closed the door behind her. "There you are," she said. "I've been looking all over." She frowned at the receiver in Liam's hand. Keeping an eye on the door, she bent down to kiss him.

"I guess, you'll find out tomorrow," Cally said, hanging up.

"I got my mid-term report card," Liam said as Franky took a seat beside him with her latest project, a dancing shawl. "Unless I get my grades up, I'll have to do summer school."

"What subject?"

"Math and English. I passed Socials."

"Don't sweat it. School's useless anyway."

"Not for you. You get good grades."

"So what? They only teach my culture once a month in a *special* class. That's why I've decided to quit school after this year. I'm going to go into the Long House next fall instead. I want to learn the old ways before the elders all croak."

"Maybe I could learn the old ways too."

Franky broke off a knotted thread with her teeth. "That should be easy. Just murder, steal, and pass on gonorrhea. Isn't that what your ancestors did best?"

Liam lay on his bed in the basement, letting the music of Mötley Crüe assault his ears. Across the room, the mirror of his dresser was draped in black fabric, blocking out his hateful image. He had turned sixteen, eaten chocolate-raspberry cake, opened presents, and almost hadn't turned down the Johns' offer of adoption.

Franky opened the door.

"I like people to knock," Liam said.

Franky rapped on the bed frame, then settled cross-legged facing Liam on the mattress. When she touched his arm, Liam thought his skin beneath her fingers looked repulsive. "My parents are disappointed about your decision."

"You can't be my sister. Not if I love you this way."

Franky placed a feather in Liam's hand. "Next summer, we'll move to Bella Coola. We'll live with my grandparents until we can afford a place of our own. They'll adore us together."

"No, they won't."

"I'll make them. I promise. They're easier to sway than my parents."

"Do you love me?"

Franky trailed her fingertips along his arms and chest. His body responded when she let her hand rest on his thigh. "More than everything," she said.

With one hand, Liam pulled her onto him. He rubbed the raven feather between the fingers of his other hand. It felt warm, like a living animal. It felt like hope.

"Guess what Franky gave me *today*?" Cally flipped through a stack of *Nature's Treasures* magazines in the school library with destructive force. When Liam didn't bite, she said, "A birthday invitation. Too flippin' bad the party was *last week*."

"She didn't mean to forget."

"Sure she did. Not that I care. It's no skin off my nose if she hates me — as long as you don't hate me too."

"Of course, I don't. We're friends."

"Then why don't you hang with me?"

"I dunno," Liam said. "Maybe 'cause we're not in the same classes anymore."

"I bet Franky told you not to. I bet she gets jealous." Cally drew devil horns on the picture of an ornithologist feeding an eaglet with a bald eagle puppet. Next she drew crosses over the eaglet's eyes and then rammed a pocket knife through its paper chest.

"I make my own decisions."

"Sure," Cally laughed. "You and me both."

"No one makes you do anything. They wouldn't dare."

"That shows how much you don't know." Cally squeezed her eyes shut. "Remember the day we met?" she whispered. "I came to your place to get away from home. It wasn't my mother my father found with my mother's boyfriend. It was me. My mother let him. She let all of them."

Liam knew — deep inside he'd known for years. "You should have told me," he said.

"What would you have done? Beaten up all the men, and my mom too?"

"I would have helped you," Liam said.

"Oh, yeah? Then you can help me now. Stand still a moment." Cally snipped at the feather dangling from Liam's long hair with the scissors.

"Stop it."

"Franky gave you that feather, so if you're my friend like you say you are, you're gonna have to prove it."

Liam batted her hand away. "Screw off, Cally. I mean it."

"You think I don't? Stand still, or else."

"Or else what?"

Cally lunged with the scissors. "Or else I'll have no one left to fucking trust."

That day Liam came home to find Starlene and Benjamin huddled together on the living room sofa. One sobbed, the other sat speechless. A woman police officer with mud on her trousers stood nearby. When Liam tried to enter the room, her male partner blocked his entrance into the room with his arm.

"Give us a minute," he said.

"I'm sorry," the female officer was saying to Franky's parents. "Both of the girls involved in the accident were yours."

"What accident?" Liam whispered, but everyone ignored him.

"Are," Benjamin said. "They *are* our girls. Good girls too." He clutched his wife's hand. "Real smart kids." Spasms jerked Starlene's mouth as she nodded agreement.

The officers exchanged glances. "The driver of the Oldsmobile was drunk," the female officer continued. "When his car hit the sidewalk where your daughters were walking, it was going ninety miles per hour. The girls' injuries were ..."

"Serious?" Starlene pled. "Say serious."

The male officer let down his guard, but Liam no longer wanted to get past him to the Johns. Instead, he went into the kitchen and found Benjamin's bottle of Pepto-Bismol. Although he drank half of the contents, the pink fluid didn't ease the burning he felt in his stomach.

He looked at the family photographs on the walls, some of which included him. The spice-bottle pattern of the wallpaper no longer seemed cheery. He touched the new stove, replaced by insurance after he'd started a cooking fire, and wished the Johns had used that opportunity to make him leave. Then he wouldn't be here now, listening to the wailing coming from the living room. Liam knew his time in the house was done. He could not live there without Franky.

He removed the denuded feather from his hair. Just as he had feared, the warmth was gone.

On the morning of the girls' funerals, Liam saw a doctor who confirmed a bleeding stomach ulcer. Done with the foster care system and with school, he borrowed a truck to move his bed, clothes, and medications into the one-bedroom basement suite Cally's mother paid for in exchange for her silence.

After settling in, he boiled pasta for a Kraft-Dinner-and-beer lunch. He noticed pale mushrooms sprouting on the apartment's baseboards. The mushrooms' conical heads grew damp with the steam from the unventilated cooking. He considered adding a few to the noodles for flavor.

"So, Liam…" Cally dished herself a bowl of pasta, added ketchup and sat on the futon to eat. "Does shacking up mean that you dig me as more than a friend?" A cheesy noodle slipped from her fork. It plopped onto the off-white futon.

Liam squatted with his back to her. He scraped a mushroom from a baseboard with a sharp knife. "I guess." With the same knife, he worried a scar on his arm until a bead of blood popped up.

"About effing time."

When winter arched into spring and the snow at the higher elevations began to melt, Liam and Cally went with a group of friends to race around the backcountry on off-road motorcycles. Late in the day, the group roared to a stop beside a river.

Disturbed by the noise, a juvenile bald eagle lifted off from the top of a tree. Beneath the tree, Liam found the bloodied remains of a rabbit mingled with bird droppings and feathers from a molt. He secured a feather, stiff with dried rabbit's blood, and attached it with the rubber band holding his braided hair.

The group gathered to listen to Cally regale them with a story of the time the effing pigs searched her buddy Patty's effing Mazda and missed the effing bag of weed stuffed under the effing seat. Liam had heard all of her stories before, so he set down his can of beer and left.

Spring runoff swelled the river. Using ferns and exposed roots as handholds, he scrambled over fallen logs and along clay banks. After traveling upstream for an hour, he found a flat spot to rest. In his backpack, under a sweatshirt, lay the book on Aboriginal food plants. He touched the book with the tip of his feather.

In that instant he spied moss-covered steps that led up an incline on the opposite bank. He crossed the river on stepping stones, ducking under a canopy of black cottonwood branches before following a trampled path. A blue tarp was suspended between four Sitka spruces by nylon ropes. Beneath the tarp, more stone steps led down a hill. The space at the bottom was flat and clear of growth. A trestle table held the remains of a meal: an empty barbecue-sauce bottle, plastic bowls, a fork, a knife.

Under a second, smaller, tarp, Liam found a stash of dry wood and a jar of matches. Beside the woodpile someone had ringed a pit with rocks. Using a match and an index page from his book, he started a fire. As he stood with his back to the heat, his eyes began to make out objects in the chaos. A curved loveseat, hewn from a fallen log, waited near the firepit. In front of the loveseat sat a stump ottoman and a plastic basin.

The love seat did not surprise Liam. His father had carved something similar once at Rae's request. The three of them had lived in the woods for one happy summer, before Rae cared more for strange men than for her family, before his father let his rage loose on an innocent bystander, before Liam began to blame himself for everything bad.

It took what was left of the day for him to tidy up the site. He swept off a padded mat intended for use beneath a tent and then built a bed of moss and cedar bows. Beside his moss pillow, he propped up Franky's photograph.

When the first stars appeared, he filled the basin at the creek and returned to the fire. An owl hooted. A stand of trillium glowed white in the darkening forest. He rested on the loveseat to watch the fire. A deeper memory surfaced — that of feeling innocent, vulnerable, and safe while nestled on a parent's lap.

Night advanced. He held his book in the firelight and read that wild ginger root, when made into tea by the Nuxalk, was used to treat stomach pain, and that Indian hellebore was a remedy for madness.

He doused the remains of the fire and then got into bed beside Franky. She smiled into his eyes and whispered until he agreed. Tomorrow, at first light, they would search. They would search until they found these cures.

"I don't feel crazy here," Liam said.

"Because you aren't," Franky whispered.

In the morning, a wet object rooting around in his ear disturbed Liam's sleep.

"I told everyone that I knew where you went, so they left," Cally said. She wiped her finger on the front of her dirty T-shirt. "Can you believe the assholes pretended to believe me? What if I hadn't seen those effing steps? I almost didn't find you."

Beyond Cally's head, deep-green firs framed a shock of vivid sky. Liam shifted into a sitting position. He'd fanned branches over his chest and shoulders to ward off the chill that lingered in the shadows. His neck ached and a purple bruise spread over the back of his hand, although he could not recall receiving an injury. Yesterday's sun had browned the rest of his skin.

Cally picked up a charred stick. She hurled it like a javelin into the forest, causing a bird to explode from the underbrush. She eyed Franky's photograph. "You're still pining after that Indian chick? She's kaput. Worm food. No way she's ever coming back."

"I guess."

Cally grunted. She sat on the loveseat, let her muscles slacken. "It's the shits, babe," she murmured, "but I'm all you've got left." The sun baked a rivulet of blood that flowed from a scratch on Cally's cheek. Liam realized, in all the years he'd known her, she'd never been unhurt.

When he joined her on the loveseat, Cally rested her head on his shoulder. "I was up all night, and I'm effing bagged," she said. "You'll have to carry me back."

Liam spread the fingers of his injured hand in a pool of light.

Already the day was hot, a false summer. "We could stay here," he said.

"For the day?"

"Way longer."

"What about the bike?"

"It can rot."

Cally squinted up at Liam. "I don't want to stay here with Franky. Competing with dead perfection's wearing me out."

A bald eagle caught a current and spiraled up past the smoky blue of a distant high bluff.

"She's gone," Liam said.

Looking into the sky, Liam saw a future, one without the burden of a past. If he tried, he could be like Franky, someone who healed damage in others, instead of like Rae, someone who caused it. And not just like Franky — like Cally too. All she had ever done was wait and hope.

"What your mother and those men did to you," he said. "It wasn't your fault, Caitlin."

"Don't call me that. You know what it means."

Liam looked into his best friend's eyes. "Pure," he said. "We are."

"STOP! DESIST! Put every ice chunk back right now," I wanted to yell when Larry Goodyle punched a hole through the last of the snow that blocked my way onto the Top of the World Highway. He parked his loader fly-like on the edge of the cliff to let me pass by. I clapped to feign enthusiasm while he grinned and patted himself on the back. The winter exile of Dawson, Yukon, from Chicken, Alaska, had unofficially ended. Impatient to go home, Larry waved me on as though I was a normal person, one who could manage the trip I had begged him to let me take — as though I wasn't my mother's daughter.

As I navigated the first few hairpin turns, trees hemmed me in and made me feel secure. The wide road meant I could hug the cliffside and have space between me and the drop-off. With all of the extra weight in the back, the truck handled well. I merely had to stay in the present and wipe away the tears whenever they clouded my vision. Considering the circumstances, it was not so much to ask.

*

The previous week my father had died of an aneurysm while lecturing on environmentalism to high school students in Tok, Alaska. Before that he had lived a life of uninterrupted bravura. According to witnesses, he clung to the lectern as though it was the face of a mountain. His last words, delivered to a hushed audience in a voice that boomed before it broke, were, "If the world was flat, I wouldn't give a damn."

Everyone thought my father died lamenting unconquered mountains, but I knew the truth. Those words were a cry of despair that referred to my crippling fear of life. Even in the moment just before death, my cowardice plagued him. He had tried with me often over the years, tried and failed — though he never tried as hard or failed as spectacularly as he did the summer I turned thirteen.

Our family celebrated this particular milestone with a coming-of-age adventure, which meant one month of one-on-one time with our world-famous mountain-climbing father. His only stipulations were that the trip had to include height, deprivation, and isolation. Rented condos in Hawaii and jaunts to Disneyland were out. My siblings Theodore, Carly, and Simone had chosen Switzerland's Haute Route, the Italian Monte Rosa, and the Corcovado National Park respectively. All three returned addicted to height and glory. All three made my father proud.

When, eight years after third-born Simone's turn, mine came, I deferred the choice to my father. The research required meant a trip to the main library downtown. I couldn't take the elevator to the third floor where the travel books were housed because the motion made me carsick, and had to pretend my dad was right when he said my desire to tackle the three flights of stairs meant I was a natural-born mountain climber. If that wasn't bad enough, just looking at photographs of things with names like *precipice* or *gorge* made me feel like I might fall.

To my relief, he settled on an easy section of the Pacific Crest Trail. In the pre-trip week that he was home, he pored over the map books and beguiled me with descriptions of switchbacks and avalanche-swept valleys. Purchases of green and purple gear were made for me. Daily, he coaxed me to circle the neighborhood with a weighted pack on my back and my new boots on my feet.

"The world is your oyster, Judith." My father would strap me in and herd me out the door. "Go shuck it."

"Let's take a road trip instead," I suggested once. "We could eat junk food and camp like Angela did with her parents last summer."

"And skip a Fellman tradition?"

"It's not like hiking is sacred or something."

His silence confirmed my suspicion. The thirteenth summer held the status of a holy holiday on the Fellman calendar, just like a cathedral grove of giant redwoods invited worship.

I thought I had won my freedom when I handed my father my report card. I had failed three classes.

"This must have taken some doing," he said.

"I have to go to summer school. I can't go hiking."

"Failure," he said, "will make you wiser."

About that, he was wrong.

We were three days, not a month, on the Pacific Crest Trail.

On the morning of the third day, we arrived at Hopkin's Lake, glittering in the bowl of a natural amphitheater coated in ice. The melting glacier fed a placid blue-green pool that in turn fed a lively stream from which we greedily drank. A fallen log, black with age, lurked dragon-like in the water near the shore, while russet peaks loomed above the dense forest.

"Don't tell me this wasn't worth it," my father said.

The view was worth every cramp and blister I had suffered getting there. My legs, once soft and weak, felt hard and Fellman strong. I had developed a system for swinging the cumbersome pack onto my back, and had almost grown to enjoy its weight. I could see myself making an adventurous foursome with my siblings instead of always being the lone one out.

"Judith. Look!" My father pointed his walking stick at a doe peeking out from behind an alder. "Watch this." Breaking his own rule about not feeding wild animals, he gathered a handful of tender bitterbrush and held it out. The doe inched forward with her hind end up and her front legs splayed out on the ground. She tested the bitterbrush with her teeth and then, disappointed, backed away to hide herself sideways behind a skinny pine.

Our laughter chased the doe away.

As we unpacked a lunch of apples and granola bars, a yellow butterfly landed on my white T-shirt. It probed the fabric's loose weave, looking for something sweet and finding my salty skin. I stood still, justifying the creature's trust until it resumed its haphazard flight.

"Happy?" my father asked.

I nodded. I had never been happier.

"Good," he said. "I want you to see it all. Everything this earth has to offer."

I looked at the series of switchbacks called the Devil's Staircase that ran up the northern side of the amphitheater. From where I stood on level ground, the route we were to take after lunch didn't seem to rise too high. For the first time, I wanted everything my father wanted. For the first time, I ached to see it all.

"Me too," I said.

We ascended with our stomachs full, and my father in the lead. I stopped often to shoot close-ups of thistles and beargrass with my coming-of-age present, a used Pentax camera. My calf muscles burned as I climbed the steep grade, but the warmth of the day, and the thick vegetation on either side of me, lulled any fears.

The world fell quiet as we neared the top, above the treeline. The only sounds were the thump of our boots on the trail and the moaning of the wind. Our view was unimpeded as my father pointed south and then northwest while shouting, "Three Fools Peak" and "The Cascades." On the crest, monstrous clouds drifting overhead shadowed tiny earth-hugging plants. As far as I could see, mountains stretched out in frozen, timeless ripples.

"Keep up," my father said. He strode on ahead, eager to see the next vista.

I stopped to shoot the shaggy head of a pink thistle that caught my eye. A yellow butterfly, maybe the same one that had tasted my skin earlier, landed on the flower. It probed the petals for a moment, then simply rested with its top-heavy body balanced on thread-thin legs.

By the time I had shot half a roll of film and looked up, my father had passed beyond sight. I called his name, but the wind that had risen whipped the word back into my mouth. I ran to catch up, letting my camera bang painfully against my new breasts in my hurry. "Dad," I called again. "Wait."

The safe, forgiving trail morphed into something threatening on the far side of an outcropping of rocks. Instead of cutting a swath through a wide expanse, it narrowed, then led across a naked slope that ended in a jumble of boulders far below.

I slowed to a crawl, but kept moving forward even when the trail shrank beneath my feet into a thin ribbon of dust. I was halfway across the section when I felt my feet slide towards the edge. My toes curled inside my boots in an effort to stay put. The world blurred, then darkened on the edges. Terror squeezed the air out of my lungs. With nowhere safe to go, I threw myself face down on the trail. Even prone, my body felt unmoored.

I moaned in terror, certain the ledge I was on would crumble away. Someone who didn't sound like me screamed.

Ages passed before I heard the clatter of my father's pack, centuries before he knelt over me. "Judith! What happened?"

"You left me," I wailed.

He tried to help me to my feet, but I resisted. "Are you hurt?"

I butted his legs with my head, almost knocking him off balance. In that moment, if he'd fallen to his death, I wouldn't have cared. "I almost fell and you weren't there."

We returned to camp under heavy cloud that arrived from nowhere to sock us in. Soon, drizzle wet my face. Under the cover of trees, my father built a fire. The doe came around, but we ignored her. I poked and probed the heart out of the fire with a stick.

"Are you okay now?" my father finally dared to ask.

"How can I ever be?" I said. "I'm a chicken. I shouldn't even be a Fellman. If I'm adopted, send me back. Get a sports model instead."

My father took my cold hands in his and rubbed them. "It's not you," he said, "I was around more with the others. I started them younger. Tomorrow we can try again."

I shuddered, from fear as much as from cold. "I'll never go back up there."

"If we quit now, it will be even harder for you next time."

"Oh, no! There isn't going to be a next time."

"I won't give up on you, Judith."

I removed my hands from his and then hugged myself. "Well, you should. I don't want to be like you," I said. And then I added the clincher, "I want to be like Mom."

When my brother phoned to inform me that he and my sisters planned to bury my father in Tok the following day, it was the first I'd heard of his death. Though I'd lived in Dawson for a decade, it had taken Theodore three days to track me down, proof that he'd never tried before. When he apologized for the short notice, I pretended to be devastated.

"The only way I can make it to Tok on time is if I take the Top of the World Highway," I moaned. Then I used my Get out of Jail Free card. "Unfortunately, the road's still closed for the season."

After hanging up on my siblings, I went to Larry Goodyle's house to break the news. The loader operator, who had climbed Mount Logan with my father in '69, was one of his most ardent fans.

"To a great mountaineer and a fine friend" Larry said as our impromptu wake got under way. He clicked my glass of rum with his over the burl table in his kitchen.

"May the old fart rest in peace," I said.

"Your father loved you, Judith. Don't you ever forget it." Larry drained his glass to hide the doubt in his eyes.

"I know he tried," I said. "But it made it hard that I'm the one most like my mother." Larry looked me over. Before her death from a tan-induced melanoma, Mom possessed a doe-like grace. With my small eyes, big nose and recessed chin, the animal I most resemble is a hamster. "Hard to like," I clarified.

Larry's bearded face wagged agreement. My mother deserted my father soon after I was born, not for another man or a burning dream, but simply to be away from his relentless idealism. She wanted to watch soap operas in peace and bleach her hair without a fight. "Kenyon had the devil's own time with the two of you," he said.

"My father wasn't always right."

"He was about as right as a man can hope to get in one lifetime." Larry stood and took my empty glass to the sink, signaling the end of his patience with me. "Your father was one of the great ones, Judith. He grabbed life by the balls and never let go. I knew it. The world knew it. Your mother, bless her soul, didn't have a fucking clue."

"He had some fine moments," I agreed. "Just none of them included me."

"Whose choice was that?"

If I was from another culture, say Japanese or Inuit, the community would probably believe I got what I deserved — an ugly lover, an even uglier home, and social isolation. I had, after all, disrespected my elder. I had moved to the Yukon, not out of a sense of adventure, but because I thought it would be the last place my father would search for me.

When Larry introduced himself a month after I arrived in town, I'd threatened to commit suicide if he ever tipped my father off. If the threat was hollow, neither of us knew for sure.

"He'd have found me if he'd tried," I said.

"I told Kenyon you were in Dawson years ago," Larry said. "He was giving you time."

"To do what? Bottom out?"

"To find it in your heart to forgive him."

"For what exactly?"

"For trying to make you exceed your reach."

I couldn't let myself cry in front of Larry, so I hid my face in the bowl made by my arms on the table. "I need to get to Tok," I whispered. "Can you open the road?"

"I'll open it, but I can't take you. My kid's coming to town tomorrow. I haven't seen Nora for months."

I used Larry's phone to call Stephen my lover. I could hear him yawn while I told him about my father's death and asked him to drive me to Tok in the morning.

"I've got plans," was all he said.

After I hung up the phone, I told Larry I would drive myself.

"Well, there's one for the record books," he said by way of a response. I noticed his eyes were wet. "Judith Fellman drives the Top of the World Highway all by her lonesome. My word! Kenyon would be proud of you, girlie."

"There's a first time for everything," I said.

"Are you certain, kid? Top of the World's treacherous this time of year." In his blue-gray eyes, I saw miles of empty space and the spin of tires. "It's got to be unflagging." He tapped his head.

"I'm not a Fellman for nothing," I said.

I arrived back home to find things still as I had left them: dirty dishes soaking in a sink full of greasy water, empty cat's dish, missing cat. I stood in the doorway of the bedroom to watch Stephen sleep. His long-fingered hand supported his face. Red blemishes the size of loonies marred the skin beneath black bristles. His legs and arms claimed both sides of the bed.

I went into the living room and made a nest of coats on the sofa.

The alarm raised hell at five a.m., an hour I rarely witnessed. I abandoned my makeshift bed, brushed my teeth and then left a note for the cat in case it returned. I packed a lunch and a Thermos of coffee. On my way out, I slammed the door twice.

The day would warm later, but early morning felt brittle. Larry had been by while I slept and had loaded the bed of Stephen's truck with sandbags. I sprayed the lock to thaw it and then climbed into the musty cab. During the five minutes it took for the thermometer to reach the lowest reading of warm, I whacked at some other woman's garter that hung from the rear-view mirror. When we met, Stephen had made it clear that all such mementoes of his prowess were sacrosanct.

I spit on the garter and then drove down Front Street, turning north over the frozen Yukon River.

I inched the truck past Larry in his loader, and continued north on the Top of the World Highway past the snow-covered campground and golf course. Switchbacks led me higher, and soon naked precipices replaced the comfort of trees. I slowed the truck, but didn't stop. In the deep slush, starting again would have proven difficult. With each mile my breath grew more ragged. I tried to regulate it as I fought off the wet blanket of panic that smothered me. It's okay, Judith," I said. "It's okay. Breathe in. It's okay. Breathe out." Sweat from my palms slicked the steering wheel. I knew that any moment my hands would slip and I would hurtle over the edge of the cliff down, down, down, to a swift and gory death. I checked my watch. Any second, my nerve would surely fail.

I'd traveled twenty-eight miles according to the odometer when I reached the reprieve of a rest area overlooking yet another scenic viewpoint. I parked as far from the edge of the road as I could. With stiff limbs, I made a sandbag sofa in the box of the truck. Peace snuck in as I sipped hot coffee and devoured a baloney sandwich. Mountains stretched out in frozen, timeless ripples, just as another, more southerly range had so many years before. The place seemed hallowed, and I felt the allure of my family's religion. I verged on belief until I remembered that I was alone on the top of the world.

Still, I was a third of the way there, and I hadn't driven off a cliff. I felt sudden strength. Somehow, I knew that I would make it. I got back in the cab, stepped on the gas, prepared to continue. My tires dug into the mud. I got out of the truck and found the boards and shovel that Larry had provided along with the sandbags. If he'd have me, I decided, I'd dump Stephen and marry the man out of gratitude.

As I dug a trench in the slush at the base of a tire, I imagined my siblings' reactions when I told them what I had done to get to Tok. They would pat me on my back and ask me all about it. "Any close calls? Were you frightened? Good Heavens, Judith! Whatever possessed you?"

"A few," I'd say. "No big deal. Nothing possessed me, I just came."

"Dad would be so proud of you," one of my sisters would gush. My sage brother Theodore would nod. Tears would flow.

They would signal looks of agreement before asking, "Are you free next summer, kid? Come raft the Amazon with us. We talked of climbing Mount Logan as a kind of memorial to the old guy. You up to that?"

My truck still wouldn't budge, so I climbed back out. The rotten boards were broken under my tires: Damn that cheapskate Larry. Tomorrow they would bury my father. My siblings and their families were gathered already, heroic in their mourning. A banner probably read, *Tok Welcomes the United Fellmans of the World.*

My back tires had dug two holes to China.

As I shoveled muck and slush, a mound formed behind me. I resisted the urge to spread it flat. The upheaval of the earth, a mountain in miniature, would remain when I was gone. It would remain when I was living large — on my own terms.

To celebrate the dawn of my nineteenth birthday, I, Cindy Delores Gourlie, balanced on a girder and considered the fine line between extreme sport and acts of desperation. As an ex-champion diver, I had superior kinesthetic awareness and planned to execute a reverse pike from Lanten, Saskatchewan's yellow water tower into the twenty inches of water that had fallen since the previous day — that is until Gwendolyn Morelos pulled up in her custom painted '59 Pontiac Bonneville that she called the Pickle Car.

She stepped out into the dwindling rain, then peered up at me. "Showtime?" she shouted.

I felt the tower's happy-face totem smirk behind my back, as though it knew I lacked the guts to follow through on the promissory note I'd left taped to the door of Gwen's mother's house.

"Don't believe everything you read," I shouted back. "I'm actually only up here to enjoy the view." To make the claim true, I gazed at the valley with its sputtering lights and Holstein-deep flood waters. My parents were out there, drinking double martinis while they zipped the family jewels and insurance policies into waterproof Baggies. As the mayor, my father was paid to pretend concern for Lanten, but I wondered if he'd thought to worry yet about his only child's welfare.

"You can't live for enjoyment, Cindy Gourlie," Gwen said. "Come on down."

"Come on down" is what my fiancé said when I demanded proof that the stripper he'd fallen for at Dolls 'N More was better-looking and a thousand times nicer than me. It's also what my father called to my mother so she could witness the moment he disowned me for becoming an embarrassment to the Gourlie name.

"If that advice is wrong for others," I shouted, "what makes it right for me?"

Gwen repositioned the ladder that I had used to reach the bottom girder. "Come down and I'll let you ride in my car."

"I already have," I confessed.

Once, in my old life as Lanten's Queen Bitch and with my old clique, I'd gone on a joyride in Gwen's newly purchased car. Our theft was motivated by the dashboard shrine that she'd created using a jaw spreader, multiple hospital bracelets and the epithet *Cleft and Proud of It*. Before ditching the vehicle in a farmer's field, one friend scorched the epithet with a lighter, another poured beer on the hospital bracelets, and I nicked a photograph of Gwen posed dressed for First Holy Communion. In it, she looked euphoric in a white gown embroidered with a picture of the Virgin Mary, but I knew better. My mother had hosted an after-party complete with a piñata and Boffo the clown for seventeen of the eighteen communicants. At my insistence, Gwen was the lone Bride of Christ out.

Now, in the growing light, Gwen looked gorgeous. Her black hair shone and her dark eyes gleamed. Thanks to surgery and orthodontics, parts of her mouth were perfect, and I wondered why it had taken me so long to notice her beauty.

I squirreled down the girders and perched at the top of the ladder. "Want to know what your mother says about me?" Gwen's mother was Holy Cross High's counselor for students A through G.

"Not particularly."

"She says I resemble lungwort. It's a plant with pretty blue flowers, like my eyes." Then I described the rest of the correlation her mother thought she saw: prickly leaves and a root system that strangled everything in its path.

"My mother's a lousy gardener," Gwen said. "What would she know?"

A narrow gap opened in the clouds far away on the horizon. Instead of touching farmland and a snaking river, the rays of light sparkled on a transient sea. Closer yet, people canoed down the streets of a residential district. The houses, built after World War II, were just big enough to fit an amputee and his wife. Now, retired dairy farmers, redundant fishermen, and ex-owners of independent bookstores inhabited them. These people favored windsocks in primary colors and drove electric scooters with bumper stickers that said things like *My Other Car is a Ferrari*. Despite their low elevation, none of the houses, including that of Gwen's mother, were protected by sandbags.

"My father commandeered a generator and two pumps for his rancher in Eagle Ridge Estates," I said. "He knows there isn't a chance in hell he'll need them."

"And you're telling me all this why?"

"I don't know. Penance, maybe."

Gwen walked back to her car. She scooped up a pickle jar full of aquarium figurines from the passenger seat, and fished out two. She climbed the ladder, then handed me a knife-wielding diver embroiled in a death roll with a thrashing shark, keeping a chubby hula dancer for herself.

"Thanks," I made the shark say.

"Feeling better?" Gwen said.

Because "yes" was the expected answer, I made the shark say this too.

"Good enough to steal some sandbags?"

"I think so."

Like Utah's Bingham Canyon Mine, Gwen's grin could have been seen from space. A fresh onslaught of rain hissed on the water. The rain played castanets with the Pickle Car's wiper blades. Gwen raised her face and then stuck out her tongue to wet it. "A toast to the good old times," she said.

I was thirsty, confused and a little hypothermic. The world tipped precariously beneath the ladder. "The old times weren't so good," I said. "Not nearly as good as I remember."

Gwen made the hula girl dive into a newly formed stream. "Be free, Cindy Gourlie," she said.

As though granting sinners absolution came easy.

ONE AM. TOO LATE FOR COFFEE, yet my mother's long coral nails tapped as she sipped a cup of sugared instant coffee to the music of Dolly Parton. Her body vibrated with guitar twang and dehydration. Footsteps in the hallway sent a violent message; Vance, my mother's lover, hated that I was there.

The lights flickered off, then on. The toilet flushed, gurgled, flushed again. "Bet that's a load off his mind," I said. My mother's face remained a practiced blank. She had lost boyfriends because of me.

I was trapped in her kitchen. Trapped by rain — I had arrived on foot without coat or umbrella, or even my purse — and by a return of childhood inertia. I needed someone to jerk my strings and make me move, but the puppet-master, my father, was six feet under on the outskirts of town. Because of my father, my mother had never developed the knack.

"Spill," she said.

Five blocks away, my husband and the only bean I had to spill slept, unaware that one-third of them was missing. She would wake soon, my two-year-old daughter. Gloria never slept long.

The day before, at the end of the world, Andy and I had been informed that sleep disturbance was part and parcel of her condition — also absence of speech, facial abnormalities, jerky gait, protruding tongue (not yet, but one day), a fascination with plastic and water, hand-flapping, frequent laughter, a permanent smile. We had mortgaged a new house in a single-family neighborhood with good schools for a child whom Harry Angelman, the discoverer of her syndrome, would have called a Happy Puppet Child.

"We met with a geneticist," I said as I shifted the green lace tablecloth toward my lap. I squeezed the fabric's nub between my wooden fingers as I recalled the guarded look on the female specialist's pixie face. Maybe some parents responded to bad news about their children with violent outbursts, but not Andy and I. We'd fallen mute, and the doctor had to suggest questions we should want to ask her. Our inability to vocalize lasted for the long drive home and all through the salmon dinner neither one of us could choke down. When it broke, our silence was replaced with inarticulate sounds uttered in separate rooms.

"It's not good," I said.

My mother, ever patient, waited.

"He said Glory might never potty train and she won't ever talk. Sound familiar?"

"Well, good," my mother said. "I suspected Angelman's. Now you can help that little darling instead of pretending everything is hunky-dory. Now you can figure out the upside."

"Pardon?"

"When your father passed, you said it was a relief we were finally out of his misery. That was the upside."

"That was the only side, Ma. I remember cousin Gerald. This isn't like Dad dying."

Vance shuffled into view. His housecoated barrel of a body blocked the only exit from the kitchen. "The offer stands," he said. Earlier on, when he'd arrived at my mother's door a moment after me, he'd volunteered to rearrange my face because I'd tried to lock him out.

"My price has risen," I said. "Two hundred bucks up front and now you have to wear a rubber."

"To the moon, Alice." When Vance jostled my shoulder, his housecoat flapped open. Unwashed trucker scented the air. He opened the refrigerator, rooted around, and came up empty.

I glugged down the last quarter of the last can of Labatt's. "Ah!" I said. "That hits the spot." When I slammed down the can, it made a wet ring on my mother's green tablecloth.

"You little shit. That's my beer."

"She's upset, honey," my mother said.

"Well, boo hoo. It's always something with Alice, ain't it?"

"It's news about the tyke," my mother said.

"What's wrong with my girl?"

Gloria was not the foul man's girl. My taunting grew barbs. "Go back to bed — Tony." Tony, my mother's other lover, didn't drive long-distance.

My mother patted Vance's butt, drew him close, and whispered something into his cauliflower ear. With a final glare for me, he trotted off like a frisky spring lamb.

She struggled to her feet. "One day, Alice," she said, "you're going to see me lonely." She made her way to the stove where a lemon-shaped timer sat. She wound it, returned, and placed the timer on the table between us. I had two minutes to unload my grief. She tipped a Virginia Slim out of its package. Her thin lips wrinkled as they held the filter.

"Okay. You want to know the upside? Easy. They can do anti-drool surgery on Glory when she's older."

"I didn't raise you to be snide."

I took in the bottle depot of a kitchen — empty beer cases stacked high, rinsed shot glasses upside down on the green rubber mat by the sink — and wondered what she did raise me to be. Last year's calendar still hung on the wall. *Dance at the Legion* and *Art's funeral* were marked in red. Debauch and death were my mother's red-letter days.

"Then how about this; she won't need much to be happy. I mean, if happiness is one of the symptoms, it figures." The timer's shrill made me jump. "Right?"

She exhaled a thin stream of smoke. "Glory's got one up on the rest of us then."

"I guess she does."

My mother tamped out her cigarette. She stood and then glided past me, smelling of carcinogens and rose perfume. The familiar combination provided strange comfort. Her hand swept my head, sparked me to life. She had the knack after all, only her knack didn't hurt. Tears of self-pity formed in my eyes. "I just wanted her to be normal, Ma."

"Bulltwity. You and Andy never wanted that."

Andy and Alice, the perfect yuppie couple, needed a perfect child to maintain what now seemed like an illusion. After five years of amicable marriage, and merely because of one flawed chromosome in our daughter, we could barely stand the sight of each other. She was right, but still, I was stunned that the woman who had refused to acknowledge the gaping crevasse in her own marriage had pointed out the chink in ours.

My mother said goodnight before disappearing into the cavern of her bedroom. Vance's baritone rumbled. Bedsprings gave way. My mother laughed.

I parted the curtains to press my face against the cold. The rain had stopped. I wound the lemon timer for three minutes, set down it outside the bedroom door, and then let myself out of the house.

At night our old neighborhood looked unchanged from the time of my childhood. One working-class family per bungalow, painted porches, hardy rose shrubs, nothing extravagant. Daylight revealed gardens gone to weed, porches that hoarded litter, and too many cars in front of each house. My father, who raged over everything, had raged to excess when I left home to marry even-tempered, diplomatic Andy. To his mind I had sold out my working-class roots for a flimsy college boy who would crumple under the pressures of life.

I jogged the five blocks to our new and exclusive neighborhood. There the houses were tall replication Victorians. Front porches sported hanging moss baskets filled with designer annuals and swings that might never be used. Small yards shared a thin strip of green space. To make room for this, a developer disbanded a court of mobile home-dwelling retirees, many of whom were my parents' friends. The developer paid residents to disperse without a fight, and most embraced the windfall. The few who went public said they feared the loneliness of dislocation. Their story didn't make the front page.

On our street, I walked past three *For Sale* signs. Despite our postcard-pretty setting, unrest ran like sewage. Transfers, bankruptcy, and divorce: these things took their toll. Even so our neighbors slept with confidence inside their heavily mortgaged homes, knowing that their children would read before kindergarten, be icons of socially conscious fashion, win athletic awards, earn honors, be beautiful or handsome or both. When grown, they would graduate with multiple degrees and then move to the United States because the wages are higher. They would marry well and buy nicer homes than these. They would make their parents proud.

They would avoid our daughter like the plague.

The sting would be ours, not Gloria's. Like my cousin, she would laugh and grin and be a whirlwind of misdirected activity. She would flap her hands for fun and offer stiff hugs and wet kisses to whoever would receive them. She would still swim with a life jacket in her twenties. She would never marry, never give us grandchildren.

But, if we let her, she would be happy.

Inappropriate joy scudded through me like the clouds beneath the smiling face of the moon. A breeze scoured the already spotless street. It felt fresh and good. I hurried, eager to be home before the clouds regrouped.

In our house, lights were on, lights and Leonard Cohen's doleful music. I opened the door on a disgruntled husband and a Happy Puppet Child. Andy swiped at a puddle of Gloria's drool that marred the perfection of his silk pajamas. "It's past one, Alice. Some people might live lives of leisure, but I have to get up for work in the morning. Where the hell were you?"

His relief as he relinquished our daughter into my arms seemed to betray the false bottom of his anger. He knew that I, as a carrier, had passed on a flawed chromosome 15 and was almost certainly responsible for Gloria's uniqueness. We'd discussed the slight possi-bility when we were trying to conceive. He'd promised his love for me and any children we might have would be unwavering, but what if the reality of Angelman's was more than he could bear? What if Andy wanted to leave us and try again with someone better? When I read his downcast eyes and rigid mouth, I saw a hint that his future plans might include such consolation.

I carried Glory into the formal living room. "I went home," I said.

He slapped an ivory wall, maybe to avoid slapping me. "Your mother's hell-hole isn't a *home* — this is."

Gloria let her soft, pliant body meld into mine just as easily as Andy's had on the day of her conception. I snuffled the vanil-la-scented curl held up by a yellow ribbon at the top of her head, and imagined a world of perpetual innocence. It seemed, in that moment, a wonderful thing that she would never feel a need to es-cape our bond.

Her baby cheek pressed against me dampened the front of my Irish linen blouse as I bent with her to start a new CD, one of my own, Handel's Royal Fireworks. "I thought so," I whispered. My gaze sought the safety of Gloria's face.

When I looked up. Andy's fingers run through his hair left it sticking up on end. His shoulders slumped as his anger drained out. "You're not the only one who's suffering. She's my child too."

I twirled around the living room to trigger a bout of our tiny daughter's bubbly, infectious laugher. The horn section signaled the triumphal entry. I helped Gloria hold out both sticky hands for Andy to catch up with and take or not, as he wished.

And while he stood in the doorway trying to make up his mind, we danced without strings.

It's 1:25 P.M. ON A Thursday, but Cricket's not dozing through metalwork class. Instead, she's upstairs in her bedroom sniffing a bottle of Ben Nye's liquid latex. The ammonia preservative gives her a heady sensation. As does the act of digging scar wax from a jar, giving the glob shape, then trying out the effect on her lower lip. For $112, charged to her father's Visa Gold, she also has wrinkle stipple, fresh scab, and castor sealer. She doesn't feel bad that she used her dad's card to buy the theatrical makeup without permission — whatever else they are, the Fairchild family is not poor.

Alexis, Pamela, and Sandra will be pleased by the purchases, but Cricket doubts her friends share her perspective — that their Friday night makeovers are necessary for survival. The other girls are one year older, but they're nowhere near as smart or as desperate.

"You're the most seriously warped chick I've ever met," Alexis once said, and the others agreed. It's true, Cricket's twisted, thanks in part to genetics. She's being raised by a father, after all, who, for Saturday morning breakfast, serves cream of wheat topped with undercooked eggs — which she claims to like because she loves him — then runs through his repertoire of leper jokes until someone gags or at least pretends to.

"What do you call a leper in a hot tub?"

"Relaxed," Cricket says, swallowing hard. She hates her sensitive stomach at such moments, wishes she didn't spend so much of her free time googling leprosy.

"Wrong. Porridge."

She'll tell Alexis how she scammed the money to pay for so much booty, but only because Alexis has her learner's license and a car — a gift from a dotty grandmother who doesn't know about graduated driver's licenses — and a car is just as necessary as liquid latex for what they do.

Because of Alexis's Impala, Cricket's not the alpha of the pack, but she doesn't care. She's something better. She's the catalyst, the one who invented Ugly Cruising in the first place, the one who came up with the kick-ass name. She's also the one who changes the rules each week to keep things fresh. And she's the one who won't let the girls quit, even though she suspects they talk of doing so when she's not around.

It's some statutory holiday, maybe Good Friday, Cricket's not sure. Her mother Wanda, who's already sluiced, interrupts the morning's leper-fest to say to Bing, "Even a blind man can see how thin your jokes have grown." She chooses the perfect moment, if exposing her callous nature is the goal. For the first time in weeks, The Grub has left the sanctuary of his bedroom to join the family at the breakfast table. In the past half year he's lost over thirty pounds, and looks like a hunched anorexic as he peers at Wanda through the 1970s Elton John glasses he insists on wearing to disguise his wide-set eyes.

To Cricket, Wanda's subtle reference to her brother's emaciated state is obvious. And The Grub must get it too, because he picks up an indelible felt-tipped pen lying on the table, cadavers himself over to the fridge, and then makes the first move in what Cricket later thinks of as the Refrigerator Skirmish.

While the three of them watch with reactions that range from alarm to incredulity, he sketches a hiccupping grub hoisting a whisky bottle to its mouth on the white surface. He labels it *bean weevil.*

Cricket admires his devious brilliance — in one simple cartoon character, he rests the blame for his present wasted state on Wanda's drinking problem. As far as caricatures go, however, the bean weevil is an inaccurate portrayal; thanks to Treacher Collins Syndrome, her brother eats and drinks through a hole in his stomach. He has a torso and all the usual appendages — arms, legs, and, she knows from the years when they were bathing buddies, genitals — but what he does lack is a nose and a chin and a voice to confront others with.

"Perhaps," Bing proposes, "the new Maytag's not the, um, *ideal* forum for self-expression."

"He's already defaced everything else," Wanda says. "Why not this too? In fact, I'll help." Pale with rage, she stomps across the kitchen, and then wrestles the pen from The Grub's hand. Beneath the bean weevil, she scrawls *Puberty = Parental Hell.*

Cricket can tell how upset her father is by the way he uses his butter knife to jab the colors of a prism cast onto the table by the morning's sharp light. "Why did the leper crash her car?" he asks under his breath.

She left her foot on the accelerator.

Wanda tosses the marker Cricket's way. "This is a democracy," she says. "Vote."

Cricket thinks for a moment before fetching the family's *Websters Ninth New Collegiate Dictionary* from the living room bookshelf. She spreads it open to the *gall • galore* page.

She copies out a definition in the place where the old fridge had twin dents in the door. Cricket had created both dents with her feet — the first when The Grub came home from his umpteenth stay in SickKids Hospital with rows of jaw-stretching metal bursting through the skin of his face, and the second when he came home from a follow-up visit eight weeks later, with stitches and an unwillingness to thrive.

Gallows humor *n (trans. Of G galenhu-*
mor) (1901): humor that makes fun of
a <u>very serious or terrifying</u> situation.

In case Wanda doesn't get what is very serious and terrifying in their household, she draws an arrow up to the bean weevil.

She pats the top of her father's balding head as she presents him with the pen. "Your turn."

In his small, careful hand, Bing, a lover of puns, writes, *This family is not a mourning person.*

Even though Bing and Wanda previously agreed they would take all of the Friday night Grub-watching shifts, they've left Cricket alone with her brother until his nurse arrives at eleven. His nurse-of-the-moments, or NOTMs, work nights, which is when he eats. Feeding is a slow-drip process that, if he allows it at all, takes seven hours, including a half-hour cigarette break, not that many of the nurses smoke. The rest of the time the family must manage alone.

Before The Grub — or Elvin, as he was named at birth — elected to forgo any more of medical science's heroic attempts to build a mouth and nose where none had originally grown, his room had sported a hackneyed cowboy theme courtesy of Bing. Their father took it as proof of his failure as a parent when, freshly home from the hospital, the still-fit Grub scraped off the Western motif wallpaper border, tore down the faux leather curtains, and tossed the ceramic cactus nightlight into the garbage bin. In the place of these items, The Grub hand-painted a wraparound view of Earth's universe on the walls, floor, and ceiling. The boldest strokes belonged to the sun which loomed on the speckled ceiling, an uncomfortably bright sight with its fiery coronas and solar flares.

"Now *that's* the big picture," Bing tried to joke in a cracking voice when The Grub let the family in to see the finished painting.

"It's a fucking cosmic joke," Elvin signed his admonishment. "Like me."

Cricket leans back in a rocking chair, willing the graphic center of The Grub's universe to overwhelm her senses, as it had at first sight. But nothing drug-like happens, so she gets up, leans over the bar of the hospital-style bed Wanda insisted on renting the week before when Elvin dropped below one hundred pounds, and pinches him awake in a bid to relieve her own boredom. "Grub," she says, "look lively." One of her father's many optimistic, but ultimately useless, phrases.

Elvin whacks her on the side of the head, though without force. When, as youngsters, they roughhoused together, Cricket sometimes worried that she'd knock off an ear or wrest off a few of her brother's fingers. Now she suspects he would like to do worse things to her; maybe lop off her head or leave her without a leg to stand on. She could hug his antagonism, it's so palpable.

Why did the referee stop the leper hockey game? There was a face off in the corner.

"I bet I can guess what you want to do," Cricket says. She presses her fingers against her forehead, pretending to receive his answer telepathically. "It starts with the letter *p*. P-O-R-N." Despite the fact that Elvin isn't illiterate and objects, Cricket has taken to reading aloud from Bing's secret *Hustler* and *Penthouse* stash during her shifts. Her belief that, because he's a male, smut will somehow spark in him the will to live has, so far, gone unproven.

Elvin shifts his gangly, teenage limbs. He lifts a hand and extends his middle finger.

"Okay, I'll read one lurid tale," Cricket says, "but just because you said please."

When she returns to his room with a dog-eared *Hustler*, The Grub has covered himself with a blanket and rolled onto his side, away from her.

She flips through the magazine before choosing one of her favorites, a poorly plotted story involving two males and an accommodating female with great clothes. To spice the reading up, she bleeps out innocent words, but ramps up her delivery of everything explicit.

Afterwards, she leaves Bing's magazine on The Grub's bedside table for Wanda to find.

"What should we do next?" she asks. "I'm open to suggestions."

"Nothing," he moves his hands enough to sign. "Go far away."

"I'd love to, but I can't." Although no one has come right out and said it, Cricket understands that she's on suicide watch.

"Stop nattering," The Grub signs.

"Hey, Wanda," Cricket shouts in retaliation. "Come see what The Grub just grew. I think it's called a woody."

What did the leper say to the whore? Go ahead ma'am. Keep the tip.

"Bitch," he signs. "If you think I don't hate you too, you're fucking wrong."

There are tears in his eyes, the first he's let her see in years. She should remind him Bing's out enabling Wanda, should relieve his mortification with the truth. Instead, she tells him to face the big picture alone. Then she goes downstairs to phone Alexis.

Alexis's Impala heads towards a popular cruise strip on Marine Drive as Cricket transforms her face in the backseat. She does her nose first. After dabbing her skin with spirit gum, she uses a small wooden spatula to layer flesh-colored latex over the bridge and sides of her nose until she achieves a flattened effect. Then she seals off all but a fraction of each nostril.

"I'm Elvina," she says before using more latex to make her mouth vanish. The joke's private — she's never mentioned her brother's legal name to the girls, hasn't even introduced them to him — but Pamela and Sandra laugh anyway.

Pamela, the least imaginative member of the clique, dabs black tooth paint on three of her front teeth. She then uses spirit gum to attach a moustache to her upper lip, just as she has done every Friday for the past two months. She mock-admires the results in the mirror. "Fuck me, I'm sexy," she says, mimicking the much cooler Alexis, who can say lewd things without sounding idiotic.

Sandra, the least confident member, copies Pamela move for move. It's obvious that Ugly Cruising makes Sandra nervous. She's plain enough, with her fat cheeks and small gray eyes, that her efforts with Cricket's theatrical makeup merely augment reality.

Alexis, who borders on gorgeous, wears a rat's ass wig to hide her long blonde hair. Before they left Cricket's driveway, she used Ben Nye's more subtle Nicotine tooth paint to make a disaster of her teeth. She also rendered her skin acne-pitted.

Why did the leper lose the poker game? She threw in her hand.

Like the others, Cricket wears a skimpy bikini top. Her rule for the night is that they all must reveal their assets from the neck down. "Think slut," she'd told the girls on a four-way call. She'd hoped The Grub, alone upstairs with his misery, had heard her raucous laughter.

Cricket finishes applying latex over her mouth just as the Impala joins the queue crawling down Marine Drive. She turns her face away from the bay side, where the tide is out and people look like hard-bodied fleas on the exposed sandbars. She catches the gaze of patrons gobbling deep-fried oysters and hand-cut fries on the crowded restaurant patios. They look, but do not understand the nature of what they see. A hefty woman, ensconced at a margarita-glass-covered table with other hefty women, points out the Impala's occupants with circus-like excitement.

Alexis pops in a CD, Dream Theater's *Six Degrees of Inner Turbulence.*

The girls cruise towards their first prey of the night, two men in an orange Mustang. Both wear wife-beater T-shirts to display their triceps. The passenger sports mirrored shades, even though the evening light is soft, not glaring.

"Hey, baby. Wanna get lucky?" This is Pamela, leaning across Cricket to shout, too stupid to know that the rules have changed yet again, that, tonight, while whorishness is fine, speech is not permitted.

The passenger turns to look and Cricket sees that something's melted the features on the right side of his head. She feels a surge of guilt, as though the fire or chemical or whatever it was that defaced him originated with her.

She discovers she's gawking only when he makes a point of taking off his sunglasses and gazing back. She sits straighter, shimmies her torso, but not even the enticement of her baby cleavage lures his gaze away from what she knows is the hypocrisy of her face.

"Dude." His voice is the soulful woof of a once-beloved dog just as its master shoots it. As the car rolls away, he says it again,

"Dude."

Pamela's laughter is senseless — she gets a joke no one has told — and it stops abruptly when a Slurpee flies through the open rear window. Cherry-flavored slush explodes against Cricket's face and hair. A group of kids from a rival high school howl together on the sidewalk, entertained by one of their number's daring. "Freakoids," another among them shouts.

The traffic snarls. Alexis leans out the window, cursing in French and Spanish at the delivery truck that's blocking the road.

Cricket bends over, dripping Slurpee. But it's the damaged man's voice that makes her hyperventilate through her blocked nostrils, not the cold of the drink. Attempting the impossible, Pamela lays a calming hand on the protruding knobs of Cricket's spine.

The Impala finally moves away from the laughing kids, dislodged from the bottleneck by the force of Alexis's impatience. Still Cricket doesn't raise her head. Instead, she presses her fists hard against her eyes. She doesn't know if she can make her eyeballs explode, but she's willing to try. She presses in, courting blue-rimmed coronas and imploding white light.

The Grub is still curled on his side when Cricket returns home. She crawls over the safety bar of his bed, and then lies spooned against him with the cold metal at her back. Although she cannot smell much through her altered nose, what does reach her is decay and disinfectant.

Don't die, she thinks.

He shifts in the bed to face her, then runs a finger across her latex mouth. "Why did you do that?" he signs.

She returns his touch with one to his stomach. "Why did you?"

"I met someone in hospital," he signs. "A girl. Meagan."

"Where is she now?" Cricket signs back. She already knows the answer.

Elvin makes the same digging motion he has made for other hospital-stay friends over the years.

Cricket wants to kiss his sweat-soaked hair with her spirit-gum-and-latex mouth. "Did you love her?"

"She's the only person I ever have."
What did the leper tell the aide worker? I have no feeling.
"Why did you love her?"
Elvin slipped on his Elton John sunglasses.
"She knew how to hope."

In the garage beneath them, the door begins its caterpillar crawl across the ceiling. Bing and Wanda have returned from their spiritual sojourn at The Fox and Hounds pub. Wanda's voice is slurred as she grumbles loudly about nothing. Cricket imagines Bing as a silent, gaping wound at her side.

Time is short, but Cricket has a plan. "Sit up," she says as she fishes a black grease pen from her pocket. She uses it on Elvin first, drawing a cheerful Happy Face smile with care, avoiding the stitch marks. Then she hands the pen to him. "You do me."

Soon both of their parents will climb the stairs. They'll look in on The Grub's universe, expecting to see the blindsiding big picture. Instead, all they'll see is the small detail of two terrified teenagers, huddled together.

SEDNA

CLIO KLYTIE WAS SURPRISED to find herself hitchhiking to work. She wasn't the kind of girl who took risks. Actually, she wasn't any kind of a girl. At thirty-eight, she no longer qualified for the g-word, even if her single, teddy-bear-cuddling status made her feel juvenile at times.

Her ride, however, still had youth on his side. He also possessed a seal-like head — liquid brown eyes, mottled skin, sparse hair — which he bobbed in time to some imagined music, and flippers instead of arms. Strange, maybe, but he seemed nice enough, and why, she decided, have instincts if you can't trust them?

"Besides which," he said as though he had read her thoughts, "you'll poke my liquid brown eyes out with your house key if I try anything untoward."

"I will?" Clio looked down at her right hand and saw the tip of her key jutting out between her first and second fingers. She dropped the key and attached Hello Kitty fob into a pocket. "But you won't try anything," she suggested, as much for her own sake as to demonstrate her faith in the youth's good intentions.

"It's more that I can't," he said. "Your life, as it stands, is a tad on the narrow side. Your present safe lifestyle doesn't leave room for you to play the victim." He tattooed a cheery rhythm on the steering wheel with his flippers. "It doesn't leave room for you to take Cuban vacations or win a lottery either, but don't worry — lifestyle choices can change."

Clio patted her chest with authority. "My life's fine," she said as they passed a billboard that read *Experience has taught us not to take our client complaints at face value.*

"So good you'd turn down a wish — if I could grant one?"

Clio thought for a moment. If she could wish to have someone's entire life, for instance, she would pick that of Angelina Jolie. But, if she had to narrow the choice down to specific attributes, would she choose Angelina's body, or her acting career? She could rule out Angelina's children. They didn't stir envy in her, even though Brad Pitt fathered some of them. Kids she could do without.

"That's a big if," she said.

"The biggest. If you need help deciding, look in there." The youth popped the car's glove compartment.

Clio rooted around. She discovered a fragment of limpet shell and some grains of sand that stuck to her palm, but nothing more. The compartment did not even have registration papers. In fact, except for an underlying smell of tuna on rye, the Datsun was void of any personal signs. No wads of chewed gum in the ashtray, no *Save the Whales* sticker on the back window, no stainless-steel travel mug.

Clio picked up the shell fragment.

"Good choice," the youth said.

"I didn't choose," Clio complained. "It's all there was."

"Compromise is all there *ever* is."

The car slowed as it tagged onto the tail end of a string of ferry traffic headed east to the mainland. They passed a scenic point of interest called Poseidon's Thigh where someone had revised the warnings on a familiar nine-by-twelve sign: *Don't Swim with the Sharks. Don't Dumpster Dive. Don't Discard Toxic Waste without Permission.* Clio longed to be free of the car and away from all the weirdness. In fact, she felt sleepy enough to wish she were safe at home in her own bed.

"Wish granted. But before we part, here's a word for the wise," the youth said. "Don't mess up when you meet my old ananaksaq. She only gives her chances once."

"What chances?"

The youth spun the Datsun's wheel. The car left the road and headed for the cliff's guardrail. Beyond the bluff, the green Pacific Ocean waited with open arms.

"Stop!" Clio screeched.

Both car doors sprung open. With a grin on his face, the youth tumbled from the seat.

Clio made a quick decision to follow suit. Her body landed safely on the floor beside her bed, but the dream about the flippered youth and his old ananaksaq were driven from her head when her temple hit a decorative cast iron salmon's fanned tail.

Clio walked to work, even though it meant she might be late. She'd woken late and felt like crap. Her head ached and her vision blurred unless she made an effort to maintain focus. The usual half-hour walk down the highway had taken her over an hour. Worse, now that she'd reached the commercial district in town, other pedestrians were giving her odd looks.

When the reflective window of the Wiley Deep Gift Shop offered her a chance to check her appearance, she took it. Her face looked wan, but otherwise all right. Her hair was blonde and stringy — nothing new there. She was still four or five inches too tall and ten or twenty pounds underweight. The only alarming feature was a bump on her head. A careful exploration of the lump told her it was the size and consistency of a moon snail.

"Oh, why do these things always happen to me?" she asked out loud.

"I'd guess, but I'm not allowed to talk to strangers."

Clio's eyes darted over to the speaker. A girl of about eight blew a pink bubble, then sucked it back in. Her small black eyes brought to mind the word *shrew*. If Angelina came upon this child in her travels, she would not bring her home.

"I think I know you," Clio said. "Your dad's a regular at the restaurant where I work. He's Jeffrey Wonder."

"Yup, that's him. I'm Darla, also Wonder. I'm on a mental health day from school."

"Schools give those?"

"Mine does for me. I'm traumatized because my mother left me. The school counselor says I'm so stubborn that I might never get over it."

"I'm sorry to hear that."

"My dad's sorry too. He can't cope with all my problems." Darla pointed to an Inuit doll behind the plate glass window. "I'm here to liberate Sedna from prison."

Clio rested a hand against the window to cut the glare. Sedna was as old as time. Her braids were the bleached gray of a dead sand dollar. Her eyes were wet beach pebbles. Each finger ended at the second knuckle in a bloodstained wound from which sprouted a miniature octopus arm, a sea star ray or an eel tail.

"Is she an old ananaksaq?" Clio wondered where she'd heard the word, and why she'd used it without knowing what it meant.

"No, silly," Darla said. "She's a *doll*, duh."

A Wiley Deep employee, a woman wearing angel earrings, made her way over to the window. Ignoring Clio and Darla, she tidied the display. Then she poked at the doll with a fingernail, apparently troubled by its presence in her store window.

"Can I tell you a secret?" Darla whispered.

"Sure."

The child gestured for Clio to lean closer. "If Sedna doesn't get home to the sea soon, she's gonna croak," she whispered. "I don't have twenty-eight dollars and ninety-five cents, so I'm gonna steal her. Kind of like in *Free Willy*."

Inside the store, the saleswoman shrugged her shoulders towards the angel earrings, then glared at the doll before she walked away.

Clio patted her pockets. "If you wait until payday, I can lend you the money." Her blurred vision made the doll's tentacles appear to wave.

"Can't," Darla said. "I'm not known for my patience." To prove her point, she skipped towards the door. "I'll have to off any witnesses, so you'd better not watch."

Clio covered both eyes with her palms. "How's this?"

"You'll be safe as long as you don't peek until we're gone."

Clio peeked. It wasn't every day she got to witness the daughter of her only suitor pull off a doll heist.

Fifteen minutes later, Clio entered the Grotto, the restaurant where she worked as a waitress five afternoons a week. She drifted past empty milk crates, stacks of flattened cardboard boxes and into the grease-enriched air of the kitchen. Monty, the chef, was nowhere to be seen and the kitchen was a mollusk vale of tears. Living inkfish, whose wise eyes seemed to size her up, awaited the deathblow in a wire-covered basin. Along the length of the wooden island, squid and octopus lay in various states of undress (de-beaked, de-pouched, de-inked). One specimen lay flattened beside a mallet.

"Tardy bitch!" Jilly, Clio's co-worker, shrilled as she entered the kitchen burdened with a tray of dirty dishes. "I was supposed to be out of here twenty minutes ago, girl."

Clio touched the moon snail near her right temple. "Something happened. An accident, I think."

"You'd better cover that nasty thing up, or you'll drive away the customers." Jilly shrugged out of a blouse, sniffed its armpits, and then stepped into a sundress. "You just missed Jeff Wonder. The guy's got it bad. He ordered a wife with dressing on the side." She reached under the sundress, pulled down her skirt, and kicked it off. "You weren't here, so he settled for a libido-boosting oyster burger."

"My Jeffrey can't eat oysters. He's allergic." The word *my* came out of Clio's mouth unbidden. He wasn't hers just because he flirted with her. The man flirted with all the staff, even Monty and Günter, the sixty-three-year-old German dishwasher.

"Oh, ho!" Jilly said. "The happy couple has gone past innuendo to the ownership stage. How'd stud muffin handle the birthmark, kiddo?"

"Fine," Clio fudged. It was too late now to admit that Jeffrey had not yet seen her naked leg. In her twenties, those years of naiveté when she had still wanted only to be wanted, she had leapt at an opportunity for romance, and look at what that had gotten her — a moment of public humiliation that had blossomed into twin phobias of public pools and physical intimacy. In her single semester of community college, Murphy Larson, top dog on campus, had invited her on a swimming date. She should have said no, should have seen it coming, the look of disbelief that skewered his face when she dropped her towel onto the pool's non-slip floor.

"That's great!" Jilly's enthusiasm jolted Clio from reminiscence. "Really. I underestimated the guy's tolerance."

The tide was so far out when Clio arrived home from work that she could walk out on the sand as far as the bend where the bay spilled into the open ocean. She'd forgotten orders, dropped a plate, and had been forced to witness Monty's grim expression whenever she entered his kitchen. She needed the calming presence of the sea.

The bay was dotted with executive homes that clashed with her solo rental cabin. Most of her neighbors were wealthy Americans who lived stateside most of the time. Clio roamed the beach alone, searching debris from storms for treasure. Once she found a leather wallet with an out-of-service number on a scrap of paper. That and a Calgary Flames jersey, a black lace G-string, a sodden jack of clubs, mammal bones, and more used condoms than she could shake a stick at.

Clio recovered a vertebra and two spindle whelk shells. The shells fit cold and smooth in the palms of her hands. Putting them down, she doodled a man in the sand. The man had Jeffrey Wonder's thick torso, stick legs, and boots. She arranged a handful of rockweed with the shells and vertebra between the stick legs. When she pressed on the end of the vertebra, the tip rose.

Clio sketched a sand-mate for the horny sandman. She made the sand-mate flat and gangly. A dark, hairy birthmark, the shape of Texada Island, covered an entire inner thigh. "Kiss," she demanded of the sand-couple.

When they refused to budge, Clio threw sand on their faces. It was then that she felt the beam of briny eyes. They belonged to a seal, basking on a rock. The creature had a grin that reminded Clio of someone she couldn't quite remember. She ran from the beach, overcome by an irrational fear of sea mammals.

The following Saturday, Clio discovered that Jeffrey Wonder lived with his children three blocks from the Grotto. Their unkempt, seventies-style house was surrounded by bent bicycles, deflated balls, stacked beer cases, and a rusted camper. When Darla had called her at the unpleasant hour of five a.m., she'd insisted Clio meet her at noon. The child had also criticized Monty for giving out employee phone numbers without permission.

"How did your boss know I'm not a stalker?" she said, then gave instructions and a warning, "Don't be late or else."

Clio tried to keep the hope out of her voice. "Will your father be there?"

"Of course not, silly," Darla said. "I'm not crazy."

As Clio approached the house, Jeffrey's twin boys skateboarded past, cursing in tandem. "Fucking A!" Besides his iffy language, the boys shared Jeffrey's low forehead, white-blond hair and unbalanced body. Angelina wouldn't adopt these children either.

On the house's second floor, Darla jerked a pair of bedroom curtains open. She mimed instructions for Clio to be quiet and come in.

As Clio entered the foyer, the child skipped down the stairs. "I've decided to show you something," she said as she stood. "It's top secret."

Clio followed the child back up the stairs. They walked in silence down a hall thick with toys, coats, and shoes until Clio pointed at a pockmarked door at the end of the hallway. "Is that your dad's bedroom?"

"Nope. My mom's. She let That Bastard share it sometimes, but not my dad. He had to sleep on the couch." Darla opened another door. "This one's mine."

Torn lace dangled from a canopy. The bed beneath was piled

with rumpled sheets and a faded Barbie quilt. Amputee dolls lay on the worn carpet outside a dilapidated doll house. Darla opened the door of a walk-in closet. She ushered Clio in and made her sit on the floor beside the stolen Inuit doll.

Yanking off a piece of cardboard attached to the doll, she showed it to Clio. "I've got the legend memorized," she said. "Sedna's father hacked off her fingers, and then tossed her into the ocean because she wouldn't get married. He wanted her to drown, but she became a sea creature instead."

"That's too bad." Realizing just how ridiculous the "meeting" was, Clio attempted to stand.

"No, it's not." Darla tugged her back down. "Sedna likes the ocean. She wants to go back, but I can't walk that far and my bike has a flat."

"I could drop her off at the Wiley Deep for you. The store owner would probably like to have her back."

"Sedna hates it there."

"I live by the sea. I could take her home with me."

"No, silly. She won't let you."

"Then why am I here?"

"My dad followed you home one day, so I know you live near the beach. You could invite us for supper tonight."

"I have to work."

"So call in sick. My dad does all the time, even if he's not. We like to eat spaghetti and Neapolitan ice cream, but no yucky garlic toast."

"Why did your dad follow me home?" Clio said.

"He thinks you'd make us a good mother."

"Me?"

"Yeah, but we don't need you. My mom's coming back real soon."

"Do you want her to?"

"Nope," Darla said. "But she has to. She promised."

Clio found it hard to believe that the Wonder boys were cuddled up in blankets, playing with their Game Boys, on her sofa. To make the children feel at home, Jeffrey had turned on a television sitcom. Instead of watching the program, Darla wandered the room making morbid statements about the bones, whale's jaw, and dried puffer fish that Clio kept in baskets.

For his part, Jeffrey seemed just as stunned as Clio to find himself in her cottage having an after-dinner glass of wine. He had dressed up for the occasion by putting on a new John Deere cap and sneakers instead of work boots.

"Great spaghetti," he said for the third time. "It's a nice change from eating at the Grotto. Plus, I don't have to leave a tip."

"What's taking you so long?" Darla whispered into Clio's ear. "It's time for plan A." In Clio's plan A, Clio took Jeffrey snorkeling so that Darla could liberate Sedna. In her plan B, Clio locked Jeffrey in the bathroom for the same purpose.

Holding out the wetsuit she'd borrowed from Monty and a waterproof flashlight, Clio said, "I thought we could go for a swim."

Jeffrey laughed. "What, tonight? In the dark?"

"I knew he'd be too chicken," Darla said with disgust.

"I just ate," Jeffrey said. "I might get cramps."

Darla pinched Clio's arm until Clio said, "Snorkeling is more like floating than swimming. I promise you'll be fine."

"If you don't go," Darla said, "I'll tell the school counselor that you're going to kill That Bastard. And I'll cry so she'll believe me."

Ten minutes later, Clio let the cabin door bang shut behind her. Under moonlight, the climbing roses glowed white. She followed Jeffrey down the shoe-strewn stairs and then along a dirt path that led to a crooked garden gate. Beyond the gate surged the age-old ocean, alive with silver birthday sparklers.

"Nice night," Jeffrey said. He took Clio's hand as they walked into the water.

Even in winter, if the water was flat and the tide in, Clio, sleek in black neoprene and flippers, waded through the eelgrass in front of her cabin. Long waves that had originated as far away as Hawaii tugged at her body as she deadman floated. She sucked air through a snorkel to watch silver schools of perch dart, crabs scuttle, and sea blubber drift. Sometimes, she dove to retrieve a crab that broke the surface of the water with its large pincher waving distress. And when swimming at night, she often caught such timid animals as eels and mud sharks in the beam from her dive light. One thing she'd never done before, though, was share the experience.

"Bend down," Clio instructed. Jeffrey hollered as water seeped under his wet suit collar. "The shock will pass," she said meaning the cold of the water, but thinking of the birthmark.

"What now?" Jeffrey said through the chattering of his teeth.

"You could swim alone to the end of the bay."

"Why the heck would I want to do that?"

"I don't know. Maybe for the bragging rights," Clio said.

To her relief, Jeffrey took Clio's bait, leaving her to drift alone. She used the time to develop a fantasy in which she and Jeffrey swam together in nothing but skin.

"Talk about coincidence," the fantasy Jeffrey said. The moonlight grew so bright Clio could see his full body even below the surface of the water. A hairy nevus birthmark covered most of his body. "Mine's bigger than yours," he said.

A child's scream interrupted Clio's satisfying moment.

Clio found Darla standing knee-deep in water, using Sedna as a paddle to agitate the phosphorescence. "Sorry," she said. "I stubbed my toe. On a rock."

"I'm sorry to hear that."

"I did it on purpose because it's Friday," Darla added. "I'm real mad."

"I don't follow."

"He used to play board games with me."

"Your father?"

"Yup. On Fridays."

"What does he do now?"

"Drinks beer, barfs, and says, 'I'll kill That Bastard. I'll kill him'." Darla peered into the darkness. "Where is my daddy?"

"See that flashlight?"

"What's he doing?"

"Proving he's not chicken."

"I already knew that," Darla said. "Sedna's the real chicken. She changed her mind 'cause the ocean's too cold. She wants to stay with me." Darla's teeth chattered.

When Clio carried the shivering child back to the cottage, the feel of small arms around her neck did the unexpected. It gave her what she suspected was a maternal thrill. In that moment she wanted to keep Darla safe above all other things. She wanted to ward off the dangers of meningitis, gossip, and solar flares. She wanted to pack the girl's lunches, drive her to ballet classes, and update her shabby bedroom with colorful furniture from Ikea. She wanted to buy her all the weird dolls she could find. She wanted to teach her to snorkel.

Under the hot spray of the cabin's Mexican-style outdoor shower, Clio's goosebumped flesh grew smooth. The cedar beneath her feet was soft with water and soap. She picked out Jeffrey and Darla's laughter in the cabin as they played the Game of Life. She dropped the towel and looked down at her birthmark. Taking courage from the vague memory of a dream, she went inside to look for a pair of shorts.

"This is you," Darla informed Clio when she returned to the living room. The child was wrapped in Clio's velvet electric blanket. She touched a tiny green convertible. "I played your turns, but you got all ones, so you're losing." She moved her own car full of blue and pink peg people. "I'm winning. I was born lucky, so I always win at games."

"Were not born lucky, Darla the big fat schmarla," one of the twins paused his Nintendo playing long enough to say.

"Was too, fart face!"

"Children, that's enough." Jeffrey said. He spun the game's wheel as Clio took a seat beside him. His hand grazed her birth-marked thigh.

Sedna lay on a towel in front of the fireplace, waving her tentacles.

Clio lifted her car with its single pink peg driver off the flat-tire/

miss-turn square. Maybe these people didn't look like Brad, Maddox or Shiloh, but Angelina didn't know what she was missing, Clio decided. She held the car above the space that granted marriage.

Darla nodded her permission.

From somewhere far beyond the cabin, came the sound of a seal's sharp bark.

Oh, Darling. What Have We Done?

DESPITE THE SMELL OF smoke in the Elizabeth Fang Playhouse, Emily Rose believed she had more pressing concerns than escape. Where, for instance, had her lover hidden the dildo? Also, did he prefer any of the other village women to her (the new bar owner, Jo-Jo Green, was a number one suspect)? And, finally, what did he plan to do to her next? In the two years of their affair, they had yet to establish boundaries. Bruises and ruined clothing were getting increasingly hard to explain to her determinedly trusting husband, who, in truth, reminded her of a fish she'd once bought because of false advertising: *Active, peaceful, and easy to care for, the Blind Cave fish makes an interesting addition to a community tank.*

Like Alan, the creature's allure had worn off fast.

With the sex toy's retrieval in mind, she tried to stand. Her head spun. Her pink panties with the daisy appliqués were down around her calves, but it seemed unlikely that they could be so effective in preventing movement. A closer examination revealed that her lover, who always came prepared, had bound her ankles together with reams of electrical tape. Worse, he had then tied her bound legs to the legs of the antique divan with nylon rope. A fun situation to find oneself in under the right circumstances, but regrettable at present. At least he'd left her hands free.

They'd argued, she remembered. He had insisted she divorce the Cave Fish and make their relationship official, something she was not prepared to do. She had an emotionally fragile daughter to consider. At age seven, River still wet her bed. The girl woke screaming from a recurring nightmare involving a bear almost every night. The Cave Fish would sue for, and probably get, full custody. Knowing this, how could she leave?

In the end, her lover had called her a drama queen — the ultimate insult. A mixture of booze and fatigue must have made her pass out, and he'd positioned the divan, with her on it, center stage and turned on a spotlight to make his point. What she needed now was a monologue, and an appreciative audience. If only she could remember the heinous scene from Marlowe's *Dido, Queen of Carthage* her twelfth-grade drama teacher (another man she'd slept with) had made her perform before the whole school. She only remembered the humiliating sentiments she had rasped out at the end, something about eternity residing in a lover's kiss.

Emily Rose had no respect for the kind of women who needed the kiss, or any other attentions, of a male to make them immortal. In her books, men made good slaves but lousy masters.

Her fierce independence did little good now; she needed her man. The smell of smoke had increased, and the sliver of auditorium visible behind the heavy velvet stage curtain glowed orange, a spreading color that meant fire, not romantic candlelight. She shouted her lover's name until her throat ached. "Horse's ass!" she added, but even that slur did not make him reappear.

Oh, why was she so demanding? After their argument, she had berated him for finishing the bottle of Cranberry Finlandia. She'd also insisted that he go out and get her something to drink, even though the liquor store was closed.

The smoke curling through the room made her cough. It was two a.m., or so the watch on her wrist said. She pictured the Cave Fish, lying wide awake in bed, watching the red numbers on the bedside clock glow, waiting for his errant wife to come home or for his daughter's nightly need for warm milk and clean sheets. She closed her eyes and concentrated on not retching.

Understanding ran like a tremor through her body: she might not survive the night. If, by some miracle, she did escape her bonds, and then the building, she'd break things off with her lover for good. She would sleep in her own bed, keep up with the laundry, have dinner on the table by six every night, and start helping River with her homework. Next summer she would ignore the men who eyed her up as she tended her perennial garden wearing short shorts and a tank top, or fished from the sweet spot on the edge of town. She would appreciate the Cave Fish's clumsy romantic gestures. Who said she needed a charmer with bright eyes and amazing stamina to be happy?

Watching flames munch the purple velvet curtain that cordoned the stage off from the auditorium proper added to her dizziness. She remembered the mood-setting candles she had lit and then forgotten.

Despite her drunkenness, she recognized that now rather than later was the preferred time for action. With some difficulty, she jockeyed herself once again into a sitting position on the divan. Scraping at the tape in search of an edge broke a fingernail. Though she strained to move her legs, the tape barely stretched.

Even if she managed to pry her legs free, then she'd have to flee the burning building in her underwear. Her embroidered cotton blouse hung from a rafter, well beyond reach. Henry had tossed it there as part of a game of hide-and-seek-the-clothing. And she had no idea where she had left her parka and boots.

Escape, however, seemed unlikely. Bronchial spasms rocked her body. After a bout of painful vomiting, she tried to roll into a ball, but couldn't.

Tears started in Emily's eyes as she realized something of what her death might mean to the people who loved her — the Cave Fish, for one. Like his namesake, he used sonar, only he used his to avoid confrontation with reality. She doubted he would be able to find a way to avoid the fallout from this. When the evidence came in, he would finally and irrevocably have to face the sad truth: he was an imperfect man in an imperfect marriage.

And as for River, the shy little girl needed her mother. Before falling into the first and last coma of her life, Emily managed to think, "Oh, Darling. What have we done?"

I Can't. I Mean, I Do

To celebrate the forty-eighth morning of her seventeenth year, River Barker opened her father's liquor cabinet with a copied key. She felt a strong affinity for a bottle of five-year-old Canadian Spirit because of the name — she was after all half-Canadian and, when the circumstances were right, spirited; but the liquid looked a little too golden to be consumed at nine o'clock in the morning on an empty stomach. A quick rearrangement of bottles displaced the essential Jack Daniels Sour Mash, her father's favorite poison (even his Wrangler jeans were held up by a Jack Daniels Whiskey Sippen' Sour Mash belt buckle). A taste for that brew, like appreciation for the strangest of her father's eccentricities, was a thing River would need more maturity to acquire.

Her fingertips next lingered on the cool surface of a Cranberry Finlandia bottle. The brand, a recent purchase, had been her mother's favorite. She pictured her father, intent upon yet another useless gesture of his undying devotion, smuggling it into the house to furtively hide it behind the sour mash. Pitiful as far as gestures went, but useful too.

She cracked the seal and sampled the sunset-colored drink. A flash of nostalgia went down with the sip; the bright hue, sweet flavor, and lingering taste reminded her of her dead mother. When the recognition made her tear up, she decided to skip her shift at Open Late Gas & Groceries and wallow in self-pity instead.

A herd of leather-bound photographs topped the liquor cabinet like cows faced into the wind. There was the proof she'd once possessed an intact parental unit. And there she was, a little kid with a button nose, green eyes and join-the-dots freckling. Amongst the formal studio portraits was one candid shot of her younger self fishing a lake beside her mother. Far more dead grayling than two people could eat were stacked between them. Mother and daughter both had long, wind-tousled hair. Despite the year, 1983, both wore peace sign necklaces, fringed leather vests and bell-bottom jeans. River's expression was open and trusting while her mother's shielded eyes seemed to conceal a secret.

Not *a,* she scolded herself. *The. The secret.*

River always thought of the phrase as displayed in full capitals like the marquee of a theater. THE SECRET starring Emily Rose Barker and - who? Mr. Tall, Dark, and Handsome, she supposed. Surely her mother would not have cuckolded her father for Mr. Short, Pasty, and Homely. Or would she have?

After restoring the Finlandia bottle to its place of concealment, she chose a familiar and watered-down bottle of Bacardi. To face the day and all that it meant or didn't mean, she would need a clear and simple tonic. To face the day, she needed more guts than she naturally possessed. Today, after all, was the semi-annual anniversary of the day that had reduced the Barker family numbers and changed the dynamics forever.

In the disaster called River's life, drinking was a stop-gap measure, an attempt at damage control. By mid-afternoon, when guilt and nausea came into play, she would feel like crap. For the moment, however, she courted the buoyancy that always came first. Her alcoholism was the one effortless thing in her life, and she viewed it as an intimate friend — albeit a moody one. Still, not all of the moods of her friend were dark and unpleasant. In fact, the first rush of warmth when she drank always calmed her fears, while the second made her feel childlike. In a lifetime of insecurity and having to grow up too fast, such moments were priceless.

Before River quit the program, her A.A. sponsor claimed that her client's problems stemmed from unresolved anger, but anger at whom? True, her mother had died in a manner that fueled ugly rumors, but if Emily Barker had entertained a man in the local play-house at the time of the fatal fire, then so what? It simply meant that not one but two generations of Barker females were sluts. And as for her father…

Kingpin Al would be home at noon for lunch, dressed for a rodeo he'd never enter, and intent upon protecting her from both herself and reality. If she wanted to be good and drunk before then, she'd better get at it.

River twisted off the bottle's lid. She guzzled, pushing past the burn in her throat to the sweet glow further down. She felt 99.9 per-cent sure that she didn't resent her widowed father just because he had chosen a ridiculous way to express his grief. In fact, she adored him, if not because of, then despite his annual commemorative ice walks on the breaking Yukon River.

Unlike the rest of the village, River knew the history behind his decision to walk the ice. While everyone else saw a man with bronc-bucking recklessness, she saw a romantic, one who'd fallen in love with a young, backpacking tourist at first sight. Before Emily's death Alan had often recounted the story for *his girls* (as he'd called his wife and daughter): how he'd met Emily on the banks of the Yukon when the sun had come as close to setting as it would that night; how they'd made an audience of two when a drunk clambered out on the ice, bemoaning his broken heart; how Alan had said to Emily, "In Everlasting the men know how to love. You should stay a while, ma'am — see if I'm telling a fib or the truth."

"That is *not* why I stayed," River once heard her exasperated mother say.

She gazed at the ring on her left hand. When she got married nine months from now on April Fool's Day, she hoped that her man, Cameron Leanard, would show himself capable of a fraction of her father's affection. Not that she expected slavish devotion — theirs wasn't that kind of relationship. You scratch mine and I'll consider scratching yours was more their style. The hard edge of their relationship kept boredom at bay, and, best of all, he didn't have a problem with her drinking.

She carried the Bacardi across the room and then plopped onto a green vinyl ottoman. The closed room had a tomb-like atmosphere year-round. Nothing changed but degrees of wear and tear and the depth of dirt accumulation. The color scheme remained brown on brown with orange accents, although the brighter hues were muted from the dust kicked up each summer from Everlasting's unpaved streets. The cornucopia-print sofa ensured that the room remained in a perpetual autumn, the walls displayed macramé hangings done in natural wool and spider webs. The room's only plant, a broad-leafed philodendron, had partially decomposed.

Did Mr. Question Mark ever stand in this room, and, if so, what had he thought of the decor? They had never met — River and her mother's lover. At least, not that she could remember. Unless, that is, he was the fishing picture's photographer. When asked about the day, her father had denied being present, and the few moments of it she remembered did nothing to shed light on the mystery. There was the burn in her thigh muscles as she squatted behind a curtain of brambles unable to do her business, so fearful was she that something with teeth and a stinger would attack her exposed bottom. And it was her mother, not a stranger, beside her in the cab of the truck during the drive home. Her mother's cool hand on her head had soothed the carsickness out of her. Someone else must have been behind the wheel, but who? If only she had not been the kind of child who didn't pay attention.

Through the closed living room window, she spied her old boy-friend Jovan Yarddog hauling a red wagon down the street. Two of his young nieces were seated in the water-filled wagon wearing filmy princess dresses over bathing suits. A third child followed, squirting the girls with his water gun.

Dismay over the where and why of their breakup the year before plagued River. She and Jovan had spent a perfect afternoon at their favorite place, a ghost settlement from the Klondike gold rush days that tourism had yet to discover. They were in the 110-year-old clapboard church, holding hands with their faces illuminated by light glowing through a stained glass window. The settlement's greatest treasure, a large-as-life wooden angel, gazed upon them with what River thought of as motherly compassion.

It was a romantic moment, but, instead of popping the question as she expected, Jovan had asked her to quit drinking. And he confessed that he'd dumped her hard-earned bottle of vodka onto a blackberry bush when he was pretending to take a leak. Now, as the opportunity to wave at him came and went, she kept her arm by her side, restrained by guilt.

Her neighbor's retired horse, Working Boy, swayed past the Barkers' post-Christmas plastic Santa. He lowered his head into the Barkers' perennial garden. Daisies grew there still, among roses of the wild variety and rocks released from the permafrost's bowels last spring. River supposed she should pick the rocks, but what the yard lacked in street appeal it made up for with hardiness.

Moved by a sudden impulse, she made her way to the front door and out onto the porch. There were vegetables in a bucket on the porch, fodder for the compost pile her father half-heartedly maintained. She plucked a hairy carrot from the lot and dangled it over the porch's railing. The horse edged towards her and gingerly took the lure between its brown and deeply grooved teeth.

River knew what she was going to do when she caught hold of the horse's bridle and clambered onto its swayed back, just not where the action would lead her. Blackflies worried a festering wound on the animal's neck and a cloud of dust rose from its flanks when she spurred it into action. She steered it across the lawn with one hand. With the other she clutched the Bacardi.

Mr. Winkwest, the horse's geriatric owner, pressed his bulbous nose against the screen door of his house to watch the horsejacking. His face remained impassive when she waved the bottle. As one of her tribe, the Raging Alcoholics, she knew he wouldn't fink about the illicit cargo, though he might stir himself enough to complain about the horse.

Five minutes later, she dismounted on the northernmost end of the village, at the site of the playhouse where a fire had taken her mother's life. She turned the horse back towards home, then swatted its rump. "Go on, take a hike. I want to be alone now." When it refused to budge, she led it to a patch of grass and let it graze.

Fireweed bloomed around the perimeters of the playhouse ruins. She plucked a bouquet of the mauve flowers, then cleared a swath along the top of a section of wall rubble before laying it down. "For Emily Rose Barker. Deceased," she said. The horse ambled over to nuzzle her body in search of more carrots.

Refracted sunshine formed bubbles of light on her freckled hands as River tipped the bottle back to drink. Remembering a toast often used by her great-grandmother, she shouted it out loud: "Here's to those who wish us well. And those that don't may go to hell."

She felt as much peace as a chronically depressed person could expect to feel, which is to say, not enough to float a boat in.

"Blink," nineteen-year-old Tom commanded his father, who was seated across from him at the kitchen table.

Instead, the old man's stiffened fingers comforted a mug's ceramic surface with its cryptic proclamation of *World's Greatest*. The coffee inside was so old it might sprout mold, but if Henry was too stupid to brew himself a fresh pot, then tough luck for him. Tom would let him drink funk.

In the living room, a panel of Aboriginal people jabbered on about something crucial, like melting ice pacts or glue-sniffing children. When Tom arrived three days ago, his father had been parked on the sofa in front of a program called *Northbeat*. The scene had made Henry seem normal, but he hadn't known enough to turn the set off when he left the room for bed that night. Tom hadn't turned it off either; he needed background noise to live his life by; even if they didn't get stations like MuchMusic in the middle of nowhere.

He hadn't minded the Yukon silence much when he was a young

hick. What with the fishing trips, ball games, and snowshoeing trips his father took him on, he'd always found enough to do somehow. They'd shared some great adventures, like the time Henry helped Tom land the seventeen-pound Dolly Varden he'd snagged with his own handmade Wolly Bugger fly. Now, however, after his teenage years in the big city, his entertainment needs were more risky and less legal.

Tom placed his elbows on the table although he'd been taught manners in his childhood. His father wouldn't care; it was his mother who'd been the stickler, and where had that gotten her? She'd never even left Everlasting except to die in a stinking hospital with her body stuck full of tubes.

Tom's hands curled into tight fists. He leaned across the table to shorten the physical void that separated him from his father. Then he tried again. "You blink for that frigging caregiver. I'm your son. Blink for me."

His father's taxidermic eyes remained fixed on an unmade bed at the end of the trailer hallway. Above the bed was a grainy photograph Tom hated. In it, his plain-faced mother sat with a tired look in her eyes while newborn Tom slept in her arms, unaware of the crap hand life had dealt him. Standing behind mother and child, old-school Henry, pre-injury, looked proud of what his sperm had produced.

A truck turned into the yard and the noise disturbed a robin scrounging through gravel for grubs.

"Goddamn it." He aimed his eyes back at his father. The visitor was the irritating caregiver who was paid big bucks by the government to do diddly-squat for the old man. She made a big deal about being connected to the family, but Tom refused to let on that he remembered the woman, who was the sister of her father's former best friend. They'd both let him down, these Chinese sisters — they'd never once called him or written him or remembered his birthday in the years he'd been gone. Nor had they stopped social services from shipping him down south when his first foster family moved, even though there was plenty of room for him in the sister's friggin' huge house.

"You're a friggin' waste of time," he said to Henry. "I never should've come."

Getting to Everlasting, Yukon, all the way from the southern border of British Columbia, had not been easy. He had tried twice before, when he was twelve and fourteen, but both times the police had caught him before he got too far and delivered him back to whichever foster home he was living in. This time, however, he was the legal age to hit the road and run out of money without anyone caring. Some rides were decent enough, a few even fed him out of the kindness of their hearts. But there were others, mean sons of bitches, who'd expected payment in kind. A ride for a ride. He'd had to jump out of one slow-moving semi and hide for an hour in the bushes. And there was the lunatic granny who stunk like cats and urine — Tom's four-hour, Barry Manilow-accompanied ride in that old biddy's creaking Camaro didn't bear thinking about. If he never heard "Mandy" again it would be too soon.

The need to see his dad had pushed him on, though. During his years in foster care, dreams of an idealized father-son reunion had kept him sane. Even though the last time he'd seen his dad, the man had been prostrate on the floor with his head caved in, and even though foster parents and social workers had used descriptions like "practically vegetative" and "severe traumatic head injury" to describe Henry's ongoing state, and even though he'd had no contact with Henry since the attack, Tom still expected a full recovery. What was one baseball bat to the head compared to all the barroom brawls and mining accidents Henry Bose had suffered and Tom had helped him bounce back from?

So much for a happy reunion; after three days home, his father's immobile face and soft, hula-dancer-tattooed arms already sickened him. He hated the sight of the old man's steel-toed boots lined up straight as arrows, going nowhere, and the familiar cleft chin and thin lips on the face of a stranger. Even as late as yesterday, he'd hoped for a flash of recognition from the old man. Tom's retelling of a few of their old jokes had fallen flat, the family photo album he'd spread open on the table before his father hadn't drawn so much as a glance, and neither had his fit of dish-smashing rage.

"Last chance," Tom warned. To prove his seriousness, he hoisted his backpack and buckled the straps.

His father's fingers shifted on the mug, but his yellow eyes held steady.

The caregiver So-Wah Fang, ridiculous with a mess of preternaturally red hair, let herself in.

"Ever hear of knocking?" Tom crabbed.

"'I hear you knocking, but you can't come in," she sang in a high, sharp voice. From her smile, it was evident that he was expected to join in the fun.

"Save it for karaoke night," he said.

So-Wah set a full laundry basket on the table. She checked the contents, handing a pair of socks and two pairs of briefs to Tom. Then she eased the old man's fingers off the mug and carried it to the sink. As she rinsed out the mug, she said, "Not leaving already, are you?"

Tom stuffed the underwear in a backpack pocket as he crossed into the living room. His plucked his shades from the coffee table and his Yankees baseball cap from the sofa. The bedding he had used for three nights could rot on the couch forever, for all he cared.

The caretaker trailed him into the room. She flicked off the television set just as something interesting was finally about to come on. "When people ask a question," she said, "they usually receive an answer."

Tom gave her his f-you look. "I'm leaving. Nothing here to stay for."

"How about staying for him?" She pointed to the old man, still immobile in the kitchen. "Your father's enjoying your visit."

The sneer on Tom's face was genuine. "He tell you that?"

"In his own way."

Tom felt blood rush to his face. His eyes filled, but just because of the pressure in his head. He shoved his shades on his face, then kicked open the unlatched door to prove his toughness.

"It's like I said," he croaked as he stepped outside into the mellow sunshine. "There's not a damned thing here."

*

River had consumed more Bacardi than was good for anyone intending to remain upright when a hitchhiking youth appeared on the horizon. He reached the Elizabeth Fang Playhouse and dropped his backpack near the surviving sign that perpetually promoted opening night of *A Doll's House*.

She watched him through a hole in the waist-high wall as he lit a cigarette. He had long brown hair, a cleft chin, dark glasses, and what looked like a chip on his shoulder.

His voice was gruff when he called the loitering Working Boy over. The animal lifted its head to peer over the wall. It snorted once, and then lowered its head back to the grass. "Screw you, too," the boy said. "I hate quadrupeds."

River considered rising to the animal's defence, but decided she preferred spying to confrontation. She watched the boy puff away on his cigarette for a while and had to stifle the giggles when he seemed to be arguing with himself under his breath. Then he made a worse mistake than telling off a horse: he lit the skeletal remains of a vine on fire with his cigarette.

"Hey!" River jumped to her feet. The wall spun, so she held on tight to keep it in place. "Show some respect."

"The plant's dead, chick." If the boy was surprised to see a girl pop up from behind the wall, he did an admirable job of concealing it.

"So's my mother." Her toe swiped an *x* in the dirt to mark the spot. "She burnt to a crisp right here."

"Mothers die."

"What would you know about it?"

He shrugged.

Keeping her body pressed against the stone for balance, River made her way around the wall. When she reached him, she momentarily forgot the boy as the long blond hair of a guitar-wielding rock star decaled on his T-shirt grabbed her attention. Forget her fiancé, she wanted to run away with the blond musician. She wanted to ride in his tour bus, and blow him kisses from the wings while he sang for thousands. She wanted to have his babies.

"You're a hunk," she informed the decal.

The youth in the shirt snorted. He also lifted his backpack.

"Wait," River begged. Her gaze rose to the youth's face. Something about him looked vaguely familiar, but she lacked the energy to figure out the mystery.

"Why?"

"I need to talk to someone other than these assholes." With a finger, she seemed to conduct an orchestra made up of a stand of birch, the base of the Yukon River, and the village of Everlasting.

"I would, but there's nothing in it for me."

"Maybe there is. First we talk . . . " The words *brazen hussy* troubled her thoughts as she stroked the plastic hair of the blond musician, then reached for the waistband of the boy's jeans.

Tom stole a glance at the ride who'd picked him up. Some of the skin on the big man's face and all of the skin on his hands looked like melted plastic. There weren't any cattle ranches in this part of the Yukon as far as Tom knew, so what was with the ten-gallon cowboy hat, embroidered skirt and hurtin' music played way too loud?

The dude had picked him up on the edge of town, saying he could only take him as far as the bridge a few miles out, but now here they were halfway to Dawson City. A pervert probably, but Tom knew how to deal with pervs as long as they didn't carry heat. He fingered his pocket, reassured by the hard outline of his jackknife. If the dude brought it on, he was in for one hell of a surprise.

"You got family in Everlasting?" Mr. Home on the Range asked instead. His eyes left the road for a moment. Tom almost felt the man's gaze burn a hole in his forehead.

"Used to. Not any more."

"Good reason not to stick around then."

"Yeah. That and the town sucks."

Up ahead a bear-cub-sized porcupine waddled down the shoulder of the road. No way he'd ask for the favor, but Tom hoped Mr. Tex/Mex would slow the truck and let him get a good look. He hadn't seen a porcupine since he was what, four or five years old? His dad had pled for the creature's life after it got into a tussle with Hardball, Tom's stupid puppy, but his mom had shot the animal.

Tom had kept a bundle of quills. Still had them packed away in one of his boxes of stuff. His last foster family had booted him out the minute he turned nineteen; they needed the bed for a paying customer, some retard with autism, but at least they'd agreed to store his things in their garage for the summer. If he didn't make it back by September 1, he bet they'd junk the lot.

They sped past the porcupine.

A song urging the listener to drink hard, party harder, and screw the consequences came on. Mr. Lone Ranger reached over with his lava flow hand and snapped it off.

"Is it drinking you don't like, or just decent songs?" When the man refused to rise to the bait, Tom added, "So, do you have a daughter? 'Cause I met a chick outside town who has the same beady eyes as you. She likes drinking and plenty more besides, if you know what I mean."

Mr. True Grit slowed the truck. "You aiming to ride shank's mare?" he said.

This was it, the moment Tom had anticipated. He shifted closer to the door, and then slid a hand into his pocket to feel for his knife. His armpits released twin streams of sweat. He tried to suck his bulging eyeballs back in; perverts preyed on fear.

Mr. Back in the Saddle kept his eyes on the road. "I'm asking if you want to walk," he said.

"Fuckin' right, I do."

Mr. Cowpoke stopped the truck without pulling over. He could park sideways across the road and it wouldn't matter — two vehicles driving the same road on the same day would constitute rush hour this far north.

Tom jumped out of the truck onto the side of the road. His grabbed his backpack from the truck bed before the jerk had a chance to drive off with it. Then he hightailed to the far side of the shoulder until a stand of pygmy pines stopped him from going any further. From the choking stink that rose up to greet him, he guessed something big had died and rotted nearby. Maybe Lava Face's last passenger.

"Hey, kid. Come here."

Tom took his time crossing the few feet. "What?"

"Besides having beady eyes, what did that girl you met look like?"

"Plastered," Tom said. "And she had a butt-ugly horse." He didn't feel compelled to add that the chick had insisted they talk for a half-hour straight before they screwed (though the conversation really seemed to be between her and his Kenny Wayne Shepherd T-shirt), or that the horse whinnied at a crucial moment, or that the chick had passed out immediately afterward.

Mr. Alamo reached across the cab to stick his hand out the open window. His melted-plastic fist held a one-hundred-dollar bill.

Tom eyed the money. "What's that for?"

Mr. Giddyup released the bill which floated to the ground. "It's traveling money," he said. "If you're thrifty, it'll get you far enough away."

From what, Tom wanted to ask, but the man cranked the wheel so hard into a U-turn the tires squealed in protest. Then he sped off.

With the one-hundred-dollar bill safely stowed away in his wallet, Tom held his nose and walked off the highway towards the smell of decomposition. He parted the bushes and peered into the shadowy gloom. The "victim" was a stump-tailed cat with the head chewed off. Each of the protruding paws had six toes.

Everything, but everything was weird about this place. Tom could not get away fast enough.

He headed back to the road and held out his thumb. Warming it up — just in case.

Mr. Winkwest's horse was in its yard, and River was in her room — on the floor, though, rather than on the bed — when Alan returned home. He allowed himself a sigh of relief. The person the hitchhiker had probably defiled could not have been River — not if his little girl was here at home, sleeping sweetly.

He lifted River onto her bed, keeping his nose away from her mouth just in case there was something he'd rather not smell. Despite the summer heat, he flounced a Cinderella blanket around her body, then tucked the edges between the mattresses to prevent her from tumbling out again. Emily had been the same — a deep sleeper who often dreamed the day away.

He pulled the pink tufted stool from River's vanity table and positioned it beside the bed. With her smallish green eyes, his daughter looked a bit like the Barker side of the family, but everything else about her, from the set of her lips to the elfin shape of her ears, was pure Emily. She also shared her mother's headstrong nature.

Alan smoothed the hair away from his daughter's face. He fought to avoid the line of thought which always took him to a disturbing place. Just because River had inherited so many of her mother's characteristics did not mean she would share her awful fate. If he had anything to do with it, Alan's beloved daughter would live to be a happy old woman.

Leaving River snoring loudly, Alan headed down the stairs. While she slept, he'd sneak the thing he needed most — a little shot of liquid courage delivered neat. Being a single father was hard work and, from time to time, Alan required assistance.

River sat on the toilet, immobile with disbelief, trying to take comfort in the dolphin wallpaper trim and tartan-patterned shower curtain. After two months away, her fiancé would be home any minute, yet somehow the stick in her hand showed blue. Her one skipped period placed her at five weeks pregnant. Obviously, she had slept with someone besides Cameron — the questions were, who? and when? and where?

Downstairs, the doorbell rang.

She had been seated on the toilet too long and had to yank her stuck rear from the seat. As a precaution, she wrapped the blue-tipped stick in paper and put it back in the box along with the instructions on how to test the urine mid-stream and the promise that the results were 99.9 per cent accurate. When the whole mess was wrapped in a hand towel, she hid it behind the bag of toilet paper in the cupboard under the vanity.

The doorbell rang three more times in quick succession; no chance now that Avon was calling. Cameron wasn't known for his patience, or his love of squalling infants, or any nurturing trait, if she wanted to be completely honest with herself. His best characteristics, invulnerability and truck ownership, wouldn't make him good daddy material.

She opened the bathroom window, but it was too small for her to crawl out of it. Besides, the fall from the second story might injure the baby.

Baby. It just couldn't be. She was too young, not to mention too irresponsible. She didn't even do chores when her father asked. She let all the fish in her mother's tank starve to death. She spent more time off the wagon, rolling in the muck, than on it, and pregnant women couldn't drink. She had a wedding to plan, and a monstrous gut would definitely put a kink in her plan to wear her mother's satin-and-pearl gown.

River turned to consider her body in the cracked full-length mirror glued to the back of the bathroom door. She lifted her top an inch at a time, hoping to see a flat stomach with well-defined abs. No such luck. Sure enough, her stomach had puffed out when she wasn't looking. Even her breasts seemed larger — they were at least a C cup now, maybe a D. Cameron, a self-declared breast man, would love the improvement if it didn't come with a small hitch. She touched one and decided it was tender.

"You are a great big ho," she told her abashed reflection. "Honestly, it's disgusting."

The doorbell had ceased to ring. River pressed her ear against the bathroom door. She heard the low hum of masculine voices, somewhere downstairs. Great — her father was home from work early and had let Cameron in. An act of mercy on her father's part, for although he tried to hide his feelings for River's sake, Alan Barker disliked Cameron Leanard. Maybe with good reason.

There was the sound of laughter — Cameron's; her father never laughed — followed by heavy footsteps charging up the stairs. River cast about for somewhere to hide. Even if it wasn't filled with dirty laundry, the wicker laundry hamper wouldn't take her weight. The linen closet had fixed shelving.

Cameron strode past the bathroom door on his way to River's bedroom. "Guess who?" he called.

She pulled back the shower curtain. Every kid who had ever

played hide-and-seek knew to check the tub, but what choice did she have? She jumped in when the footsteps headed back her way. She held her breath, hoping her fiancé would keep going back down the stairs, back through the front door, and straight out of her life.

Instead, he opened the bathroom door she had neglected to lock. "Peek-a-boo!"

River turned on the shower just as he poked his head past the curtain. The cold spray got them both.

Cameron stated the obvious. "You're dressed!"

"I'm showering in my clothes because…" River let the water flatten her hair against her scalp as she waited for a reasonable lie to form. When one didn't, she gave up. "Because, I'm pregnant." She turned off the water, reached past the curtain for a towel, then wiped off her dripping face. "It's not mine," she added.

A vein throbbed in Cameron's forehead. "Then whose?"

River chose a time-honored response posed as a question. "The milkman's?"

A fat brown bear dozed behind the fence that cordoned Everlasting's dump off from the rest of the Yukon. River and Cameron watched the animal. Despite the unexplained details of River's announcement, and more than a few fights, they'd come to an agreement to continue with their relationship, such as it was. Now they were seated in the cab of his fire-engine-red truck on some version of a date. Their sobriety-induced boredom was evident — marked by Cameron's rapid succession of yawns and River's half-closed eyes. Bear watching rated just below drinking on the unofficial list of top ten things to do in Everlasting; still, it had limits as entertainment. Even the bears, with their slumped shoulders and apathetic mauling of garbage bags, seemed uninspired.

The not so happy couple weren't there only for the wildlife viewing. They had sought out the quiet of the dump in order to nail down final plans for their wedding, re-booked for October because of the milkman's baby. So far River had agreed to ignore the stripper hired for Cameron's stag if he wore the tux she had rented in Whitehorse. It was an easy compromise as Babelicious didn't inspire much jealousy: everyone in town knew about the woman's game leg and droopy right boob.

"I'm also gonna wear my boots," Cameron insisted. "Not those spit-shined pieces of crap you bought for me."

"Then I get to have pink balloons for the reception. Five hundred of them."

"You can have a thousand as long as I don't have to blow them up."

"You won't have to. Someone who loves me will help."

"Good for them."

After a time of silence Cameron gave River's shoulder a friendly squeeze. He nodded towards the dump. "There's how we pay for a tropical honeymoon," he said.

"With garbage?" The word *garbage* evoked images of festering pork chops and green mashed potatoes. River's stomach flopped. She groped for the window's handle and cranked it, but the breeze she admitted filled the cab with the dirty-diaper stink of landfill.

"With gallbladders, baby. Bear gallbladders. I told you I made an Asian connection when I was in the States." With one arm, he hoisted an imaginary shotgun. He took a bead on the head of a bear snuffling through garbage. "Splat," he said. River imagined the fur exploding. Cameron veered to the cub sniffing the air. "Bam! Gotcha!" he said.

"Touch one hair on the head of a bear," River managed between gulps designed to keep down her lunch, "and our wedding is off."

Ignoring her distress, Cameron shifted closer on the bench seat. He rested a hand on her thigh. When she didn't push him away, he lunged with the other hand to fondle her crotch. "I'll just touch fur. Promise."

River wriggled away. "Stop it! I'm gonna hurl." With a hand pressed against her mouth, she lunged for the open window. When she finished emptying her stomach, black mascara puddles ran down her cheeks and a string of mucus hung from her nose. She mopped up the mess with an oily paper towel pulled from the glove compartment.

"Now that was truly gross. Don't think I'm going to kiss you in that condition."

"I hate being pregnant. Hate it, hate it, hate it!"

"Don't blame me, baby." Cameron folded his arms across his chest. "I didn't shoot my sperm all the way to Everlasting from Alaska."

"I bet you shot your sperm far enough."

"Now that's the pot calling the kettle black."

"You're not a kettle — you're a dung beetle."

He grabbed her wrist with both hands. "If you don't want an Indian burn, apologize."

"Never."

He twisted his hands in opposite directions. "Last chance."

"Ouch! I'll never apologize to you. Not for anything. Not even if I'm wrong."

"Fine, be careful walking home." Cameron released her wrist. He reached across to open her door, and then shifted his bulk over, crowding her size-six body to the edge of the seat. "Bears love junk food."

"That's it! The stupid wedding's really off this time."

"Then give me back the ring. There are plenty of women who'd be glad to wear it."

"Like who? Babelicious? Maybe she'd like to hang it from a nipple."

Cameron hip-checked her out of the truck and into the pool of vomit.

River hurled her engagement ring into the truck. It sideswiped Cameron's chest before wheeling to the floor, where it landed on the litter that bore messy testament to the couple's vehicular courtship. "Worm!" she said.

"That's my girl." Cameron shut the passenger door. Then, with a smirk on his face, he locked River out.

Dressed in a Wonder bra and maternity slip, River shivered in front of the open bedroom window. She needed a wider vista than her childhood bedroom in order to put some perspective on the probable course of her future. If, and this was a big if, she didn't run from town screaming in terror in the next five minutes, she would become Mrs. Cameron Leanard at the stroke of noon. From there, the future got even murkier. There was a reception to get through, and then forty or fifty years of marriage.

Working Boy ambled down Croesus Street, intent on enjoying the mild spring weather after a long, cold winter. The animal's legs and belly were caked with mud. As Mrs. Cameron Leanard, she'd have fewer opportunities to hijack Mr. Winkwest's horse, though possibly more reason. She realized, too late, she'd miss the horse as much as she'd miss her room, the oasis of girlishness she'd been so anxious to leave behind.

River's few good memories of her mother were stored in the small space. Emily had put up the wildflower wallpaper, faded everywhere except the spot where River had removed a crayon masterpiece. They'd gone together to Whitehorse, mother and daughter, to purchase the now-threadbare Cinderella bedspread, plastic chandelier, and pale pink lace curtains that clashed with the outside of the house. The pristine artefacts of girlhood had once transformed a tawdry motel room into a palace for a whole weekend. Surrounded by so much pink, River hadn't minded much when Emily left her alone each night. New sheets and frilly pillows kept the fear at bay.

River patted her belly, imagining the quiet, thoughtful daughter she would produce and the times they would share — girl time that did not include strange men at their motel door (was one of them Mr. Question Mark?), crotchless underwear hung in the bathroom to dry, or pacts of secrecy.

Emily's wedding dress and veil hung from a hook on the wall as it had for the past year. The puffed sleeves and beribboned bodice matched the dress of the waltzing Cinderella on the bedspread. River crossed the room to touch, for the thousandth time, the gossamer tulle and smooth pearl beading, both tinged slightly yellow. She looked from the gown to the humiliating maternity cocktail dress she would have to wear in front of the whole village in less than an hour. A lilac tent worn over borrowed heels was the best she could manage on short notice.

After postponing the revised wedding date three times, Cameron, the dung beetle, had insisted on having the ceremony on the original date of April 1. Now, here she was, about to marry one week before the baby was due, and during the Yukon's mud season. Worse, all morning River's Braxton Hicks contractions had grown longer, stronger, and closer together. She had tried taking a warm bath, walking, and resting; all to no avail. She wasn't too worried about giving birth prematurely; everyone and their dog had warned her that first babies always came late. But, if the painful contractions persisted, she might have to groan and flinch her way through the vows.

She wriggled into the nasty lilac dress, clasped on Emily's fake pearl necklace, then went to find her father who, she suspected, had dipped into the whiskey before breakfast. If she found the courage, she would confess her fears and ask him to lend her the money for a one-way airplane ticket out of the north.

At five minutes past twelve, River looked up at her father, who had just given her away in marriage, with tears in her eyes. "Don't move," she begged. He knelt at her back, his body and the new mist-gray Stetson purchased specifically for the wedding partially blocking her from the view of the forty-eight guests who had come to watch her marry Cam Leanard but were being treated to a live birth instead. She was sprawled on the crimson carpet at the front of Saint Agreta's Anglican Church in a pool of her own water.

She groaned out loud as another Braxton-Hicks-that-wasn't moved in a wave of pain through her lower body. If she could only stop writhing, she'd tear off the sodden maternity hose she'd foolishly worn. She'd also unzip the back of her dress and not care who could see her bra. "I can't," she said, and then, "I mean, I do." Her water breaking had interrupted a pivotal moment in the ceremony.

"You heard the girl," Cam said to the Reverend. "It's a done deal. We're out of here."

"Please," River panted to her father. "Take me home."

Alan stroked the hair away from her face. "Do you think you can you walk to the truck?"

"She means *home*, dufus," Cam said, strangely unaware of what was about to happen. "As in *home* with me. Her *husband*, you know."

"Please, Daddy. Help me up."

"I'll do the honors, if you don't mind," Cam said. He grabbed one of River's hands and yanked. When she didn't rise to her feet, he added. "I'm not saying you're chunky, babe, but some bears weigh less. You'll have to help me out here."

As Alan helped River to her feet, she let out an involuntary groan. The last few contractions had been two minutes apart and forty-five seconds long. She'd never make it to the hospital in Whitehorse now. She knew she'd have to deliver the baby at home.

"What's your problem, old man? Are you having a hard time letting your little girl go?" Cameron moved into Alan's personal space.

"Shut your pie hole and move aside," Alan warned.

River looked up on time to see her almost-husband grin. "Make me," he said.

While Cameron and Alan fought it out, River waddled down the aisle toward the exit. If she had to, she would crawl through the mud all the way home. And she wouldn't push until she was back in her bedroom, snuggled up in the Cinderella bedspread, no matter how much she felt the need.

She slowed when the next contraction hit, but didn't stop. A group of boys at the back of the church sang, "*Here comes the bride, big, fat and wide.*"

Spurred to action by the song, three women moved towards River. The Aboriginal midwife, Mary Yarddog, hustled up first. She instructed the town's matriarch, busybody Agnes Everlasting, and Lenore Leanard, Cameron's scantily dressed mother, to form a circle around her for privacy. The town's male paramedic arrived, but was shooed away.

The midwife removed River's hose, before checking out the situation. "Don't push," she said. "Your perineum's not ready."

Cameron's mother rearranged the low neckline to conceal a black lace bra. "Be careful with that girl," she warned Mary, "she's got my first grandkiddy in there."

"Pshaw," Agnes said.

River's worry that Cameron had inexplicably told Agnes about the milkman was bunted aside by another contraction. She squatted, then pushed, unable to stop herself. Remembering her prenatal classes, she visualized the cervix opening and the baby coming down. She put her all into the effort and felt skin rip.

"See," the midwife scolded. "Now I'll have to sew you up."

River bellowed like a bull in heat. Mary caught the slippery body that popped out.

"Jackpot!" Cameron's mother shouted. "It has a penis."

Agnes Everlasting adjusted her bifocal glasses as she bent in closer to look. "Doesn't look like a Leanard to me," River heard her mumble. "There's too much chin."

Applause thundered in River's ears, blocking out the baby's cries.

A Worm in Tequila

On the morning of her son Mattie's second Christmas, River Leanard came to the conclusion that there were only two good things besides herself and her child in the Leanard residence. One was Cameron's eighteen-year-old brother, Wainwright, and the other was a grimy bowl she'd found at the back of a kitchen cupboard as she prepared for the day's celebration.

That morning, River had seen Wainwright's naked torso. His back and neck were hooked like the handle of a cane. Scar tissue as fine as spider's web covered his shoulders and arms, but none of the scarring was fresh. Whatever he'd suffered, he had suffered it in the past, when he was small enough for someone to torture without fear of reprisal. River stifled the urge to rescue him after the fact. She reminded herself that, no matter how pitiful his past, the young man wasn't up for adoption.

She took the bowl to the sink and scrubbed it with warm, soapy water. The glass was black with an opalescent sheen. The edges of the bowl were fluted and, best of all, a standing kangaroo was stamped into the base. It made her think of wonderful, warm places, far away from Everlasting.

River dried the bowl, filled it with water and set it on the counter. Then she added the piece of holly Cameron had cut for her that morning. The effect of a green leaves and red berries against the bowl's sheen gave her joy, a sensation she had forgotten existed.

With her father about to return with Mattie and the truckload of elderly guests River had insisted on inviting, she turned her attention back to the Christmas dinner preparations. There were bowls of chips and dip, bottles of pop, gherkin pickles, a dish of canned cranberries, a plum pudding soaking in rum, and a turkey roasting in the oven. Soon she would start peeling potatoes and carrots.

She gave the air a hopeful sniff. Instead of turkey and the floral air spray she had used, however, the house stank of bear. After their wedding, Cameron had taken to hunting and taxidermy with a vengeance. He'd skinned out five brown bears in the back yard, then spent endless hours scraping out the skins and sewing on backings of red felt. The furs now hung on the living room walls. Worse, hoping to create a trophy, he'd boiled a bear skull for days on the stove, until the steam had permeated everything.

She didn't have to go into the living room to know how stupid the Leanard family's mix of treasures looked. A stuffed weasel grappled with a blood-flecked rabbit under the coffee table, and a beaver family, consisting of father, mother, and one kit, sat on their haunches nibbling red plastic apples in a corner while a raven hovered over their heads, anxious to pluck out their eyes. Lenore's crocheted doilies and her porcelain baby doll crying under glass failed to feminize the room.

River dreamed of moving into a home of her own, but Cameron had either lost his job on the municipal work crew or quit (he refused to give a straight answer to her questions about the circumstances), and her wages at Open Late Groceries & Gas barely paid the room and board Lenore charged. Still, by going without necessities, River had managed to squirrel away four thousand dollars, which she kept in a cookie tin in the freezer — almost enough money for a down payment. She'd keep saving and suffering until she got her son, brother-in-law, and husband — if he learned how to behave — out from under Lenore Leanard's awful thumb.

Wainwright sidled into the room. "My gramps brought that all the way from Australia," he said. "He gave it to my mom, but she won't use it. She says it's ugly."

"Sometimes things are so ugly they're beautiful." River spoke with Wainwright in mind. The youth had unevenly sized eyes, hardly any chin, and bad teeth.

"I'm gonna go to Australia one day," he said. "I'm gonna live in the outback and farm sheep."

"Let's move there together," River said. "You, me, and Mattie."

"Not Cam?"

"Nah. He wouldn't want to leave his bears."

Cameron entered the kitchen a moment later. He dumped a large box on the counter beside the kangaroo bowl. "Wrap this up for Mattie will you, babe," he said.

"What is it?"

"Have a look-see."

River removed the lid to reveal a black leather biker's jacket, matching chaps and a German-style helmet.

"Those are genuine replicas," Cam said. "And check out the stainless hardware on the jacket."

"We already bought Mattie's gifts," River said. Dread made her heart race.

"So, I got a deal."

"How much?"

"With shipping and taxes, just shy of two hundred bucks."

River clenched her fists. She knew the only possible answer, yet had to ask the question. "Where did you get the money?"

"Your half of the dough's still in the freezer, so don't get pissy. Buy yourself something nice. Like maybe a keg of beer."

"I don't want beer, you bastard," River said. "And I don't want to be stuck here forever. You stole *my* money!"

"Can we can still go to Australia?" Wainwright asked.

"Is that what you were squirreling our dough away for? A fucking trip to Aussie land?"

"Australia, Siberia, or Timbuktu. I don't care where I go, I just want out of this house."

"Bitch," Cameron said. And then he flipped River around and broke her nose.

River felt safe holed up in the garden shed, seated on a fifty-pound sack of steer manure, as she doubted Cam had sufficient imagination to search for her there. Two of his discarded bear skins kept her warm, and she had found clean rags to stuff up her nose when the bleeding wouldn't stop. If Cam hadn't claimed her remaining two thousand after their fight, then that was how much money she had to spend on a divorce lawyer. It might not be enough, not if she had to fight for full custody of Mattie.

River grabbed a hoe to brain Cam with if necessary when a knock sounded on the door, but it was Alan who ducked his head to enter the shed. He held a steaming plate of turkey, potatoes, and carrots. His eyes narrowed as he took in River's condition. "Call me an idiot, darling. I believed that yellow-bellied man of yours when he swore you were sleeping off a sick headache and didn't want to be disturbed."

"Did my other guests show up?"

"Yup. Jo-Jo helped fix the grub," he said of his sometimes girlfriend. "Everyone's chowing down like pigs at a trough."

"Even Cam?"

Alan grinned. "Nope. Wainwright told Jo-Jo what happened, so she chased the bastard off with a carving knife. If I'd gotten to him first, he'd be gutted, trussed, and roasting in the oven. Do you want to press charges?"

River shook her head. She took the plate, dipped a finger in the gravy and mashed potato, then licked it. It tasted like bloody Christmas. "I didn't think anyone would find me here."

"Well, you did leave a trail of footprints in the snow."

"Oh."

"That nose looks broke up."

"Yeah." River squinted and tilted her head. "I'm a Picasso."

Alan took a seat on the manure beside her.

River covered his legs with the fur. "If Mattie and I come live with you, can we bring Wainwright too? I think Lenore beats him." She touched her swollen nose. "Or maybe it's Cam."

"Can you prove it?"

"No," River said. "It's just a hunch."

Alan wrapped his arm around his daughter. "All you can do is make the offer."

"Have you ever noticed, Daddy, that some things are so ugly, they're just plain ugly?"

"I shouldn't have let you marry that jerk."

River shrugged. "Who knew?"

Alan rested his head in his hand. "I did," he said. "I just didn't know how to tell you."

River kissed her father's bowed head. "Don't feel bad," she said. "I knew too."

The roll and crash of bowling balls, the sting of nicotine-rich air, the buzz of conversation — familiar things failed to calm Tom as he drank alone at a table in the loft of a bowling alley. He blamed the canned carols and fire-retardant tree with multicolored flickering lights set up in a corner of the room. Such trappings of the season triggered the recall of childhood memories he'd prefer to live without. The gift-wrapped toys and turkey slices of the past gave rise to longings that could only end in disappointment. If he wanted to see Santa on Christmas morning, he'd have to watch a special on TV. He'd been small the last time his old man donned a ratty old red suit and secured an even rattier white beard to his face before handing out booty. Even smaller the last time Henry faked sleigh bells and reindeer feet prancing on the roof at two in the morning, then feigned ignorance with a mischievous grin plastered across his face the next morning. Ho, ho, ho.

In the two and a half years since Tom's return home and

subsequent flight, he'd kept nostalgia at bay. He didn't regret his decision to run, though he did, from time to time, wonder if the old man was still blinking up a storm for his Chinese caregiver without a thought in his head for the son he'd forgotten.

Tom fingered a cigar, a Romeo Y Juilieta full-flavored Cuban and a luxury at ten dollars a pop. His lucky cigar would be saved and smoked after the provincial bowl-off that he planned to win in the New Year. His desires were simple: booze and tobacco, cash in his pocket, and the company of easy women. Of the four, he usually had an excess of the first two, a condition that limited his ability to procure enough of the third and fourth.

A familiar-looking blonde-tipped brunet sauntered toward his table, disturbing his reverie. She wore a tight pink T-shirt with glittering letters that advertised her as a *Bowler Babe*. Besides Tom and his table, nothing of interest was parked at the far side of the loft, and so he took her approach as an intentional attempt to cause a ruckus. At least he'd get an up-close glimpse of her new boobs.

"Hey, sexy," he said to break the ice. Not exactly a stunner as far as opening lines went, but her name escaped him. The woman had been his first serious girlfriend, and he hadn't run into Stacy, Macy, Lacy since the night they had split up after a few weeks of inspired shacking up — the night Tom had broken her heart, or vice versa. There'd been plenty of women since her time, and Tom no longer remembered how that particular cookie had crumbled, just that it had.

"Shh!" Stacy, Macy, Lacy rolled bovine eyes towards a small, stocky man paying for drinks at the bar. "I'm a married woman now." As she held out a diamond-studded wedding band, her new and improved breasts tried to wag their joy, but failed.

Tom looked from her sparkly chest to his half-empty glass. He'd need another whisky sour, and soon.

"You blew your chance, baby," she said. "I should have called the cops."

Tom remembered. He'd screwed up, busted her flimsy Ikea furniture in a jealous rage. He took a swig of his drink and stole a glance at Stacy, Macy, Lacy's face. Not so much as a glimmer of lust left there. But then their breakup had been a few years ago. Time flew when other people were having fun. "No big loss," he said.

"Asshole. You'll always be lonely, you know."

Tom angled his glass in the direction of the cash register where the new groom postured rooster-like, a cold beer in each hand and a challenge in his undersized eyes. "At least I won't be hitched to a loser." Tom lifted a finger from the glass in order to flip the man a bird.

"He'll kill you!"

"Well, you know what they say. A change is as good as a rest."

Stacy, Macy, Lacy may have had her faults, but one of them wasn't exaggeration. The new groom came at Tom like a locomotive in heat. With the man's fifth punch, Tom's jawbone shattered. The frayed ends of a live wire snaked through his brain in a private light show.

"Gracy," he tried to say as he slumped against the railing.

Spurred on by the intoxicating sight of someone else's flying blood, Rooster Eyes punched again. This time Tom fell over the railing in slow motion. A bowling ball hurtled past as he landed on his back in lane three. A million miles away his ex-girlfriend's face blanched and her mouth stretched into an O.

So that's what the old man felt, Tom thought. *It could be worse.* Then he thought nothing at all.

In the weeks after his fall from the bowling alley balcony, noise got to Tom. He noticed, for the first time, how the racket of seedy streets went on 24-7. There were sirens (police, fire, and ambulance), and fights (fist fights, cat fights, lovers' spats). Women screeched at children, men barked at , and dogs howled at the moon. Cats bred with noisy abandon, and his neighbour in the corner unit played Shania Twain CD's hour after hour with too much bass. Sometimes there were gunshots or arrests made outside his window and every night drag racers kicked up a stink. Every last decibel of noise made his head pound.

At his lowest point, during a painkiller-induced nightmare, Tom offered his right testicle in exchange for an hour of silence to a group of rat-faced creatures, but didn't get a taker. Instead, they chewed a deeper cleft into his chin until the weird chick from the Yukon came in like a dirty-blonde Lucy Liu and karate-chopped the rodents off, saving him from a gruesome death.

If noise made him crazy, his wired jaw made him crazier. His mouth felt crooked, and he doubted his unsympathetic doctor's assurances that she'd put all the pieces back in the right place. The blender he had bought to purée his meals packed it in when he threw it against the kitchen wall. The sight of the turkey baster he used to squirt tepid chicken broth into his mouth made his skin crawl, and he had taken a hammer to his last baby bottle of yams when Shania's song "When You Kiss Me" threatened his sanity. Now he'd have to survive on instant potatoes and Very Berry Jell-O — if, in fact, he decided to survive at all.

With the loss of his two hobbies, bowling and breaking hearts, time moved slower than a worm in tequila. To make up for the deficit, Tom lounged at his kitchen table and sucked rum and Coke through a straw. Pushing aside a mess of unpaid bills and an eviction notice, he found a full bottle of Empracet. Shaking out three tablets, he crushed them, refilled his glass with whiskey, and added the powder. A half-smoked Cuban cigar lay on the table. The tip rested beside a crescent moon scorched into the Formica. He slipped the cigar between swollen lips and lit it.

With his drink and the cigar, Tom moved to the couch and switched on the television. He surfed past commercials for leak-proof diapers, roach hotels, and Mother Nature's gasoline until he chanced upon an old Yukon documentary on CBC. Although the frigid North was the last place he wanted to think about, he watched spellbound as the camera panned a ridge of violet-hued mountains. He'd forgotten about the Yukon's beauty, how it made him feel like a man in steel-toed boots was tap dancing on his chest.

"Prettiest dog-gamned place on earth," his father used to say. Purposefully changing the letters around. "Go to town" was "to to gown" and "whip your butt" became "bip your whutt", though Henry had never resorted to corporal punishment. Henry claimed he could make his son mind without resorting to child abuse, unlike other fathers he knew.

Tom still had a sweet tooth to prove it.

Still Henry hadn't been a pushover. He always claimed exercising his bragging rights didn't make a man a braggart. In his prime, Henry took top spot in everything he did: work, play, and drink. And, if other men felt threatened by the Bose superiority, well then, thuck fem.

The scene on the television screen faded to an aerial shot of Helpert Mines, Everlasting, Yukon, the place where, until Tom turned six, his father had worked.

Thuck fem too.

In the years before Tom's birth, Henry dug copper in Ontario, uranium in Saskatchewan and zinc on Vancouver Island. He settled for marriage and gold in the Yukon, having vowed off working underground after a cave-in spared him but killed two of his co-workers. He never shook off the taste for the dark, however, and claimed to prefer Everlasting's long winter nights over the sunlit summers.

Tom knew and hated where the documentary was going; years before, he had watched it start to finish in the trailer in Everlasting with his mother and father. A G.I. Joe doll claimed half of his attention, but he heard the smug foreman explain the workings of the mine. He also heard his mother's quiet sobs.

When his mother said the man in the shoot should have been Henry, Tom was too young and ignorant not to ask why. Instead of answering, Henry told Tom's mother to shut her yap or he'd shut if for her. It was the only time Tom had ever heard his father threaten his mother with violence. Then Henry hurled his drink at the beloved TV, breaking the screen — just like Tom did now.

As Coke and Empracet dribbled down the TV cabinet onto the carpet, Tom relived the afternoon he'd gotten into the cups with one of Henry's old co-workers, who'd given up mining and taken up cake assembly in a southern baked goods plant. He learned from the man that his father's demotion from foreman to grunt came because he had the gall to do what every other red-blooded man at Helpert itched to do to the owner's pretty little trophy wife — he banged her.

And then, the real crime, he bragged about the deed.

Munchausen by Proxy and Bubble Gum Tylenol

Four-year-old Mattie Barker was playing inside Open Late Groceries & Gas when a Chevy Silverado parked in the shade around back. In the Chevy, community support worker So-Wah Fang pocketed her keys. She cast her eyes in the direction of her client, slumped in the passenger seat. The ends of her geometric haircut swung toward the man like knives as she gave a sharp tug on his seatbelt.

River had finished off a bathroom break by parting the curtains to peer outside. She blushed at the sight of So-Wah's client. The weird mystery of Henry Bose baffled her. She could not recall having slept with him, yet Everlasting's limited gene pool made it impossible to escape the fact that her son's yellow eyes, wide forehead, and cleft chin shouted the Bose name. Since becoming a single mother, the question of her son's paternity had taken on a greater significance.

River dried her hands on a towel and scurried to her place behind the candy-filled counter in the store. Mattie made bubbling noises as he plowed a toy loader through a mound of sugar spilled on the floor. He was still thin and pale after a recent bout of the flu. His play, though contented, was too subdued. The door swung in and bells tinkled, interrupting River's thoughts. So-Wah stepped inside.

"The usual please," she said.

"As in poison?" River asked.

So-Wah placed a hand on a slim hip. "I'll purchase my cancer sticks without sass from you, girl. I have a democratic right to smoke, no matter what the pantywaists say.

So-Wah switched her attention to the boy. "Hiya, kiddo."

Mattie pointed to a tabby tomcat, stretched out underneath a comic book display. "Cornflakes has got six toes on each paw."

"That's right," So-Wah said. "Cats need six-toed paws to catch songbirds and near-extinct mammals. It's a fact of nature."

River unlocked the cigarette case. "My son starts school next year. He'll get teased if you teach him lies."

The boy's thin lips trembled. "Mamma thinks cats have five toes. Tell her."

"All I know is that my cats are all six-toed," So-Wah said.

"My buddy Sam's cat is too! We counted!"

"So-Wah, people will think he's addled. He'll fail preschool."

"Don't worry, kid. I've seen plenty of addled and you're not it." The caregiver winked at the boy and then clicked across the hardwood floor on high-heeled sandals. "Change okay?" She dumped a baggy of loonies on the counter.

"You never heard of Interac?" River removed a carton and placed it beside the coins.

So-Wah sliced through the wrapper with a star-bejeweled fingernail. She faked dismay when individual packages, decorated with a smoker's ghoulish grin, fell out. "Speaking of gingivitis, I've got old Henry Bose out back in my truck."

"So?"

"So come outside and say hello."

River rang in the purchase. She passed So-Wah her receipt and then looked past the caregiver and into the customerless store. "Next?" she said.

Attention:

Councilors Jim Prime and Augustine McAudrey

Re: possible Internet advertisement

The village of Everlasting (population 174) offers all the services and amenities a traveler needs, including one hotel, dining facilities, post office, liquor store, propane and gas, grocery store, nursing station, pharmacy, volunteer fire and ambulance services, and police.

Located on the Yukon River between Dawson and Mayo, Everlasting can be accessed by either boat or car. It is the perfect departure point for an adventure holiday. Hunting, fishing, and canoeing are popular summertime sports. A host of other activities can be enjoyed year-round. Local inhabitants include artisans who produce a wide variety of arts and crafts for sale. Renowned Aboriginal carver Jovan Yarddog calls Everlasting home as does Alan Barker, a.k.a. Kingpin Al of CBC documentary fame.

Everlasting on the Yukon River, your perfect holiday destination.

Screw truth in advertising, boys. We need tourists.

Sincerely,

Her Royal Highness

Mayor Elizabeth Fang felt a sense of accomplishment as she sent off the email. She'd fulfilled an official responsibility and could now lounge with good conscience for the rest of the day.

She stood in the dining room of her three-thousand-square-foot log home folding a stack of dragon-embroidered towels. Having lived in Beijing for the first nine years of her life and various Yukon villages for the next thirty-seven, her decorating style was an odd synthesis of East meets North. A moose head presided over a delicate hutch with inlaid chrysanthemums, and twelve bamboo chairs waited for guests around the gargantuan oak table.

As she folded, she watched over her yard where sixteen colony-style kennels provided shelter for her Siberian husky brood bitch and the dogs she'd kept from the bitch's last two litters. Two males, Yao Ming and Yuan Shihai, moved off from the pack. They circled each other for hierarchy until Elizabeth rapped the glass of the large bay window. When she rested her hand on a hip, the dogs slunk apart.

Elizabeth was bent over, depositing the towels into the china cabinet where she kept linens instead of a table service, when she heard So-Wah's Chevy pull into the yard. As always, the arrival of her sister stirred the dogs into a ruckus, a bad habit Elizabeth had not been able to break the animals of. From the evidence of their breath, she suspected, but could not prove, that So-Wah regularly slipped the dogs forbidden treats of teriyaki jerky.

The sisters had always lived together. Neither had married, although So-Wah had come close once with a prospector named Sourdough McDougal and, before his injury altered him, Elizabeth had cherished an unrequited passion for the widower Henry Bose. For the most part, both women were content with the arrangement.

So-Wah's light footsteps crossing the porch were followed by a heavier pair. The front door opened. "Everyone decent?" The sound of So-Wah's shrill voice reminded Elizabeth of their father's mother who had lived with the sisters until her death at ninety-six. The tiny woman had persisted in perching on toilet seats to do her business despite the sisters' explanation of Western habits.

"As decent as I'll ever be." Elizabeth modulated her voice,

aiming for Westernized blandness.

"Pity me," So-Wah said as she entered the house with Henry Bose tagging along. "This afternoon I have to clean the Leanard pigsty. That horrible Lenore comes home from hospital today."

Elizabeth eyed Henry up, comparing the living man to the image she carried around in her imagination. As always, the two men canceled each other out, leaving behind nothing but an easy-to-ignore shadow. She turned her attention back to the conversation at hand. "How's Lenore's cancer?"

"Not as virulent as she is."

"Coffee's still hot." Elizabeth moved towards the sideboard. She poured three coffees from a silver decanter suspended over a lit tea candle.

"Thank heavens for small mercies." So-Wah flopped onto a delicate bamboo chair. "Some days I hate my job."

"Then quit."

"I can't. Some days I love it."

"And how are you today, Henry?" Elizabeth said as she handed the man a translucent china cup and guided him to a chair. The cup looked ridiculous in his bear-paw hand. Hard to believe her body had once craved the touch of those hands to the point of distraction.

"He's peachy," So-Wah answered for him. "We stopped by the gas station this morning. River had a fit when I suggested she come out to the truck and say hello."

Elizabeth's blew a wisp of steam away from her cup. "You know I hate to be a busybody, but maybe it's time we forced the issue. Her boy's got a grandfather he should meet." She moved to the window. When she rapped on the glass at some perceived misconduct on the part of the dogs, four of them looked up before trotting out of sight.

"Sure, but how?"

"Damned if I know. That girl doesn't make things easy for people."

"Maybe she doesn't know." So-Wah peeled the red polish off a pinky fingernail. "She was hitting the sauce pretty hard back when

Tom made his brief appearance."

Elizabeth smirked. "Everybody except Alan knows. She just doesn't want damaged goods for her baby's grandfather."

"You think?"

"River's ashamed of her family's history," Elizabeth insisted. "As the mayor, it's my job to perceive these things. Believe you me, it's a simple matter of pride."

"What about Tom-Tom? Shouldn't he be told he has a son?"

"I bet he'd flip if he heard you use his old nickname."

"It's a shame how surly that boy turned out. When he was here last, he treated me like something you'd scrape off the bottom of a shoe."

Elizabeth turned to Henry. "What do you think, old pal. Should we track your boy down and tell him he's a daddy?"

A crystal doorknob held Henry's undivided attention.

"Track him down how?" So-Wah asked.

Elizabeth moved to the sideboard. She opened a drawer and removed a map of Canada which she spread open on the table. Beside it she placed a portable telephone and a red felt pen. "Directory assistance. Start in western Canada and work your way east. If Tom Bose's listed anywhere in this country, you'll find him."

"Why me?"

"Because, as the mayor of Everlasting, it's my job to delegate."

When the red-haired woman returned Henry to his home, she followed him inside. She used his bathroom, then wandered into his bedroom. "Good boy!" she said. "You made your own bed today." She chatted on, but he found it difficult to pay attention. "The sky's the limit now. Maybe one day we'll see the old Henry again. Why not shoot for the moon, hey?"

Henry felt something fuzzy land in his right eye. He blinked it away.

The woman thanked him for agreeing as she made noise in the kitchen. Then she handed Henry a tall glass filled with something murky. "It's a brainpower-improving cocktail of dang gui, walnut, dragon tooth and rou cong rong," she said. "Drink up!"

Henry tried, but the fluid wasn't coffee or juice, it was something that tasted awful.

"Down the hatch." the woman picked up the glass and held it at his lips until he gulped it all down. "You want to do more than dress, eat, and sleep, don't you?"

He did do more — Henry tied the laces of his steel-toed boots, prepared instant coffee with sugar and cream, poured cereal and milk into a bowl, used a microwave to heat TV dinners, washed his hands after he used the toilet, locked the door at night, unlocked it each morning, and, sometimes, remembered flashes of the man he once was.

Henry was changed in more ways than anyone knew. The brawling, joking womanizer was long gone, replaced by his truer self, a person who was both humble and sensitive. If he could speak, he might tell the woman not to sing as she rinsed the glass, that the haunting love song caused him pain.

"Sore is my heart with yearning!" she sang.

Sore was his heart. Sore was his heart.

She quartered a pear and placed it on the table in front of him. "Eat your fruit."

Henry did not acknowledge her comment with a blink, nor did he reach for the pear. He preferred to eat alone. She clucked her tongue in disapproval. "If you get bunged up you can call Roto-Rooter to clean you out. I'm not giving you an enema." She pinched her nose. "They stink."

Oh sore, sore was his heart.

"I want you to think about making the move into town," the woman said as she filled his Thermos with boiled water. "Neither of us is getting any younger. I could keep a better eye on you in Everlasting, and to be honest, I'm getting tired of the long drive." He felt the heat of her hand on the back of his head, and then she was gone.

After that, time passed slower. Between the woman's visits Henry felt lonely. He entertained the notion that his trailer floated mid-air, that hand-over-hand the slant-eyed woman hauled it back to earth each morning. Small things regulated the tempo of his existence: a clock's tick, his heart's erratic beat.

Henry angled forward. His fists formed the shape of a heart. Pear scent, sweet and juicy, tickled his nose. His fingers closed in on a section of pear. His mouth slackened. Drool pooled. He ate. The words *Roto-Rooter* popped in and then out of his head. As did the words *dragon tooth* and *boy*.

As he finished the pear, a sound issued from the bedroom. *Emily*, he thought. Rising, he shuffled down the narrow hallway. With his head cocked, he considered the unpainted wood and rusted screws that made up his bed's headboard.

Henry's stomach growled.

His mind wandered to lustful thoughts of instant noodle soup and the coffee he could make with water from his Thermos. He turned towards the door and a flash the color of a young woman's hair appeared in his peripheral vision.

Henry let the water in the Thermos cool. Night fell. He became a living statue immersed in the cool blue light of the moon. Night waned as black turned to gray turned to gold. A finch trilled. Fat and sassy, a wheat-colored rat slipped through a hole, eager to bed down for the day.

Henry Bose, Emily Rose Barker's other grieving lover, waited on, his old heart sore with yearning.

Twenty-six hours after spring thaw released the ice of the Yukon River, Kingpin Al set his fourth beer of the day on the table. Through a cloud of smoke, he viewed the crowd in Jo-Jo's Bar & Grill. There were the usual suspects: smelly prospectors, proud municipal employees, underemployed adventure guides, and a few chronically depressed housewives. There were also some tourists and the press, identifiable by their stealthy glances at his scarred hands and face, their good haircuts, and the synthetic nature of their clothing.

If it weren't for the crowds gathered on his behalf, he'd probably call the damn thing off. He was getting old, and Kingpin Al Day hadn't shifted anyone's opinion of events as he'd hoped it would — instead it had given old rumors an unnaturally long shelf life.

"Piss or get off the pot, Barker," town matriarch Agnes Everlasting shouted. Alan's great-aunt, Elspeth Ferment, snored open-mouthed on the seat beside her.

Alan shifted in his chair, checking for numbness in his legs and butt. He'd sat at his table, reliving the night of Emily's death, since the bar opened at nine that morning. Too long, yet not long enough to find a fresh perspective.

News of the fire had come via telephone courtesy of Elizabeth Fang just after three a.m. He'd been in bed, wide awake and anticipating Emily's return home while fighting back the demons of suspicion. If he'd been man enough to keep his wife under control, Emily would not have died that night.

As Elizabeth spoke, he remembered thinking her somber tone did not bode well for him. "Alan," she said, "please tell me Emily's home."

"She's not."

"Oh, Lord. I don't know how to tell you this."

"Try straight out."

"Okay, okay. A fire has destroyed the playhouse earlier tonight."

"What's that got to do with my wife?"

"The fire crew found a body inside."

"Emily's right as rain," Alan said, not believing it himself. "She's having a spa night with a girlfriend."

"I hope she is, but yesterday she dropped by my place to borrow a playhouse key," Elizabeth said. "She said she wanted to rehearse alone."

Alan arrived at the playhouse too late for anything except a show of bravado. Onlookers had gasped when he'd fought off the volunteer fireman who tried to restrain him. He'd charged the still-hot building, prepared for anything, even death, if it meant finding another body, that of his wife still alive against the odds.

Instead of martyrdom, however, he only achieved third-degree burns on his hands and face when the floor gave out and he fell through to a hot spot in the basement. And then, when he returned home from the Burn and Plastic Surgery Unit in Vancouver General Hospital, he heard the vicious rumors.

Emily had not been alone or rehearsing. The candle that had fallen over onto a stack of papers and started the fire was one of eight. A melted sex toy was found in the ruins.

The names of possible lovers were bandied about by the police until airtight alibis were established for each of the men. In the end, foul play was ruled out. When the fire was ruled accidental, Alan committed himself to the onerous task of rehabilitating his wife's reputation. In the spring after her death, he invented Kingpin Al Day.

Which, at present, a bunch of drunks were growing impatient to witness.

"Well folks." Alan projected his bass voice to be heard above Jim Cuddy's plaintive request to be "The Last to Know." "I know you're all waiting on me."

Conversations ceased and bodies shifted to give their owners a better view.

Jo-Jo Green took advantage of the sudden lull to urge her man to "Take it off. Take it all off!" to which someone added a drum roll. Her wicked grin revealed a four-leaf clover painted on the right incisor. If he survived the next hour or so, Alan would have to discuss the gravity of the day with her. He would not have Emily disrespected by anyone close to him, no matter how understanding and warm-bodied that anyone was.

Alan silenced the crowd's twittering with his trademark burning glance. "If I planned to strip," he said with a meaningful look for Jo-Jo, "it would be for the first time in public." When the laughter subsided, he added, "In fact, as you can tell by the burned bits, I'm wearin' the same blue jeans, cowboy shirt, and stetson that I wore the night my wife died."

The chastised crowd held its collective breath.

"You all know who I'm doing this for?"

"Emily!"

Alan's eyes misted at the name. "Say it again. Slowly this time. Say it like you mean it."

He noticed tears forming in the eyes of some of the women as the crowd complied. "Emily Rose."

"Yeah, you know." He paused for effect before shouting, "Come on then! What the hell are we waiting for?" The crowd stood with him. Some of the women sang "She'll be coming around the mountain" as he led the surge of bodies out the swinging doors and onto the boardwalk.

Despite the late hour, the sky blushed pink around a horizon-hugging sun. Kingpin stopped the crowd to let three little Indian kids ride one rusty bike past the Bar & Grill. Then he signaled the all clear with a wave of his arm. Over eighty pairs of boots slogged across the muddy street.

When they reached the riverbank, Kingpin stopped to size up the enemy. The ice flow seemed to skate down the waterway at a breakneck speed. Some of the chunks were bigger than his truck. His throat dried out and his sphincter tightened. He knew, all too well, what he'd gotten himself into.

No turning back now. He took a tentative step onto the steep bank, then slid, arms flailing, to the bottom. Needing time to regain his composure, he pretended to adjust the laces of his mountain-climbing boots. Then he stood tall — the heartbroken lover with his heart pinned to his sleeve. A Romeo courting death for the sake of his lost beloved. A giant of a man. A hero.

Chants of "Kingpin" rose and fell.

"Show time!" he shouted.

Forsaking land, he leapt onto a slab of ice as it butted momentarily against the shore. His weight redirected the slab's trajectory back into the bulk of the flow. The ice tumbled and churned around him, upending the slab. His legs dipped into frigid water as he heaved his body onto a car-sized chunk of ice. The ice waffled, but he held tight.

The idea was to ride the ice, while keeping his position in front of the crowd. Kingpin Al Day was not a solitary endeavor. An audience, the larger the better, was required.

For the next twenty minutes, he fought for his middle-aged life.

"Enough, Kingpin," a spectator finally bellowed, granting him permission to call it a day.

"Come on in, Daddy!" River echoed.

Alan rode a twirling chunk of ice to shore. He grasped his daughter's hand and let her haul him ashore. Once again, Kingpin Al Day officially ended. As he knew they would, the crowd went wild, almost drowning out the sound of whispered lies.

River entered the Everlasting Health Center with Mattie in tow. She waved to her banged-up father on his hospital bed before shepherding the boy onto a chair beneath a poster listing Alcoholics Anonymous meeting times, times she knew by heart. The boy scooped up a brochure on genital herpes from a coffee table and fished a crayon out of his pants pocket. "Surprise me with a masterpiece," she said.

As she approached Kingpin Al, he seemed dazed and exhausted from his ordeal on the ice. He also looked older than he had that morning. Each Kingpin Al Day seemed to add a decade to his life. A few more seasons and he'd look venerable.

River touched her father's hand. The scar tissue was too smooth. "How're you feeling, hero?" she asked.

Alan smiled. "Dried out and flat. Like roadkill."

"Deer or deer mouse?"

Instead of answering, River tapped her father's bruised hand. "You look like a bloody pincushion. You'd think that Phyllis would get good at IVs. You know, what with all the practice Everlasting's dehydrated drunks provide."

"I stayed on the ice one minute and twenty-seven seconds longer today than I did last year. Beat my all-time record by forty seconds."

"You did yourself proud."

Alerted by her patient's attempted laughter, Phyllis Mounteraunt, the clinic's Nurse Practitioner, poked her head out of an office. A pen was balanced above each ear and she held a third. "Five minutes, River. The hero took a beating, didn't he?" She waggled the pen in her hand at Alan. "He needs his beauty rest."

"Be careful, Daddy," River leaned over to whisper into her father's ear. "Word is that Phyl's a nymphomaniac."

"My lucky day. Maybe she'll have her way with me while I sleep."

River feigned a swat at her father's arm. "I'm telling Jo-Jo you said that."

"Go right ahead. She won't believe you. She knows I'm a one-woman man."

River bit down on her tongue to keep from blurting out, "Yeah, but which woman?" She liked Jo-Jo and felt for her, but the barkeeper's short skirts were no match for the Emily's sanctified memory. A pity. River was used to her motherless state, but Mattie needed a decent grandmother, someone other than Lenore.

Phyllis coughed in the office. River wondered how much of the conversation she would hear and how much she would pass on. That's how they could entice the tourists — with a sign proclaiming Everlasting as the home of the world's biggest rumor mill.

Mattie interrupted. "Mamma?" he said as he handed his mother the brochure. "I'm finished."

River turned the paper upside down and then side to side. When she had it upright once again, she figured out that the squiggles of line represented a stick man family. One stick child nestled between three stick adults. Only the child had full facial features and hair, the rest were bald and lacked noses. A wild-eyed cat pounced off to one side and a yellow smirking sun threatened to plop on the stick people's heads like a sunny-side-up egg.

"Nice," River said. She touched the largest stick man. "Who's this?"

"That's Dad." Mattie rubbed a finger over two hunchbacked figures. "And that one's Uncle Wainwright — he's got a sore back. And that one's Grandma Lenore. She's old and cranky."

"Lenore's not *old,*" Alan said. "We went to school together."

"Where are Grandpa and me?"

The boy took the paper back. He turned it over as though searching for the missing family members. "Disneyland?" he said with hope. Seconds later, a gurgle rose in his throat. His face blanched.

"Honey?" River said. It couldn't be, but it was. Mattie was sick. *Again.*

To prove her suspicion, the boy retched.

"Phyllis," River shouted to the nurse. She touched the back of her hand to her son's forehead. She turned to her father. "Mattie's getting hot again."

The nurse jogged the ten feet from the office and peered at the boy. "There's a nasty flu going around."

"Lately it seems like he gets sick every single month," River said.

"You know the last set of tests didn't show anything abnormal, River."

"I know."

"But, if you're still worried, we could send him back to White-horse for another round, just to be sure." Phyllis turned to Kingpin Al. "Think you'll be up to driving them in this week?" Everyone in town knew that River had failed her learner's test three times before giving up on the hope of becoming a driver.

"I'd rise from my deathbed to help my grandson."

"You aren't dying, Dad."

Mattie stepped away from his mother. He wiped his mouth with the back of his hand. "I'm okay now, Pa-Pa. You don't have to drive me nowhere."

"Poor brave baby," Phyllis cooed.

"Do you aim to turn my grandson fey?"

River hoisted the boy onto her hip. "Can we stay here tonight?"

"He's better off in his own bed if it's just the flu. Keep him well hydrated and topped up with Tylenol and you'll both be fine. I promise."

It seemed to River that Mattie melted as she carried him along the sagging boardwalk. The fight had drained out of him during the fifteen-minute journey from the clinic to the opposite end of town. Normally a four-minute walk, River struggled to take each step with the boy's heavy body weighing her down. His cheek pressed against her neck felt like a steaming dim sum dumpling.

For the first few blocks he had wrapped his legs around her waist, but now they hung limp and his boots banged against her knees with each step. The courage with which he usually began each bout of illness had given away to lethargy. Though it had felt mid-grade when they began the walk, now she guessed his temperature at one hundred and four, a searing heat that would steal away a little more of his childhood.

If Mattie hadn't already been bruising the heck out of her legs with his Spiderman boots, she would have tried to do the job herself. Going home had been the wrong decision; she should have insisted on staying at the clinic in sight of Phyllis, Gravol suppositories, and intravenous fluids. It seemed unfair that her mind shut off whenever Mattie needed her to make clear, logical decisions about his welfare.

She reminded herself it probably was just the flu again. Mothers could take care of their children's minor illnesses at home without going into a panic. Except, when other mothers did seek out medical help, they didn't have pediatricians in Whitehorse snidely suggest they might have Munchausen by proxy. Nor did they pass out in the Whitehorse library after discovering what those weird words meant — that they manufactured their children's illnesses to get sympathy and attention.

River had stayed sober, learnt how to cook healthy meals, and taught Mattie to read with an expensive phonics program she was still paying for, but these accomplishments weren't enough. The facts were that, although Mattie didn't have any symptoms of fetal alcohol syndrome, except maybe failure to thrive, she'd been drunk during his conception and several times in the first few weeks of pregnancy. Whenever she passed the liquor store, caught people whispering, or saw idiotic Henry Bose riding past in So-Wah's truck, she believed in her guilt anew.

"Mommy." Mattie's voice tickling against her the base of her neck disrupted her self-flagellation session. "I want..." His voice trailed off into an incomprehensible whisper.

When she hitched his body higher, he tried to wrap one leg back around her waist, but failed. "What pumpkin?" When he got through this bout of illness, she would give him anything within her limited means to give — a new Lego set, Rollerblades, a baseball mitt, a pound of candy. "What do you want?"

"...my daddy," Mattie said.

Turquoise paint gave their old, permafrost-twisted house a deceptive appearance of youth. The front porch listed to the southeast.

There was an antique porch light to guide the wayfarer home, its glass cracked and the metal rusted through. River climbed the front stoop of the home where she had lived all but the two married years of her life, breathless and on the verge of tears.

She rested Mattie on the porch to slip off his rubber boots. They were adorable and innocent with their flying superhero decals. When he started kindergarten in the fall, she wondered if he would still wear the boots and his red nylon cape over blue pajamas, or if peer pressure would make these things uncool. One thing was certain: he wouldn't wear them if Cameron had his way. That dung beetle discouraged childish imagination and innocence. If River had stayed with the man, he would probably have the boy smoking cigarettes and getting tattoos of naked women by now.

She removed her own boots, heavy with spring mud, then lifted the boy and put him down on a chair in the foyer. As always, the smell of dust and loneliness greeted her as she entered the house. To the left, the living room maintained its museum status although Alan had agreed to remove the dead plants when the toddling Mattie developed a taste for soil. The only other change was the addition of photographs, both professional and amateur, all of Mattie at every conceivable stage of cuteness.

She entered the kitchen in search of children's bubble-gum-flavored Tylenol and a thermometer. Kingpin Al Day curios littered the kitchen table. The newspaper clips, pins, videos, and other paraphernalia were evidence that Alan had needed to psyche himself up before the day's ice walk, although he would never admit his fear or misgivings to River.

With a plastic syringe and the bottle of Tylenol in hand, River made her way back towards the foyer. Mattie whimpered as she made the Herculean effort to get him up the stairs, down the hallway and into his single bed with the cowboy motif sheets, a gift from Alan.

She gave Mattie a dose of medicine, then wet a face cloth in the bathroom sink and used it to wipe the sweat from his face and chest. She checked his temperature every minute until it fell from 104 to 100 degrees Fahrenheit. Then she turned on the baby monitor she kept for use on such occasions, and went downstairs.

While coffee percolated on the stove, she forced herself to look through her father's ridiculous memorabilia. The collection seemed at odds with itself. Cheerful buttons in bright pink with the words *For Emily* shared company with faded newspaper articles offering graphic descriptions of the fire and state of Emily's corpse. Fortunately, the reporters didn't quote any of the town's meaner residents who called Alan a crispy critter and Emily a hockey puck.

River had yet to forgive Alan for allowing her to sleep through that tragic night. When she woke the next morning, instead of Alan, Mr. Winkwest was in the kitchen making breakfast. The old man told her the facts of her mother's death and father's injuries, then tried to calm River's hysteria with a plateful of apple cinnamon pancakes. River had knocked the food from his hand and run all the way to the playhouse. She had held an irrational expectation that she would find her mother. Instead, she encountered a lake of ice guarding the theater's charred remains.

She collected Alan's memorabilia and tucked it out of sight in a cupboard. She had more immediate things to cry about.

Although it was only seven o'clock, she was dead tired from the turmoil of the day, yet she didn't dare sleep. What she needed was company to keep her awake. For Mattie's sake she knew she should call Cameron, but when she picked up the address book it flipped open to the Y page. She placed a finger under the only name listed, that of Jovan Yarddog penciled in with a beginner's handwriting, proof that their friendship had blossomed in grade one. Since her divorce, Jovan had begun to infiltrate her thoughts and even, it seemed, to shadow her movements. Just yesterday they'd stood in the same line at the bank. And the week before, he had been carving a log into a bear in his yard when she drove by as a passenger in Alan's truck. Suddenly she longed to call him.

She lifted the receiver, hesitated, and then restored the address book to the drawer. She pressed speed-dial and got her ex-husband's answering machine. "Mattie has another fever." She paused, wishing she could take back the information. One day soon, she would tell Mattie that Cameron wasn't really his father.

And then, when he asked who was, what would she say? *Oh, some guy* wouldn't cut it as an answer.

The message machine beeped the end of the time to leave a message. She pressed speed-dial a second time. "We're upstairs," she said. "Leave the booze outside and let yourself in."

Mattie, who had slept through a night of high fever and his mother changing the sweat-soaked sheets twice, woke to the sound of loud snoring. It was morning, and his father lay on the floor by his bed, an empty bottle tipped over by his head so that it looked as though the contents had poured into his ear.

Cameron mumbled the word *bear* as he rolled over, away from the bottle. The word made Mattie look for his teddy, which he spied on the dresser across the room. The stuffed toy, which had once belonged to his mother, was missing both eyes and one paw, but its cuddles always made Mattie feel better when he was sick.

"Bear!" Cameron said again. This time his eyes flew open in what looked to Mattie as surprise. They darted around in their sockets a few times before the eyes closed again. Mattie waited for his dad to wake completely and get him his teddy, but he started snoring again instead.

"Mom," Mattie whispered. His body felt as hot as a chicken pie right out of the oven, so hot he could burn someone's tongue. And his stomach felt like it was going to barf. The plastic bowl his mom always left on his bedside table for emergencies was on the floor next to the empty bottle.

Mattie rolled to the edge of the bed and let his body fall to the floor. He needed his bowl, but didn't have the strength to crawl over his father's body. A gurgle rose in his throat, and then a thin stream of liquid gushed from his mouth and onto Cameron's neck and chest. Mattie gasped for breath between spasms.

Cameron's arm flung over the boy, then pulled him in close to his chest which made Mattie even hotter. Through his tears, the boy saw a smile on his barf-covered father's face.

"Teddy," Mattie cried without hope.

"Big effing bear," the sleeping Cameron replied.

Good Food, Good Friends, Good Family

For one glorious summer day, River was free to do as she pleased. To celebrate Mattie's graduation from kindergarten, he and Alan had journeyed to Dawson with plans that included Robert Frost's poetry and Chinese food. A warm southern breeze, possibly the last of the season, flowed in through an open window to tug at curtains and clothes. Mindful of wilderness safety, she filled a canteen of water and pocketed a Mars bar. After writing a note for her men, she secured a jacket around her waist and then headed out of town on foot.

She waved at Mr. Winkwest who sat on a rocker on his porch door watching the inactivity on Eight Street. The geriatric Working Boy lay on his side on the dirt that stood in for a lawn, dreaming horsey daydreams. "I'm on foot today," she shouted to reassure man and horse.

Mr. Winkwest sipped from a paper-bag-covered bottle in response. "That Injun asked me to pass on a message."

"Which Indian?"

"The one who carves statues."

"Jovan?"

"If you say so."

"Well, what's the message?"

"Angel."

"Angel?"

Mr. Winkwest nodded. "Yup. Angel."

"That's it?"

"He said you'd know what he meant. I warned him you weren't no clairvoyant, if that's what he thought, but he didn't listen."

River thanked the man, then crossed the town. Leaving a one-word message with her neighbor was the closest Jovan had come to reinitiating communication after years of silence, and his boldness thrilled her.

Ten minutes later, she reached the edge of town, where there was a dark hole in a blaze of green. As she drew close, she saw that someone else had taken the trail that morning: the mud held fresh shoe prints and a spider web was in tatters. After a moment's hesitation, she plunged in. The beauty of the day and her heightened mood seemed to promise immunity from bears, or even Big Foot, if he existed. She followed the footprints up and over a rockfall, where their outline quickly faded.

An hour later, after a run past a bear-flattened patch of berries, and more than one fall, River reached the settlement. She made her way down to a pebble beach. The languid Yukon River rolled past as she squatted to wash the sweat from her face and dirt from her hands. Clean and fresh, she stood to face the settlement, which was shrouded in eerie silence. Beech tree leaves fluttered like green and gold butterflies above an old schoolhouse. Other buildings survived in varying states of decay. A few had collapsed, and the smell of wood rot hung heavy in the air.

Other than her private times with Mattie, River had rarely experienced such happiness since she and Jovan were children together.

A bell tower straddled the pitched roof of a white clapboard church. The bell was missing, but vibrant stained glass glowed in the mahogany-trimmed windows. She tramped up the broad stairs. Inside, the carved angel offered greetings with wings raised for flight. She patted its sky-blue gown. It was exactly as she remembered: the comforting presence of the angel, the delicious cool of the building after a hike, and the beauty of stained glass reflected on glowing wood.

A crunch made River's heart skitter. She tiptoed towards the sound and saw Jovan resting on a pew with his bare feet pointed towards a window and an apple in his hand. One black braid whirl-pooled on his chest. The floppy fishing hat he wore was the same one he had worn for years. With a mischievous grin, Jovan extended a second apple and said, "I thought you might be hungry."

Their meeting had the feel of a happy dream that, after years of nightmare, River had just woken up to. Jovan's smile with its one chipped tooth produced a live current that arced towards her. Its heat rushed through her body and scorched the floor beneath her feet.

In taking the apple, she made good and sure to touch his hand longer than strictly necessary.

By an unlucky coincidence, Cameron Leanard arrived at the abandoned settlement just as true love ignited within the church. He had a killer hangover and five minutes to spare. A rendezvous had been arranged with his American contacts, and the pack on his back held dried bear gallbladders stored in zip-lock freezer bags soon to be smuggled to lucrative Asian markets by way of the Top of the World Highway and the Anchorage International Airport. For his part in the decimation of a species, he would be well reimbursed.

As he paced the beach, a powerboat approached. He controlled his anxiety with plans of cold beer at Jo-Jo's Bar & Grill and a romp in the sack with Kendra, the Bar & Grill's newest waitress. Wiping sweat from his palms onto his jeans, he walked towards the boat as it beached.

Inside the church desire revved through River's body like a twenty-horsepower engine. The apple forgotten where it had rolled to the floor, she concentrated on kissing Jovan Yarddog. "Let's do this forever," she said. "Let's never, ever stop."

He blocked her lips with a hand. "There's a boat on the beach."

River captured his braid. She wrapped it around her neck and cinched him in tight. "Ignore it."

"Probably tourists," he said. "Hold that thought. Seeing a half-naked Indian on the beach should scare them off."

Cameron caught a glint of sun on something metallic in one of the guy's waistbands as he relinquished his backpack to larger of the two very large men in the boat. They were packing heat, he realized.

"Go easy," he warned them. "There's a year's work inside. I don't want it falling in the drink."

"What'ja think we are," Goliath snapped. "Fucking retards?"

Before Cameron could finish assuring them he thought no such thing, that in fact, he was sure they were both frigging geniuses, the driver gunned the engine.

"Hey!" Cameron dashed into the water. "Assholes! Where's my money!" He lobbed a rock after the departing boat.

"Next time, come alone," the driver shouted.

Cameron turned towards the inexplicable sight of Jovan Yarddog jogging down the beach towards him. River, his own ex-wife, emerged from the chapel, buttoning her blouse.

"Were those guys bothering you?" Jovan asked.

The Indian's face glistened with Cameron's ex-wife's saliva, but the bulge in his pants was a joke. No wee willie was going to satisfy River, not after time spent with Cameron's considerable tool. Barker and Yarddog — what a piss-poor couple they'd make.

"You'll pay for this, Yarddog," he said.

"For what?"

"For her too. Mark my words, Indian. I'm gonna make you pay!"

River's feet felt cold in their white ballet slippers. Her nerves, never the strongest, were completely shot. Her skin crawled, and she pictured bundled nerves actively fraying at the ends. In the hopes that a change of view would help, she draped the frothy tulle of her mother's wedding dress over one arm and then tiptoed to the window of her bedroom.

The street below was empty except for Working Boy who ambled down the center of the road with an off-center sway to his arthritic hips. Not a good sign, she decided — the day called for a parade, with rose-covered floats, giant helium balloons, and a marching band.

As the horse veered left on Goldwell Avenue, Mattie appeared in the yard below. Dressed in a borrowed tuxedo, with his blond hair slicked back, he headed for a dirt pile with a toy loader.

"Matthew Alan Barker," River said. "Get back inside this

minute."

The boy grinned up at her before trudging around the side of the house where he kept a reserve dirt pile. River guessed his strategy, but lost the will to hinder his play even though it would mean a dirty ring-bearer.

River sighed and let the curtain fall back in place. The chronically ill and undersized child deserved whatever fun he could muster up. The Whitehorse doctors had sent him south to Children's Hospital in Vancouver where a specialist had diagnosed a rare blood ailment. Not just rare, but weird too. When she told people details, River could see the disbelief they were too polite to voice. Just like a werewolf, Mattie's well-being fluctuated with the cycles of the moon. During the full moon, his white blood cell count rose to normal levels, only to fall as the moon waned. Without a cure, the only hope of staying healthy lay in caution and good luck. And so, River and Jovan had planned their wedding to take place during the time of a full moon.

Mattie had decorated a card with a picture of a stick person in bed with a thermometer in its mouth, a full moon, and the words *Keep Out*. It hung by a string from the doorknob until it was needed again. The commitment to stay in Everlasting instead of moving to Whitehorse, where Mattie would have been isolated for a week each month in the hospital instead of in his bedroom, had proven difficult to make. In the end, a town meeting decided things. Phyllis, along with River, would oversee the care of Mattie during the boy's down times, and the villagers of Everlasting would take every precaution to keep their colds and viruses away from the Barker door. So far, so good, although his frailty and retarded growth remained serious complications of the disorder. Mattie had not caught anything contagious since his diagnosis, a fact for which River was both grateful and proud.

She stepped back from the window, then fell backwards onto the faded satin-and-lace spread of her childhood bed. Mattie's cot was an arm's length away. She stroked the cowboy quilt with its musty boy smell.

A rap on the door interrupted River's reverie. "Five minutes, darling," Alan said at the door.

"The door's not locked, Daddy." River rose from the bed. "Come on in."

Alan wore the same suit he had worn to River and Cameron's wedding. "You're a vision," he said. "If only your mother was here to see this day." The words were also a repetition. Last time he spoke them, a vision of her future as Mrs. Cameron Leanard had overwhelmed River. The vision of violence, of living in poverty, of sharing a house with her husband's unbearable mother had proved accurate.

But Alan's suit, his rah-rah speech, and the church where the ceremony would take place were where the similarities ended. She had chosen a prettier color for the wedding decorations (sea-foam green instead of pink), she wasn't nine months pregnant, and the groom was a far better model. Jovan was kind, gentle, and fun. He'd make a great father.

"I'm all thumbs," Alan said for the second morning-of-the-wedding time. "Could you knot my tie?"

She should have thought to buy her father a new suit, should have printed out a list of forbidden phrases, should have held the ceremony someplace totally alien like Houston, Texas or Wawa, Ontario.

"Nervous, honey?" Alan asked.

"Not so much." *Dread* seemed to best describe what River felt. But her fear was of the institution of marriage, not of spending her life with a mild-mannered artist. Second time lucky, River hoped as she twisted the maroon silk of his tie with her icicle fingers.

With his ex-wife's wedding slated for noon, Cameron had to hurry. Chartreuse ribbon and gold-flecked wrapping paper waited on his bedroom dresser while he knelt in the closet digging through boxes. At the bottom of the third box, he found a card with two embossed silver bells and the words *For the Two of You*. He opened the card and snorted as he read out loud. "'Dearest River and Cameron, Here is wishing you a long life of happiness together. With love, Alan Barker (Dad).'"

Alan's need to add "Dad" in parenthesis had cracked Cam up years ago. Now it cracked him up to think of River opening the card. The fish mouth she'd make as the joke hit home. The tears she'd try not to cry. The horror she'd experience when she opened the gift.

He stuffed the card into a mint green envelope and addressed the envelope to Mr. and Mrs. Jovan Yarddog. Next, with his jackknife, he severed the string that dangled a shriveled bear's paw from the ceiling rafter. He placed the souvenir into a blue Birks box. When the box was wrapped and tied with the bow, he put it into a plastic bag along with the card.

Cameron found Wainwright sprawled on the living room floor, drinking a can of Coke and watching a rerun of *I Dream of Jeannie*. When Wainwright was eighteen, he'd confessed a crush on Barbara Eden; the mileage Cameron had gotten from that secret was awesome.

"Hey, Wain," he said now, "I've got some cash with your name on it."

Wainwright rubbed his sallow eyes with his fists. "I'm watching Jeannie."

"Shit, dude, stop slavering. The chick's an old cougar now. She's had so much plastic surgery, her tits ride on the top of her head."

"That's a fib."

"A rerun's worth more to you than this, retard?" Cameron blocked the television with his body and fanned three twenties in front of his brother's face.

"Holy mackerel! That's enough to buy one of those genie lamps."

Cameron jerked the money away. "The favor first, dude."

Although the route to Jo-Jo's Bar & Grill via the old Everlasting cemetery led Wainwright out of his way, he took it. Cameron had commanded him not to get caught on the mission, and what Cam commanded, Cam got — most times, anyway. When the brothers were kids, Cam had always gotten the treats in the bottom of the cereal boxes and eaten most of the cereal too.

He even got the private bedroom at the top of the house, the one with the secret closet that looked like it was just part of the wall until you slid open a panel. The room had a ceiling beam for hanging things from. Wainwright still remembered the time Cam hung him up — by the feet, not by the neck, 'cause even idiots know hanging from the neck can kill you dead. The cord broke, and good thing, because all day had passed and Cam might not have let him down for weeks. Their mom, Lenore, said it served him fucking right for always playing Cam's Patsy. No use telling her they didn't play any games called by girl's names. She'd just have said, 'There's facts, boy, and there's truth.'

A truck took the turn down Croesus Street and headed straight for Wainwright. He felt the smile plop off his face like a frog spooked into a pond. Then he felt the prickle of fear start the slow crawl up his back. If someone he knew saw him now, the mission'd be in jeopardy. Here he was stuck on the open street. No bush to duck into for camouflage. No ditch to lay flat in. A failed mission meant no cash for sure. Maybe worse; when Cam got mad, he got real mad.

He swung the bag behind his back to hide it as the truck, full of gawking tourists, not locals, rolled past. He considered giving them the middle finger the way Cam did, but chickened out.

With the threat past, Wainwright returned to his previous line of thought. Too bad Kingpin Al hadn't shot Cam in his sleep like he used to promise he'd do, back in the good old days when River and Mattie still lived with the Leanards. Then Wainwright would have gotten the upstairs bedroom. Just as he worked up an image of his Flying Fortress, Tomahawk and Blue Angel airplane models flying against the sky-blue bedroom ceiling, he reached the entrance to the Everlasting Garden of Eternal Rest. Clarence Zalubniak sat on a camping stool at the foot of his dead mamma's grave, rearranging of her plastic flower collection. The stool was so low his stomach had to rest on his knees like they were a tea tray. "Out killing time?" he asked Wainwright.

Wainwright pretended the question was meant for Clarence's dead mamma so he wouldn't have to answer. He wasn't worried about Clarence seeing Cameron's present, because old people didn't count for shit in the world. That's what his grandpa Leanard had taught him just before he died, when the old man's skin had begun to stink like week-old meatloaf. "Old people don't count for shit in this world," he'd said. "Remember that boy, when you get as old and crippled up as me."

Wainwright wasn't old, but he was sort of crippled with his crooked back, so he already remembered.

His grandpa had been a World War II hero and Wainwright's hero too. He flew a plane that dropped some bombs right on the enemy's heads, which helped win the war. He also took Wainwright fishing for grayling and hunting for wildflowers to press in the family bible. Then he got old and not worth shit.

There was no pretending what Clarence Zalubniak said next wasn't aimed his way. "Heard you Leanards aren't welcome at the Barker-Yarddog wedding this afternoon."

"Am too," Wainwright said. "River invited me herself. She called me up on the telephone to do it."

Facts ain't the truth. She *had* called him up with an invitation, though only to go get a burger at Jo-Jo's, her treat. While he wolfed down his burger platter and apple pie, she said that if she could have one special guest of honor at her wedding, it would be him. But she couldn't invite one Leanard and not invite them all. And she couldn't invite them all.

"Why not?" he said.

"Some things don't make you stronger," she said. "They just kill you."

Wainwright said it was okay; he didn't want River dead.

"Well, then. Suppose we'll see you there," Clarence said.

"Yup," Wainwright said. "You'll see me for sure. I'm the special guest of honor."

Kendra, Jo-Jo's newest hire, balanced at the top of a ladder tacking a sea-foam green crepe paper heart to the wall, when Wainwright slunk through the doors of the Bar & Grill. "The sign says we're closed," she said. "Can't you read?" Her words were mean because Wainwright could read, though not very well, so he decided to listen to the sound of her voice, which was nice.

"I don't want to order nothing."

"Nothing's exactly what's available."

A table near the base of the ladder was filled with steaming smorgasbord. Wainwright sidled closer. His mouth gushed in preparation for eating. Kendra's face was turned towards the wall. If he used stealth, maybe . . .

"I've got eyes in the back of my head," she warned, as she climbed down from the ladder. She turned to face him when she reached the bottom. "I'm done in here." She wiped her palms on her apron to show how done. "Which means you have to vamoose."

"I've got to leave this present for River," he said. River wouldn't like that it came from Cam, but she would like the gift which Cam said was the shiny black kangaroo bowl.

Kendra had both of her hands on her hips like she didn't believe him. She had nice legs sticking out of her waitress skirt (not as nice as Jeannie's), and a cartoon turtle tattooed on her ankle. Wainwright liked Kendra's turtle, but Cameron would like her big boobies. He had always been mean to River about her flat chest. He bragged his next wife would rival Dolly Parton.

"This gift is from my ma," he said as instructed. "Cam may not hold truck with River anymore, but Ma still does. Once a daughter-in-law, always a daughter."

"How big of her." Kendra filled a china plate with cheese chunks, Caesar salad, and a white roll. Then she passed the plate, along with a fork and green napkin to Wainwright.

"What's this?" he asked.

"The nothing you didn't order."

The salad was the best thing Wainwright had ever tasted, better even than the burger River had bought him the week before. He stuffed his mouth before asking, "You married?"

"Do I look insane?"

"Got a boyfriend?"

"Depends who's asking. You?"

Wainwright blushed. "Nope. My brother. He's got the hots for you." If it wasn't true yet, maybe it would be soon.

"Then my answer depends upon which of the rumors I've heard about him are true and which ones aren't. For instance . . ." Kendra topped up his plate. "Does your brother, or does he not, beat his women?"

"Not…" Wainwright said. He shoveled in a mouthful of bun to stop his mouth from finishing the sentence. He doubted she'd agree to be his new sister-in-law if he said, "Not anymore. He quit after busting River's nose."

Henry Bose's new place was a toad of a home, a squat dwelling into which his six-foot-four body barely fit. To pass through doorways he had to stoop. When seated on the loo, as he was now, his knees pressed against the opposite wall, making it hard to do his business. Instead of rolling out from a holder on the wall, the toilet paper perched on the back of the crapper — if he managed to take a dump, he'd have to twist his aching back to reach the paper.

"Say goodbye to the old place, Henry," the slant-eyed woman had said earlier that day. She honked as they drove away from his home of twenty-five years with the back of her truck piled high with boxes. The gooey sweetness of the chocolate-covered cherry she had brought him filled his mouth, making it hard for him to hear her words. "Do you know why you're moving?

Henry blinked once because he hoped that's what she wanted and because she had given him chocolate, but yes was a fib. At that moment, he couldn't even locate the word *moving* in his head. He knew which parts of his body hurt — his lower back, head, and right elbow — and that it was time to drink coffee. He didn't know anything else.

"It's because of your heart," she said.

Henry's heart . . . oh, yes. His sore, yearning heart.

"You'll be easier to keep an eye on in town," she added.

Henry's heart raced. The word *town* caused him great anxiety, although he could not explain why. But maybe town wasn't all bad. Maybe town was where Tom was lost.

A teenager had turned up once, claiming to be Henry's little boy.

When the impostor finally left, Henry felt relieved, but the trick left him shaken. There were questions he needed answered, but no longer possessed the skills to ask: When, for instance, would the real Tom come home? And why had he run away? And would the heartache of waiting kill Henry?

His back gave the expected twinge when he twisted around to reach the paper, so he left the roll on the floor by his feet. Because his bar of Dove soap was missing from the sink, he washed his hands with plain hot water, glad the slant-eyed woman wasn't around to nag him about the spread of germs.

A few steps took him out of the bathroom and into the kitchen. The toad house was three small rooms: the bathroom, a kitchen and a closet-sized bedroom, nothing else. His bed was too big for the room, so the slant-eyed woman had set up an army cot in there instead. The kitchen was the same dusty yellow as a pair of gingham curtains that had hung in his grandmother's farmhouse, curtains he somehow remembered with sudden clarity.

As it had in his trailer, the kitchen table sat in front of a window. He took his usual seat, hoping for the comfort of the familiar, but the view beyond the window was too different. Instead of a rusting car on rims, there were a street, a sidewalk and crooked houses. And instead of birds and the odd bear, there were people, more than he could count on one hand.

The woman had left meat loaf in the fridge for his lunch, and instructions to "Eat-it-up-soon." But the fluttering in his heart had reached his stomach and legs. He couldn't sit and eat when he wanted to move. His fingers twitched, his foot tapped. Rising from his seat, he made for the toad house's front door.

Outside, *town* waited.

A moment later he crossed the street to where a row of dusty trucks lined the curb out front of Saint Agreta's. He climbed the stairs and opened the church's front door. The otherwise empty foyer held floral arrangements, and the lilies in them made him sneeze. Drawn by the sound of laughter, he pushed through the inner sanctuary doors and then stepped inside. When no one seemed to notice his presence, he let the door swing shut behind him.

The pews teemed with people dressed in their Sunday best. At the front of the church, a man in a black suit roared with laughter. A bride and groom were locked together in a kiss. The word *funeral* popped into Henry's head.

The couple were flanked by candelabras. Henry watched the flames until they made him nervous. When one flared up, endangering those present Henry headed down the aisle, intent on performing heroics if need be.

At the halfway point, the slant-eyed woman grabbed his arm. "Henry," she hissed. "Go home. You weren't invited." He blinked once to reassure her of his good intentions.

The couple at the front ended their embrace.

Henry shook the housekeeper off and tried to speak. It couldn't be, but the woman kissing the man was his very own Emily Rose. She had not waited, as he had, for their reunion.

Then Henry noticed an even more heart-breaking thing. His son young Tom, dressed in a suit, stood at Emily's other side holding a pillow.

Strangers spoke words intended to stop him as he stumbled forward again. When he reached the front, he knelt in front of the boy. Then he said the only word he had spoken in decades, "Son."

"Help!" Emily croaked.

Two Indians in navy suits caught Henry from behind. He tried to fight them off as they lifted him to his feet, dragging him away from Tom.

The slant-eyed woman warned them about his yearning heart, but they didn't seem to hear.

As the men hustled Henry through the sanctuary doors, he watched Emily sit on the floor in a crumpled heap. "It's no fair," he heard her say. "Other people get to have boring weddings. Why don't I?"

It was true then, River thought as she took off her wedding dress in her father's house, the terrible thing she had suspected for years. Her beautiful boy was half Bose. A tremor of disgust ran through her body. But how had she come in contact with Henry? After visiting the Elizabeth Fang Playhouse, had she ridden Mr. Winkwest's horse to Henry's dump on the outskirts of town? Had she knocked on his trailer door or just waltzed in uninvited? Had she forced herself on the poor brain-damaged man? And why, oh why, oh why?

She picked up the skirt of her sea-foam green going away suit, and stepped into it. If people could die of shame, she was a prime candidate. She had survived the ceremony and the formal photography session afterwards, but still had a wedding reception to get through before she and Jovan could leave for the anonymity of Banff. And, unless she could convince Jovan to relocate after their honeymoon, she'd have to get through fifty or sixty years of living in Everlasting among a bunch of tongue-wagging busybodies.

She couldn't do it — not sober.

River finished dressing, took a final look at the sheltering bedroom, then opened the door, being careful not to let the hinges squeak. The fan was on in the upstairs bathroom, which meant Alan would be indisposed for the next few minutes, but if she wanted to be well on the way to drunk before he could stop her, she'd have to hurry.

The spare key to the booze cabinet was still stuffed up the hollow leg of the kitchen table, where she'd hidden it years before. She opened the cabinet door, twisted off the lid of a new bottle of Bacardi, and got down to the serious business of rotting her guts.

Five minutes later, when Alan came downstairs, he took one look at River at the kitchen table with a partially consumed bottle of Bacardi. Then he removed a bottle of whiskey from the open cabinet and carried it to the table.

"So," Alan said as he took a seat.

"So."

"Some wedding."

"Yup," River said, "bottoms up."

An hour later, River stumbled alone into Jo-Jo's Bar & Grill for her wedding reception. She stopped at the entrance to take stock of the situation. The wedding guests were milling about, looking hungry and bored. Alan's seat was empty. Although he hadn't brought up the fact that one of his late wife's rumored lovers had claimed paternity of his grandson during their shared drinking session, he had declined to attend the reception, citing personal reasons. Mattie sat beside Jovan in the chair meant for River. The boy had covered the white paper tablecloth with crayon drawings while Jovan chatted with the members of his family who took up the bulk of the table to his right. The set-up placed Sam Coyote, one of Jovan's nephews, at the table's midpoint, a fortunate placement River decided — at least she wouldn't be the center of attention.

"Aunty River," Sam and some of the younger Yarddog family members began chanting when they spied her.

River tried, but failed, to hide behind a plus-sized guest.

"Hey, Mrs. Yarddog!" Jovan called out, "For a married woman, you sure are one foxy chick."

The compliment, or the plus-sized guest's strong perfume, knocked River flat.

When dinner was announced, Jovan's mother placed a hand on River's unsteady shoulder to keep her on the chair. "Don't budge," she said. "I'll fetch you a plate." She returned with two scoops of potato salad, a mass of quivering perogies topped with onion and sour cream, four slices of honey ham, a pile of hot wings, a buttered roll, and lasagna. "Eat up," she said. "You need the carbohydrates and protein — people will stare until the bride sobers up."

River looked and, sure enough, everyone's eyes were pointed her way. She closed her own against the sight. If she had to, she would eat her whole meal blind.

She jabbed her fork into what she hoped was the food on the plate, and then lifted it to her mouth.

"Here's a bib," Jovan said.

After dinner, River let Jovan lead her to the gift table. She hadn't yet opened her eyes, so he sat her on a chair and propped her elbows on the table. "Hang in there, love," he said when she groaned. "When we get to the hotel, I promise to wash your face each time after you vomit."

"I'll do the same for you," River said. "If you ever go on a bender."

"I won't and I love you."

"Excuse me, love birds. Care for some coffee?"

River opened her eyes to see Kendra standing in front of her holding a full pot. If she moved in closer, the waitress would block her completely from the guests' view. River motioned with a finger until Kendra stepped closer. "Don't tell anyone," River stage-whispered, "but I'm sloshed out of my gourd."

Kendra filled a cup with coffee. "You don't say," she said.

"Yup. When I'm drunk, people expect a show," River said. "That's why they're gawking. They want entertainment. But I won't give it. Not this time."

"You might want to drink your coffee black then," Jovan suggested.

"Weddings are hell," Kendra said. "I don't know why people insist on having them."

"I gave birth at my last one," River said. "That was worse."

"It's shameful!" Agnes Everlasting said to Elspeth Ferment from a nearby table. "Falling off the wagon on her wedding day."

"Ignore the old bag," Kendra suggested. "Maybe you should open your presents to take people's minds off of you."

"Great idea!" River said. She held a box aloft. "Thanks, whoever. We needed one of these."

"Careful," Jovan warned. "Might be fragile."

"I know. I've done this before. Remember?" River ripped the envelope to remove the card. "For the two of you," she read aloud. "Dearest River and Cameron." She tore the ribbon and paper from the present and dumped out a severed bear's foot. "Daddy?" She tried to locate Alan, forgetting he was sitting at home in a state of denial. "Why?"

"Oh," Kendra said. "Shit."

One month into her second marriage, River Barker-Yarddog stared at a blank wall in her prefabricated home. All the *stuff* in her new life overwhelmed her. Jovan was a pack rat. The chaos was necessary to

his art, he claimed. Hadn't she notice that he liked random place-
ments of objects before they were married? Didn't she see the po-
tential value of old running shoes, deer skulls, broken plates, and
miniature pine cones? How else did she expect him to earn a living?

River grasped the handle of her coffee mug, and with her other
hand scribbled *Mrs. Jovan Yarddog* in the dust Jovan had made while
sanding a woodcarving on the table. She sighed for no one's sake
but her own.

"I wish . . . " she started, but had to stop. She didn't know what
she wished for. Perfection, she suspected. A perfect refuge.

The front door swung open and her gorgeous, tall sexy husband
entered, bringing with him the smell of autumn.

"I saw two wolves," Jovan said. "Up by Medicine Creek." River
watched his muscles flex as he unlaced his hiking boots. "They were
eating a moose calf."

"Did you ask them to share?"

He wrapped his arms around her shoulders. "Miss me?"

"Maybe a smidgen. I considered masturbating."

Jovan nibbled her ear. "Cheeky girl. You should have come with
me. We could have made love outside."

"In front of the wolves."

"They wouldn't care," Jovan said. "It's not too late. We can still
go for a hike if you want."

"No way. I can't leave this dirty house. It's my sanctuary."

"If you're still hiding from our neighbors, don't sweat it. No-
body else will be outside this early in the morning. Everyone else is
asleep in their beds. Hung over. Chasing dreams."

"Uh-huh. And I bet I know what they dream about."

"River Barker-Yarddog is not that important . . ." Jovan kissed
her neck. ". . . to anyone except me and Mattie."

When his hair swept down around her face, River pressed into
that dark place, a wild creature in its burrow, hidden and safe. His
skin smelled of mossy animal lairs. She should have been born a
wolf. Then she could roam the wilderness on moonlit nights. She
could chase down rabbits and eat them raw. She could hide with her
pups in the comfort of a cave. She could bite any human who dared

to come close.

"Let's move out of town," she said. "Let's build a cabin in the woods."

"Let's go wake up Mattie and go to Dawson. Get some Chinese food. Five Spice Noodles and Barbequed Pork. Yum!"

"Let's make a baby first."

Jovan called her bluff.

Tom lay in bed and stared at the call display as his phone on his bedside table rang for the third time. He had to give it to Elizabeth Fang: he'd moved five times since she first tracked him down, yet she'd found him again every time. She never had anything of importance to say. Everlasting's gossip meant nothing to him — he disliked the people who lived there as much as they disliked him, the supposed updates on Henry's mental and physical state were never updated, and her lame attempts to remind him of his, apparently idyllic, boyhood pissed him off. Their short conversations generally ended with him telling her to go screw herself.

Sherri, his girlfriend of less than a month, stirred on her side of the bed. It would likely be late afternoon before her body metabolized enough of the gin she'd consumed the night before to allow her to function normally. He wouldn't be with her if the camouflage of dim lights and an alcoholic blur hadn't given her a glow on the evening they'd met. In the morning light, her skin showed the ravages caused by a bad diet, poor grooming, and, to his shame, by Tom's own rage.

He'd never hurt a woman before, but the night before she'd told him that she'd left her husband for his sake. Tom didn't give a flying fuck about the jerk. What pissed him off was that she'd handed the coke addict full responsibility of the couple's two- and three-year-old boys. If they were holy terrors, Tom might have been more inclined to understand Sherri's point of view. But they weren't. They were the kind of kids his mother used to call "little angels." The kind of kid he'd been before all the shit with his dad went down.

Blood had dripped from Sherri's swelling lip when she asked, "Why don't you let Corrie and Billy live here if they mean so damned much to you?"

"Screw off," Tom said.

Sherri hadn't gotten off the floor where his punch had landed her. She sat with her head bowed saying, "Fucking hypocrite," under her breath until Tom had to either leave or kill her. When he returned, she was in his bed, sleeping as though nothing had happened.

Detox, a toy poodle pup Sherri had bought for fifty bucks from an acquaintance who fenced stolen purebreds for a living, yapped at the phone. Tom resisted the urge to boot the animal off the bed. The dog had nipped him when he came home, then kept him up until dawn with its whimpering. He lifted the receiver and barked into it. "Give up, Elizabeth."

"Tom-Tom. Always defensive when all I want to do is chat."

Detox rolled onto her back and released a dribble of urine. "Fucking animal," Tom said.

"Pardon?"

"Not you."

After a pause, Elizabeth said, "I'm calling for a reason. Things aren't good with your dad."

"Tell me something I don't know."

"You need to come home."

Tom glanced down the hallway of the single-wide trailer he'd rented from a farmer. The open-plan kitchen and living room had the same decrepit, barely lived-in look that his father's rooms had had on Tom's last trip north. The view out the window, though more lush, was similar to the view from his father's bedroom window — a gravel driveway, rusting vehicles, weeds. "I am home," he said.

"So-Wah found your father unconscious in his bathroom last week. With his weak heart, Henry's not going to live forever."

Tom muscled out the pang of anxiety the news caused him. "When he passes," he said, "be sure to give the family my condolences."

"If that's how little you care, you don't deserve him."

"Earth to Elizabeth — I *don't* have him. Never have."

The pup's needle-thin teeth pricked the skin of Sherri's hand, waking her. "Who're you talking to?" she asked as she rubbed sleep from her eyes. The cut on her lip reopened, exposing wet flesh.

"No one."

"If it's another woman, tell her she'd better watch her back." Sherri plopped the puppy onto her chest. "Who's Mommy's baby?" she said. "You are. That's right. You're my little darling."

"Do you ever wonder if you're wasting your time on me," he said into the receiver. "Has it occurred to you that maybe I just don't care?"

"It *is* another woman!" Sherri made a failed attempt to grab the phone. "I'll kill the bitch."

"If you mean that, I'll stop calling," Elizabeth said. "Just say the word, Tom, and this will be the last time you hear from me."

Tom listened to Elizabeth breath on the other end of the line. Hers were the shallow, rapid breaths of someone in distress. He should say the word, should tell her to go fuck herself once and for all. Instead, he picked up the puppy and dropped it off the bed, against Sherri's protestations.

"Go home to your fucking kids," he told her.

Then he hung up the phone.

"Sweet holy Moses!" Tom's seatmate on the Vancouver to White-horse bus said. "I've got elephantiasis already! Last time I made this trip, they had to carry me off the bus." The elderly woman popped a peanut into her mouth and then offered Tom the bag. "Sitting makes my legs puff up like shrimp chips in hot oil."

Tom ignored the woman, wishing to hell she'd just shut up. He zipped his black leather jacket against the cold. The chill in his body matched that of his mind. If he got any colder, he'd freeze in place.

"Here, dear. If you won't have a peanut at least share my blanket. With the prices we pay to travel, you'd think they'd heat the bus." The woman dealt a section of down quilt onto his lap. "Where're you headed?"

Tom shut his eyes before answering. "Home, I guess."

"Good on you. You should talk to my daughter for me. I said to her, would it kill you to make the trip home just once before I die?

And do you know what she said?"

"Why would I?" Tom said.

"'Yup'. That's what she said. It would kill her. Honestly, sometimes I don't know why I bother." The woman munched another handful of peanuts before adding, "It wasn't me she had all the trouble with. It was her father."

As the engine chugged up a steep grade, Tom concentrated on the warmth spreading beneath the woman's blanket. He tried to picture a reunion with Henry, but the years had erased his father's image, and he came up blank.

In the early hours of morning, the Greyhound bus dragged its haunches to a stop. Hydraulic doors glided open. A ribbon of fresh air teased Tom awake. The hour, four-thirty a.m., felt queasy and he considered skipping breakfast to save his limited cash.

His seatmate woke with a start. After cracking the stiffness out of her neck and back, she jostled Tom. "Pit stop," she said. "And none too soon. I could hold my own in a pie-eating contest right about now." Somehow Tom had claimed most of the woman's blanket for his own use while he slept. He restored it all to her lap without an apology. Then he eased his body into the aisle to join the slow shuffle of passengers.

"Bringing up the rear," the woman chirped.

After the confines of the bus, the vast space outside felt too brisk and unreal. Mackerel clouds swam upstream in a phosphorescent sky. Cassocked trees surrounded the truck stop. Tom shivered in his thin jacket as he walked past gas and diesel pumps towards a carved grizzly bear that guarded the entrance to a log restaurant.

The restaurant's windows reflected the passengers, loaded down with chattel and heads bowed against the chill as they funneled into the restaurant. Taped to the window, a sign advertised the *Early Bird Special*. Three eggs, two sausage links, three strips of bacon, hash browns. and coffee cost $8.95. Tom moved to the lee of the building and lit up his last cigarette. Beside the first, a second sign read *Help Wanted*.

An hour later, the Greyhound took to the road, minus one

passenger. Elbow deep in grease-clotted water, Tom didn't pause watch it go.

The newly christened Charity Barker-Yarddog disturbed a luncheon held in her honor when she hooked a finger into the side of her own mouth, then tugged for all she was worth. Until that moment, she had not realized how cruel the world could be, and the shock made her wail in indignation. Her cries drowned out the conversations going on between the friends and family members who had gathered to celebrate the baby's arrival.

Mattie, who possessed an uncanny talent for calming his baby sister, wasn't able to help. A guest, Agnes Everlasting, had arrived with a cough and runny nose, forcing the boy into isolation in a third-floor bedroom.

"These things should come with a manual," Jovan joked as he tried jiggling the car seat in which his daughter writhed.

"She probably has colic," a Yarddog cousin surmised. "Dip your finger in whiskey and let her suck it. That'll calm her down."

"Now there's a wise suggestion," yet another cousin quipped, "considering . . ."

"Considering what?" River said, as she carried a bowl of potato salad in from the kitchen. "Who her mother is?"

"I was going to say, her age, but have it your way."

Charity yowled louder.

"Stop that racket!" the party's hostess, Elspeth Ferment, demanded. The oyster burger in the old woman's hands trembled. "Shut that dog up!"

"It's not a dog, Mrs. Ferment. It's a baby." Jovan's mother placed her mouth near the old woman's ear and spelled it out, "B-A-B-Y."

"I don't care if it's a ferret. Shut it up!"

River lifted Charity from her car seat. Still fussing, the infant groped with her mouth, desperate to find a nipple. River lifted her shirt and dropped the cup of her nursing bra.

Jovan's sister shrieked. She plastered a hand over her seven-year-old son Sam's eyes. "For crying out loud, River," she said. "At least cover up with a blanket."

Jovan tucked a section of the table cloth into the neck of River's shirt, making a tent over the baby. He smiled widely. "There we go. All decent."

"It's just a breast," River said.

"What did that strange person just say?" Elspeth demanded.

"It's just a B-R-E-A-S-T," Jovan's mother shouted.

"What is?" Elspeth jammed an oyster burger into her toothless mouth. She spoke through the food. "The dog?"

"No, aunty. The breast."

A breaded oyster plopped from Elspeth's mouth. The guests watched as it bounced from the table to the floor. The seeded top of the Kaiser bun fell from the old woman's hand. Jovan's mother handed her another burger.

"Hey, Aunty River," Jovan's nephew, Sam Coyote, said. "You should have called your baby Chanel Number Five — so she could be named after perfume like my uncle Jovan."

"Charity's a good sight better than River, at least," Agnes Everlasting said. The old woman sneezed to punctuate her words.

"What's wrong with my name?" A tiny bit of the day's pleasure evaporated from River's heart.

"Not a goddamned thing," Alan said.

"It's a lovely name." Jo-Jo rested a placating hand on his thigh.

"It's a filthy hippy name," Agnes declared.

"Fools!" The force of old Elspeth's word sprayed gummed potato salad across the table.

River pushed her plate aside. "My mom wasn't a hippy and she bathed every day."

"A loose cannon, more like," Jovan's sister said.

"Enough!" Alan slammed a palm down on the table. "I will not have talk against my wife at this table."

Jo-Jo withdrew her hand from his thigh.

"Bunch of damned fools," Elspeth said. She opened her mouth again, but instead of an insult, nothing came out. Her eyes bulged.

"If she's choking," a Yarddog cousin observed, "someone should pound her back."

"Aunty Ferment?" Alan rushed to the old woman's side. Her

hands trembled at her throat. He helped her slide onto the hard-wood floor, letting the upturned Kaiser bun cushion her head.

Charity came unlatched from River's breast. She whimpered, but her mother didn't notice.

Alan took the old lady's paper-skinned hand into his own. "Hang in there, Aunty. Don't leave us."

When Everlasting's volunteer paramedic arrived, he found Elspeth Ferment's body covered by a tablecloth embroidered with the words *Good Food, Good Friends, Good Family.*

River sat on a sofa with Charity sound asleep on her lap. The paramedic had to look twice because River's plump breast was fully exposed and leaking milk.

Stranger yet, Agnes Everlasting hunched over the table and muttered something about the "damned blasted cold" as she tried to ignite a bowl of potato chips with a filigreed lighter.

"I'm so sorry," Jo-Jo said as she helped Alan reload her truck with the remains of the catered meal. She longed to hop out of her cherry red skirt and into something somber and sexless, something the Queen Mother might have worn to a ladies' luncheon. She tightened red lips over her tooth with its painted cap, hoping to hide the four-leaf clover's shameless optimism.

"I'd like to cancel our Friday date, Jo-Jo."

"Of course. Take some time. Just don't cancel me indefinitely." Jo-Jo watched as he stacked empty potato salad buckets into the back of the truck. "Alan?" she said.

"I don't know." He offered her a cooler bag. "This will have to fit up front."

"What don't you know?" Jo-Jo took the bag.

"About going on any more dates. What with my aunt's death coming on the heels of Emily's."

Jo-Jo stared. "You can't be serious."

Alan nodded. "I am."

Jo-Jo took a deep breath. "Have you heard how the Carrier tribe got its name?"

"Can't say as I have."

"It was because of their women. Decorum demanded that widows wait to remarry, so they loaded up backpacks with their husbands' cremated bones and carried them around for three years. It was ghoulish, but effective."

"Your point being?"

"Emily's bones just chased off your only suitor," Jo-Jo said.

Sy Mon

A belt of driving snow pelted the kitchen window of Mound Mansion, the derelict house left to River by Elspeth Ferment. River stirred a pot of bubbling spaghetti sauce, content to be inside with a warm fire, the rich smells of cooking, and her family around her. Mattie was immersed in *The Wish List,* and Jovan played with five-year-old Charity to keep her out of her mother's hair.

"Up, Daddy!" Charity begged for the hundredth time.

Jovan swung his daughter up in the air. Then he snuggled her close for a hug.

"Don't tickle, Daddy," she said. "I want to show you something in private." Charity loosened his braids and arranged the hair around both of their faces to make a tent. She held up her hands. "See?"

"Opposable thumbs! Way to go, Pumpkin! Proof you're part of a higher species."

"No, Daddy. The other things. On the end of each finger."

"Fingernails?"

"Dead stuff."

"Charity," River said. "If this topic occurred to you because of your brother's health, apologize this minute."

"I'm sorry, Mattie," Charity sang.

"Again," River warned. "And, this time, mean it."

"It's okay, Mom," Mattie looked up from his book to say. "I just ignore her."

"You listen to your mother," Jovan said. "Or else the tickle monster will come and get you."

Charity shrieked until Jovan stopped tickling.

"Down, Daddy," she said as she wiggled free. She tore the shrink wrap off a new CD that Jovan had brought in with the mail. "Hard rock!" She whirled around the kitchen like a ballerina on speed. Jovan bounded across the room, grabbed Mattie from the chair, and turned him upside down. While he strummed the boy's stomach like a guitar, Charity careened across the room towards them.

River turned off the heat beneath the sauce. She wiped her hands on the apron and then walked over to the table.

A guitar-wielding man was on the cover of the CD. River read the song list on the back, then flipped the case over. Something about the singer niggled. His face, with its cleft chin, looked oddly familiar. If she'd been a groupie, that might explain the familiarity, but she'd never attended a rock concert in her life. And she could count the televised music sessions she'd watched on one hand. It wasn't the man's music that triggered this sense of memory, she didn't recognize any of the song titles. It was the man himself.

She almost jumped when a voice in her head said, "You've touched that hair."

River looked closer. The hair in question was long and blond and oh so soft-looking. "Did I?" she said out loud.

"Did you what?" Jovan asked.

River carried the case over to the stove, where she would have more privacy. Was it possible that she'd also kissed that mouth (a not entirely pleasant experience, because the mouth had tasted of coffee and cigarettes)? Yes, it was. Was it possible she'd done even more? Yes, it was. She'd met a hitchhiking rock star at the ruined Elizabeth Fang Playhouse. And, in front of Mr. Winkwest's horse, they'd screwed.

And there, as proof of her memory, was a distinctive cleft chin

— one exactly like Mattie's. Stupid old Henry Bose had not sired Mattie, after all. She could hardly believe that she held in her hand, the name, address, and guitar riffs of her son's honest-to-goodness father.

And the man was a star.

"Jovan," she said, holding out the cover for her husband to see. "This guy . . . it's him."

"Him who?"

River carried the CD over to Jovan. Then she whispered the answer in his ear. "Mattie's father."

Whistling wind was an incoming missile. "See!" Mattie said. "When the enemy attacks, my guys can hide in here." The blizzard's gloom shadowed a Lego universe of outposts, planets, and ships that Mattie and Sam had constructed in the mansion's foyer.

"I made a castle." Sam dropped a handful of Lego men into a box and then rammed it with a dragon figurine.

"You're supposed to be playing spaceships. Not knights and dragons."

"It's an outer space dragon." Sam rammed the box again. The side caved in and Lego men tumbled out.

River came into view at top of the stairs. "Can you bring me some towels please, darling?" she said. "They're in the dryer."

Mattie stood. He peered through a clear rose in the stained glass window that framed the heavy oak doors. His stomach rumbled. Sam's dad, Chuck, was in town for a visit and he had gone out with Jovan the night before. They had not yet returned.

The house was low on groceries, so for lunch Mattie had prepared a can of tomato soup with water while his mother stared out of the window. She refused to eat the soup even though going hungry was bad for people. Later, while he washed the bowls and spoons, River had canceled her afternoon shift at Open Late Groceries & Gas, even though the family needed the money. Something was wrong with his parents, but Mattie couldn't guess what.

Removing the android figure from the driver's seat, he placed his Lego ship on a stair and went into the kitchen. He stopped the dryer and removed two towels. As he climbed the stairs to the second floor, he snuggled the towels against his stomach. Heat soothed the queasiness caused by his newest medication. With his free hand, he made the android fly.

River took the towels. "Is your dad back yet?" she asked. When Mattie shook his head, she set the towels on the lid of the toilet. She turned to Charity, who was seated in the tub. "Okay, Pumpkin. Time to rinse."

"I want my brother to rinse me."

Mattie sighed as he set the android on a shelf. He gave his sister a cloth to place over her eyes, and then filled a margarine tub with fresh water from the spigot.

"Not yet!" Charity doused a handful of bubbles under the water. "See this?" The five-year-old stuck a foot on the lip of the tub. "Size three. My cells are replicating and I can't make them stop. Pretty soon, I'm going to be huge."

"Charity," River said. "Don't be mean."

"I'm not, Mom. I'm not bragging. I want to stop growing, just like Mattie."

"You rinse her, Mom." Mattie retrieved the android.

Charity flopped onto her stomach. She pulled the plug and then inserted a finger in the drain to slow the torpedo of water. The tip of a bubble berg broke off from the pack and floated past her face on its way down the drain. She snatched it up with her tongue and mimicked an adult tone, "Naughty girl. Eating soap will give you diarrhea."

"Out." River offered the towel.

Charity hopped from the tub. She posed dripping and naked in front of the bathroom's full-length mirror. "Faith, Hope, and Charity," she intoned. "But the greatest of these is Charity."

When he returned downstairs, Mattie found his ordered universe replaced by chaos. Sam had left, Jovan sat on the floor in his place, struggling to remove his boots, and the front door was wide open. Wind and sleet whipped through the room. Lego bricks scooted across the hardwood floor. The universe as he knew it had ended.

"Don't ever drink," Jovan said. "It sucks big time."

"Is that what you were doing all night?"

"Yup. First and last time. My head feels like it's stuck in a leghold trap. I don't get why people do it."

"Mom's upset."

"Me too."

"How come?"

Jovan pulled Mattie onto the stairs beside him. He put an arm around the boy's shoulders. "I'll never be a famous rock star or anything, but I'll always be your dad. Is that okay with you?"

Mattie rested his head against Jovan's broad chest. He skin smelled sour, the same way Mattie's other dad Cam's often smelled, but nice too, like cedar and fresh dirt and paint. "A-okay," he said, meaning it.

"Freeze the balls off a bull out here," Cameron said when Mattie opened the door to his knock. He kicked the snow from his boots, then strode into his ex-wife's decrepit mansion as though he owned it. Mound Mansion was just one more thing River had stolen from him though divorce. The loss of Mattie was worst though; the only time he got to see the boy now, it was from a distance.

"Mom," Mattie called. "Dad's here."

"Rat-fink," Cam teased. "Don't you want some father-and-son time before the shrew wreaks our fun?"

River appeared at the kitchen door that led into the foyer, holding a celery stalk balanced upon a flat of eggs. "Your dad is upstairs, Mattie. The intruder you're talking to is someone who gives pieces of dead animals for wedding presents."

"Once a dad, always a dad," Cameron patted the boy's head. "Right sport?"

Mattie nodded before moving beyond reach.

"Please leave," River said.

"This isn't a social visit."

"If I have to, I'll have my husband toss you out." River turned and walked back inside.

"I saw your randy Indian whooping it up at Jo-Jo's last night,"

Cameron said as he followed River into the kitchen. He was within spitting distance of her when he stopped. "I doubt he could toss a salad today."

River turned to face him full on. "I'll toss you out myself."

"The girl still has spunk."

"Guess you didn't knock it all out of me."

Cameron backed away a few steps. "I'll admit hitting you was a mistake, River. But what we had wasn't all bad."

"Enough of it was."

"Whatever. I'm not here to hash over old times. Mother sent me. She wants to see the kid."

"No way," River said. "She's sick. Why can't you grasp the simple fact that Mattie's fragile?"

"My mother isn't contagious. She's dying. They've sent us hospice volunteers to see her through the last few weeks. You know Mattie's the only person she ever managed to treat right."

River crossed the room. She ran a finger down a wall calendar and tapped the twenty-third, at the end of the week. The full moon came the day after Jovan's birthday. "Tell Lenore if she hangs on for a few more days, we'll come."

"What if she can't?"

River shrugged, as she circled the twenty-third in red ink. She picked up a broom and started to sweep. "They can say their good-byes over the phone. Now get out of my house, or I swear I'll break this over your head."

"That's your mother for you," Cameron said to Mattie. "She likes her men better with brain damage."

In honor of Jovan's thirty-second birthday, a fire burnt in the hearth of Mound Mansion. Happy noises issued from the kitchen where a children's table had been set. In the dining room, a potluck dinner of honeyed ham, bowls of roast potatoes, green beans with bacon, and moose ribs circled the table.

"Frittered brains anyone?" Agnes Everlasting said. Her skeletal arms wobbled with the strain as she held a heavy dish aloft.

River relieved her guest of the dish with a sigh. She set it on the table, then stood and cleared her throat to get everyone's attention just as she had been planning to do for the past week. Rather than tell the family members about Mattie's paternity one at a time, she'd decided to drop the bomb on everyone at once. And now, like it or not, the time had come to act, because Jovan had excused himself from the table to use the washroom. He didn't believe her theory about Kenny Wayne Shepherd, and she doubted he'd appreciate her strategy.

"I have a confession to make," she said to start things off. She hugged her torso for moral support. "You're all aware that I used to have a drinking problem."

"She was a greedy fish," Agnes clarified for everyone's benefit. For the umpteenth time, River wondered why the old bag's inclusion in family gatherings was mandatory.

"Thank you, Mrs. Everlasting," River said. "I'm sure you're right." When no one laughed, she soldiered on. "Because of my drinking problem, I couldn't remember who Mattie's father was for years." When no one looked surprised, she held up the Kenny Wayne Shepherd CD cover for all to see. "The details are kind of fuzzy, but I now know for certain that his biological father is this musician. He's from Shreveport, Louisiana. I think he hates horses."

Someone passed gas behind River. She turned to see her nephew Sam standing in the doorway. His grin said he'd heard everything.

"Out," Sam's mother ordered. "And don't tell Mattie what you just heard. Your Aunt River was joking. She has a freakish sense of humor." After the boy left, she quietly asked, "So, River, where did you meet this man?"

"At the Elizabeth Fang Playhouse." As River admitted the truth, she realized how ludicrous it must sound. No wonder Jovan had looked liked he'd been shot when she told him. "I mean at the ruins."

Jovan's sister reached across the table to serve River's plate with a heaping spoonful of frittered brains. "I hope you appreciate the symbolic nature of my gesture," she said.

"He was trying to thumb a ride," River explained.

"Don't rock stars ride in tour buses?" a Yarddog cousin asked.

"Obviously not all of the time," River said. She sat down, defeated. She felt her face burn. She'd expected support, if only because she had a sick son and was married to Jovan, whom everyone adored. She could tell from the variously gleeful, angry, and embarrassed expressions, however, that not one of the people gathered bought her story.

"His chin does look like Mattie's," Jovan's mother said in a conciliatory tone. She placed the CD face down on the table.

"Bullshit," Agnes Everlasting said. The old woman rose trembling to her feet. "We all know the paternity of that poor, unfortunate child."

Extra-large servings of chocolate birthday cake flanked the computer in Mattie's bedroom. "I'll write the address and you sign the letter," Sam said. Mattie agreed, although he worried that Sam's plan somehow wasn't fair to Jovan. He would have liked more time to digest Sam's confusing information, along with the double serving of dinner he'd eaten.

With the stub of a well-chewed pencil, Sam printed: *KWSB FAN CLUB, P.O. BOX 1036, Blanchard, Louisiana 71009* on an envelope. After searching the Web for information, the boys had ordered two signed T-shirts from the Kenny Wayne Shepherd Band's 2005 tour, *The Place You're In.* They also added a piece of commemorative art from his CD *Trouble Is . . .* to their cart. Sam paid for the goods with his mother's credit card, which he liberated from her purse when she was too busy eating candied yams to notice.

"You're so freaking lucky," Sam said, when they finished the letter. "My old man's a slob. I'd trade him for yours any day."

Mattie felt doubtful about the letter, even though he and Kenny Wayne did look a tiny bit alike. Sam had hidden in the kitchen after his mother sent him away, so Mattie knew about the other father candidate as well. Henry Bose was the old man who had called him "son" at his mother's wedding. Henry looked a lot more than a little bit like Mattie. They looked a whole lot alike, even though Henry was old. The thought of Henry being his real dad made Mattie sad, though he didn't know exactly why.

"Do you think Kenny Wayne will write me back?" he asked after sealing the envelope.

"You bet! He'll send you an autographed photograph for sure. And concert tickets. He'll even come see you. And he'll get visitation rights at summer and Christmas. You'll get to tour with him! Drugs, sex and rock and roll!"

Mattie looked at the Internet picture he had downloaded to put up on his bedroom wall. His possible father had a few tattoos, but one was of a cross. Mattie liked how he smiled in some of the pictures. He wished what his mother has said could be true. "I don't think he's that kind of rock star," he said. "Besides, my mom's kind of protective. She won't let me go anywhere. She always thinks I'll get sick."

"She won't have the say-so," Sam said. "My dad lets me drink beer and smoke when I'm at his house and my mom can't do nothin' about it. It's the law."

Sherri stood at Tom's open door, her kids in tow. They'd grown since Tom saw them last. Corrie, the elder, held Detox, now a middle-aged dog. Billy, despite being at least seven, had had snot running down his face. His big eyes stared straight ahead, empty of emotion. Sherri's face was a riot of colors — from the deep purple of fresh violence, to the faded yellow of ancient history.

She'd made the trip from Vancouver to Whitehorse without a stop. Fear of being followed by her husband drove her. He'd beaten her really badly this time, and she was afraid he'd start in on the boys. She didn't have friends, money, or hope outside of him. She loved Tom, she said, would do anything for him. They needed a safe place to stay.

"So go find it."

"If you make us leave," Sherri said, "I'll pack Billy and Corrie back in the car. And then I'll drive straight into the nearest lake. They don't know how to swim."

Tom gave Sherri one night.

Sherri's and Detox's sleep-drugged bodies were covered with Tom's only spare blanket. Billy sat on the couch at his mother's feet, sucking his thumb. Corrie hunched in front of the television which wasn't turned on.

"You dudes hungry?" Tom asked.

When neither boy answered, Tom left them in the living room while he fixed supper. He cut boiled hot dogs into pieces, placed them on two plates, then squirted on ketchup. He added a mound of the pre-peeled baby carrots his last girlfriend had left in his refrigerator to each plate. He rounded the meal out with pickle-flavored potato chips. The drink options were beer or water, so he ran the tap to make the water cold, then filled two glasses.

"Come and get it," he said.

The boys approached the table with caution. Instead of taking their seats, they stood looking at the plates of food.

"If you don't like hot dogs," Tom said, "too bad. I wasn't expecting company, so that's all I've got in the house."

"Can we eat in there with our mom?" Corrie asked.

Billy pulled his thumb out of his mouth. His big eyes towards the living room spoke agreement with his brother.

"What are you? A couple of momma's boys?"

"No," Corrie said.

"Then eat up."

Tom settled the boys at the table, then went to speak his piece with Sherri, but both she and Detox were gone. She'd left a pile of the boys' belongings on the couch. Among a few articles of clothing, and even fewer toys, were their birth certificates, medical cards, and the contact information for their social worker. Topping it all was a note which read, *I always liked you.*

The boys appeared in the entranceway. "Billy can't eat carrots," Corrie said.

"No?"

"Me neither. It's rabbit food."

"Did you know your mom was gonna split?" Tom asked.

Corrie nodded his head. "Are you going to be our new dad?"

"Do I look crazy?"

Billy raised his hand, waiting for Tom's permission to speak.

"Yeah, kid?"

"We eat Kentucky Fried Chicken."

Lenore didn't plan to get her knickers in a twist over a tickle in her chest. Except for the bladder cancer that would kill her sometime in the next few months, she was healthier than a horse. She'd managed to beat a recent bout of flu before it could beat her, and, with the help of a morphine patch, she felt well enough to prepare for a visit by her one and only grandchild.

Reverend Sebastian said the dying had a sacred duty to say good-bye to their loved ones and pass on mementos by which the recipients could remember the dearly departed. And since Mattie was the only person left on earth who Lenore could stand the sight of, and Reverend Sebastian was the only person on earth she had ever trusted, she was damned well going to say her goodbyes and hand over some goodies.

"Wainwright," Lenore shouted. "Hustle your lazy ass in here and help me dress."

"Do you think I have all day?" she said when Wainwright finally appeared at the door. The sight of her second born slinking into the room as though he expected a knock on the head ticked her off. He could use some of his brother's backbone. Sometimes she thought he wasn't even hers, that the hospital switched babies on her. It didn't seem possible that such a wimpy — not to mention un-attractive — sample of humanity could have come from her womb. "What were you doing out there?" she demanded. "Twiddling your thumbs?"

"Watching my show," Wainwright said.

"Well do that on someone else's time. I'm ready for my massage therapy, and then you've got to help me into my best dress."

"Does it hurt bad?" Wainwright asked. He took a tentative hold of her knobbly right knee.

"It's none of your beeswax if it does. Enough massage." She kicked to dislodge his hand almost before he began. "Now pick up the Kleenex from the floor. I want things to look extra nice today for my grandbaby."

"That nurse person said Mattie couldn't come over."

The way Wainwright got upset by things he was too stupid to understand was another thing that pissed Lenore off.

"She said he might get sick."

"Well, for your information, Phyllis changed her mind," Lenore said. "And, no, she didn't see the need to inform the likes of you. Okay?"

Using one finger and a thumb, Wainwright picked up the tissues Lenore had coughed into that day. "Okay," he said.

So-Wah parked her truck on the street outside the Leanard house. She made her way through the snow to Alan's truck. "Never thought to see you grace this driveway again," she said as she climbed in the passenger side uninvited.

"The kids are saying their goodbyes."

"Hard to believe, Lenore's finally dying." So-Wah slid a cigarette from its package. "I won't say it bothers me."

"Me neither. Is there a purpose to this visit?"

"Actually, yes. Something's been on my mind for years, and I've decided the time has come to speak."

"Don't let me stop you."

So-Wah brought the cigarette to her lips and lit it. "Okay, I'll be blunt. When she died, Emily was with Henry Bose. They were having an affair."

"Get out of my truck."

"If you didn't know, wouldn't you show a tad more surprise?"

"Out means out."

"Lenore's not the only person dying. Henry's heart could stop any day. There's a woman and a boy who have a relative they should acknowledge before it's too late."

"I trust my wife."

"Trusted. Past tense. That trust is to your credit, but sadly un-earned on Emily's part."

"You're saying that the girl in there isn't my daughter? That the boy isn't my flesh and blood?"

"I'm sure River is all yours. But I'm afraid you have to share

Mattie with Henry."

"Lying bitch! Get out."

"Can't you ever just cry, Barker? No wait — don't answer that. I already know the answer. Enjoy your pity party."

"My wife and daughter did not sleep with that man."

"Of course not. Only Emily did. River slept with Tom, Henry's son."

Alan pressed his head against the steering wheel. When his tears began, So-Wah said, "We'll talk. When you feel ready." Then she let herself out of the truck.

Lenore's bedroom smelled of honey from the glycerin swabs used to moisten her dry mouth, but also of death. The sick woman reached up from the bed to pat River's flat belly. "Why hasn't that randy Indian knocked you up again? Maybe you should send him my way. I could teach him a few useful techniques."

River stepped back out of reach.

"Don't be tetchy. I'll be good." Lenore patted the bed. "Let me see my boy. Come on, child. Let your old granny feast her eyes on you."

River reached for Mattie's hand. "He shouldn't get too close."

"Nonsense." Lenore patted the bed with increased force. "That's the good thing about cancer, it's not contagious." She laughed alone at her joke.

River caught Mattie's eye. With a nod, she gave her permission. He perched on the bed as close to the edge as he could without falling off. River resisted the urge to grab his hand and pull him to safety.

"Cat got your tongue, boy?" Lenore said after a few seconds of silence

"He's not used to seeing you sick."

"This isn't sick. This is dead." Lenore's laughter became a racking cough. She spit phlegm into a tissue and dropped the wad on the bed. "Good boys know their grannies can't make them sick. Isn't that right, honey?"

"Yes, Grandma," Mattie said.

"We need to go," River said.

Lenore grabbed Mattie's arm. "Look what I've got here." She shifted a wooden cigar box from the far side of the bed and then flipped the lid up. From among the men's rings, cufflinks and small photographs, she scooped out a medal with a faded ribbon. "This was your great-grandpa Leanard's." She pressed the medal into Mattie's hand. "He was a war hero."

"Shouldn't that pass on to Cameron?" River said as she signaled for Mattie to come. "Or better, to Wainwright?"

Lenore glowered. "It's mine to give to whomever I damn well please."

"They're your sons."

"Those boys are the bane of my existence. Cameron's hardly ever home anymore, and Wainwright would have moved in with you years ago if I hadn't threatened to kill him if he did. I should have drowned them both in buckets of water the minute they were born." Lenore closed the lid of the cigar box. She shifted it to Mattie's lap. "It's all yours, love."

River herded Mattie towards the door without saying goodbye.

In the living room, she removed the cigar box from her son's hands watched by five sets of glass bear eyes. Wainwright cowered in the doorway. "Take this," she said. "It's yours."

Wainwright hid his hands behind his back. "Cameron won't like that."

River found an antiseptic wipe in her purse, then cleaned Mattie's hands. "He doesn't need to know. Hide it."

"Where?" Wainwright took the box.

"My house," River said. "You can stay there too, if you're ready to move."

The new sign hung on the inside of Mattie's bedroom door read *Isolation. Do Not Enter.* A similar sign hung on the outside of the door, but the one Mattie could see was decorated. He'd drawn the desk in his classroom, his purple mountain bike, and two lines of children above the words *Red Rover, Red Rover send Mattie right over.* Charity contributed a flying stick person with braids that hung past the bottom of her feet. "So you can still see me when you're in jail," she'd said when she'd shown him the drawing.

Mattie's room didn't feel like a jail cell, at least not always. He enjoyed the first few days of isolation. There were library books to read — this time it was the complete Edge Chronicles series — and his Uncle Wainwright usually delivered an airplane or car model kit for Mattie to make. But day four had arrived and the fun had worn off.

His mom had been called in to work. Because she was the only one allowed in his room during isolation, she usually stayed home, but today someone had an emergency. When she was there, they'd tell each other corny jokes, play I Spy, and tell jokes to help the time pass. She had to wear a paper mask over her nose and mouth, and when she tried to kiss him good night through the paper, the rustling made them laugh.

Something smacked against the window so hard it left a small crack. Mattie got up from where he was resting on the bed, expecting to see an injured bird flutter on the grass below.

Instead, he saw Sam throw a second rock, which fell short. "Did I break something?" he asked.

"Only the window."

"You'd better not fink."

"'Course not, dweeb."

"I'm goin' over to Vanessa's house."

Vanessa Dolby, the new girl in school, had moved to Everlasting from the city. She had purple streaks in her hair, and could sing almost as well as Miley Cyrus. The week before, she'd sent a note telling Mattie he was cute.

One of Sam's rocks landed in the eaves. "Wanna come?"

Mattie thought of his mother trying to kiss him in her paper mask. She was a worry wart — everybody said so. He bet he didn't really have to stay in jail to stay healthy; he only had to be extra careful. But there was something else he wanted to do more than he wanted to kiss Vanessa Dolby. "Sounds cool," he said. "I might come later."

*

As Mattie sipped the thick cup of coffee that Henry Bose had put on the table in front of him, he tried not to choke or scrunch up his face. Even with heaping spoonfuls of sugar, the drink tasted terrible. But if Henry was his father, then Mattie didn't want to let him down.

When he knocked on the door of the tiny house, Mattie had almost hoped no one would answer. But after a few seconds, he heard someone lumbering around inside. A moment later, Henry opened the door. The old man just stood there, staring without blinking, so Mattie had to invite himself in. "For coffee," he'd said because that had seemed like a grown-up thing to say, and paying a visit to his PF (code for Possible Father) by himself was a grown-up thing to do.

Henry didn't use a coffee maker like Grandpa Al, or put a pot on to percolate like Mattie's mom did every morning. Instead, he poured some hot water from a Thermos into a dirty mug with the words *World's Greatest* printed on its side, dumped in some brown powder from a jar, then handed Mattie the cup. He had to find his own spoon and sugar, and seat himself at Henry's table.

"I'm a lefty," Mattie said to start the conversation. The list of traits he might have in common with the PF were jotted on a piece of paper that was crumpled in his pocket. "What are you? A lefty or a righty?" When Henry didn't respond, Mattie spent a few minutes studying the hula dancer tattoos on the PF's arms. He wondered if the same girl posed for both pictures, and if she had had to dance to whole time.

"I've never been to Hawaii," Mattie said next. "But I'm going to Australia with my uncle Wainwright one day. We're going to get a pet kangaroo."

Mattie didn't want to stare at the silent PF any longer, but there wasn't much to see in the kitchen. No pictures of people on the wall, not even an interesting calendar. Mattie liked calendars with *Far Side* cartoons best, but even sunsets and moose photographs were better than nothing. The PF was tidy at least — something his mom would like.

"I bet you hit your head on the door jams a lot," he said to break the silence. "This house is pretty small."

Henry turned his eyes on the coffee mug with such intensity that Mattie felt compelled to slide it across the table to him.

"I can't stay long," Mattie said as Henry emptied the mug with a series of loud swallows. "My mom doesn't know that I'm here. She gets kind of upset when she hears your name. She thinks my dad's a rock star, but I got proof that she's wrong. Everyone else thinks it's you, and I guess they're right. You have the same chin as me. And we both have gold eyes, which is kind of rare, my teacher says."

When Henry didn't answer, Mattie took the empty cup to the sink, rinsed it, and set it upside down on a towel. "Well," he said. "I'd better get going."

When he reached the door, Mattie paused to look one last time at the man. If he was Mattie's father, he sure wasn't going to be much fun to know. But some people couldn't help being boring.

"Son," Henry said.

"Yeah. I guess."

"Tom."

"No. That's not me. I'm Mattie. Mathew Alan Barker-Yarddog."

The man blinked and somehow Mattie knew what the blink meant. He was not the man's son. A kid named Tom was. "I guess it's just an accident that we look the same," he said.

When the old man didn't blink again, Mattie understood that he couldn't because of the tears flooding his eyes. The tears looked like they'd been there all along, just waiting for a reason to fall. They didn't look like they'd stop any time soon.

"Well, so long, Tom's dad," he said. "It was nice meeting you."

And even though the Not Possible Father couldn't say so, Mattie knew they both felt the same way. They felt the way you feel the moment you know you've made a new friend you could trust. They felt relieved.

Cameron wasn't in church for the good of his soul. He was there, for the third time in his life (the first being some relative's funeral and the second his wedding to River) out of desperation. He wanted to see Mattie.

Unfortunately, even though Mattie's isolation week should have ended the day before, neither the boy nor River was there to witness Cam's sacrifice. Instead, Mattie's sister Charity sashayed up and down the center aisle of Saint Agreta's unfettered while her lazy father snoozed in his pew.

Charity, black braids flopping, approached his pew at the back where Cameron sat. With her dirty face and goblin grin, she looked exactly like her mother.

"Little terror," Agnes Everlasting, his seatmate, said in a whisper loud enough for much of the congregation to hear. Then she hooked the child with the crook of her cane, then threatened to have her excommunicated. "My grandfather, Lloyd P. Everlasting the Third, built this church in 1896. Everlastings built this town." Grasping the back of the child's neck, Agnes directed her gaze to the front of the sanctuary. Carved beneath a dollar sign on the pulpit were the words, *Safe in the Everlasting Arms.*

Cameron felt a rush of affection for the old hag. "Hellfire, kid," he chimed in. "That's what you have coming, little girl."

After church, Cameron bundled up in a hat, scarf, and coat, then schlepped along the icy boardwalk. The sermon, with its mention of punishment for his enemies, had brightened his mood, and he welcomed the intrusion when Agnes, despite her age and infirmities, caught up with him three blocks from church.

"You look like a smoker," she said as she attempted to rearrange her ratty fur coat and layers of sweaters, possibly for maximum heat retention.

Cam wondered what a smoker looked like — tough and manly, or something a tad less pleasant. He confessed to enjoying the occasional social cigarette when he drank.

"So you surely have a match or two to spare in one of those coat pockets."

If Cameron had been a churchgoing man, he would have known that Agnes Everlasting liked to start fires, usually, though not always in the fireplace. And he would have heard Reverend Sebastian warn the congregation not to let her beg, borrow, or steal their books of matches, Bic lighters, or propane blowtorches.

But Cameron Leanard wasn't a churchgoing man. And so, when asked for a small favor by someone he considered a like-minded crony, he didn't think twice about delivering.

As Henry finished the last bites of the hot roast beef sandwich So-Wah had brought him for lunch, light flickered and glowed in his kitchen window. He picked up his plate, licked it clean of gravy, and considered the phenomenon — he had seen something like it before, but where and when escaped him.

A smell reached him next — something sharp, acrid, and thicker than air. Its heaviness irritated his lungs, forcing him to gulp down lukewarm coffee. He needed to relieve himself, but the thought of stuffing himself into the uncomfortably small bathroom, where the smell might follow him made him, put off the moment.

The words *Emily* and *fire* entered his thoughts just as the front door slammed open. A tiny woman swallowed up by a yellow fireman's suit and helmet peered inside. Black smoke billowed around her and Henry could see rearing flames in the distance. "We're evacuating the street," she squeaked. "Grab a coat and get." She nudged Henry until he obeyed.

The buildings on the other side of the street were on fire. A fire truck was parked close to the burning church. Henry remembered enough about such vehicles to know this one should be spraying water. "You might be safe at Jo-Jo's," the firewoman said as she pointed down the street. "Or not. Oh, hell."

Flames had spread to the front of the fire truck. A door opened and a fireman bailed out.

"Hey, John," the firewoman shouted at the escapee. "Who didn't get that electrical problem fixed when they were supposed to?"

"Screw off, Bonnie," the man shouted back.

"You still here?" the firewoman said when she turned back towards Henry. She gave him a push to get him moving. "Hustle your butt unless you want to be a hockey puck," she shouted as she power-walked in the opposite direction.

He had once heard Emily called hockey puck, but why and by whom?

The smoke and flames confused Henry. He could no longer tell which of the three identical toad homes was his, although that hardly mattered. He didn't want to go home.

There was a person he needed to find — a boy who, because of the fire, might be in danger of becoming a hockey puck. A boy who looked like his son, but wasn't.

Henry had to find and save the boy named Mathew Alan.

Mattie rubbed an icicle across his forehead. He felt hot and fluey and had missed Sunday school again. To cheer himself up, he hummed as the Coldwell Street side of the Everlasting Garden of Eternal Rest passed by on his left. Twang, twangity, twang — he enjoyed the metallic sound of his fingers dragging along the chain-link fence. With his free hand, he held Charity's cold thumb.

Her breath rose in the air when she begged, "Come on, Mattie. Let's climb the fence."

"Better not." He fixed a critical eye on the structure. "Trespassers will be prosecuted" he read. "That means going to jail." Mattie, who liked graveyards, had been inside the fence once, when his great-great-great-aunt Elspeth died. He had found it a lonely place, unlike the old Everlasting graveyard, which held most of the village's dead children.

The pair continued on and turned right on Croesus Street. They walked until Charity disentangled her wrist from his fingers. "Look." She pointed to one of her stocking legs.

Mattie considered the quarter-sized hole in the wool, which continued to unravel as he watched. The skin beneath turned pink, yellow, and blue in turn. "Try to plug it up with your thumb. Those colors might be frostbite. And zip your coat."

"No way. All everyone will see then are this ugly coat and those." Charity glared at Mattie's brown snow boots, which were on her feet.

Everything around them became hazy without warning as he strained to see his own cramped feet. He caught a humiliating glimmer of pink. "We should trade back," he suggested.

"How?" Charity asked.

The haze cleared as quickly as it occurred, but now both Mattie's and Charity's legs were sunk into the ground up to their knees.

"Quick," Charity said. "Jump." Both children did, which restored them to level ground.

They soon reached the old Everlasting graveyard, askew from a century of permafrost. Toward the front, an ornate railing surrounded a small mausoleum. Charity sucked the tip of a braid. "If I experience a biological disaster," she said, "I want one of those."

"They'd have to close the door on you. And it's dark inside." To prove his point, the mausoleum's door shifted until they could see a section of black inner space. "Let's keep walking, okay?"

Their boots ploughed through ice, splintering it into fragments. Mattie picked up a piece. He sucked it to cool his hot throat.

"Don't eat yellow snow," Charity said.

Mattie checked his ice. "This isn't snow."

"But it's yellow."

Mattie checked and, sure enough, the ice had turned yellow. "I think I'm going to be sick," he said.

"You already are," Charity pointed out.

The pair stopped beside a hummock of barren brambles. Blue shadows littered the snow. Melting ice dripped from withered leaves while meltwater ran beneath the slush and ice. Mattie rubbed ice crystals from a stone slab engraved with his name. "That's for when I'm old," he explained.

Taking Charity's arm, he led her along a track of grass between two rows of wooden crosses. They stopped at a headstone carved with trumpets and a pair of sexless angels.

"Mattie," a disembodied voice said. "I'd like a private word with Charity if you don't mind." Somehow he recognized the voice as that of his dead grandma, Emily Rose.

Obediently, he stepped away. He noticed steam rising from beneath his feet. He stripped down to underwear and then rolled in the slush.

"Let's go." Charity charged towards him a moment later. "Grandma Emily is a big fat meanie! I hate her guts."

Mattie sat up. "What did she say?"

"It's none of your beeswax. I'm not spoilt rotten and I do so love you. I want to go home, right now."

Emily Barker's headstone heaved. The children ran past the bramble bush and alongside of the mausoleum with its now-open door. Mattie tripped and fell. "Get up!" Charity yanked on his arm. "Get up, Mattie! Don't die." Hands caught him by the ankles and dragged him towards the mausoleum. He cried out for his mother.

Mattie rose in River's arms. She carried him away from the graveyard, away from winter altogether, and into a summer field of poppies. They rested on the soft summer ground, just the two of them. Sun warmed their faces. A light breeze blew. "My darling," River whispered. "Hold on. The ambulance is coming."

Wainwright urged Charity to put on a sweater and socks.

"I don't think the fire will reach us," Jovan said.

"It can't," Mattie thought. He felt a smile tug on his lips. They were all safe together, here in Australia. And soon they would see the kangaroos.

After watching days of news coverage on the fire that had decimated much of Everlasting, Tom hitched a ride into the village with a taciturn ex-miner. They arrived to find what remained of the place seemingly deserted. No Trespassing signs guarded missing buildings. Overturned trash cans rolled on their axes in dirty snow. Tom passed the blackened Goldwell, Caravan, and Croesus streets without guessing the gold-rush optimism of the names. On Croesus a lone dog growled on the edge of a yard and a flag glowed in a bedroom window of a surviving house.

Streetlights flickered as Tom's ride drove past Camel Alley. The alley ended at the doors of the community center where Tom had attended a Halloween dance when he was nine years old. Despite Henry's pledge to Tom after the theater fire that he'd knock off the hard stuff, he had come to pick Tom up dressed as a wino, with an authentic drunken swagger.

"I watched my dad take a baseball bat to the head in there," Tom told his ride. "At a kid's frigging Halloween party. I remember the guy's name was Grant Burch. He replaced my old man as Helpert

Mines foreman, but that's not why they fought. The real reason was a dead chick — someone named Emily. Grant had a crush on her, and he blamed my dad for her death. My dad went into the fight smart and come out dumb. What kind of prick does a thing like that in front of a man's kid?"

His ride cast a glance his way. "Fuck," he said as he pulled the truck to the curb and parked. "You're Bose's boy."

"Yeah. So what?"

"So I'm a prick," the man said. "Get out."

Mud-caked trucks, some with scorch marks, ranged the length of Jo-Jo's Bar & Grill. A crudely painted sign advertised the establishment as a *SAD Free Zone*. Shrugging off a chill as he entered the smoky dining room, Tom obeyed the *Please Don't Wait to be Seated* sign held by a free-standing cardboard waitress. He poured himself a cup of coffee at the bar and then took a seat near a television mounted on brackets that hung down from the ceiling. He watched a fishing program until a woman approached with a menu.

"Are you Jo-Jo?" he asked.

"Unfortunately," she said. "Keep helping yourself to coffee. I'm only offering lousy service today. On the plus side, I'm having a fire sale. Everything's half price."

"The service might be poor," Tom said in conscious imitation of his father's lost bravado, "but I like the way it walks."

Jo-Jo rested a hand on her hip. "I'm way too tired for a fling, buddy. We close shop at the end of the week and there's a freezer full of burger patties left to grill. If you want anything else, you'll have to use your imagination."

"Looks like I came to town at a bad time."

"Everlasting on the Yukon River," Jo-Jo quipped, "your perfect holiday destination."

Two overcooked burgers, a side of fries, coleslaw, and six fingers of single malt Tyrconell were settling in Tom's stomach when the door of the Bar & Grill opened. He watched Grant Burch saunter in.

The man took the cardboard waitress for a twirl then made his way past groups of diners to an empty table next to the one which Tom occupied. He turned a chair, straddled it, then said, "Look who's sticking around town like an unwanted burr."

Jo-Jo approached with the coffee pot and a menu. "Hiya, Grant." She looked from the man, to Tom, and back. "I'll serve you tonight," she warned, "but keep in mind you've used up your quota of trouble this month."

"My intentions are friendly. Bose and me were just going to do some reminiscing about old times. Right, pal?"

"You're a Bose? Good Lord," Jo-Jo said. She stared at Tom's face. "This might explain a few things."

Nearby conversations petered out. People looked Tom's way.

He stood and put on his coat. Feigning nonchalance, he asked for the bill.

"Not so fast." Grabbing Tom's collar, Grant hissed, "I'm going to let you in on a little secret: Emily Barker and me had a good thing going before she died. Your old man should've paid for what he did to my woman. And he would have — if a snot-nosed brat hadn't provided him with a bullshit alibi."

"If this is going to turn ugly, take it outside, men," Jo-Jo said.

"Fight!" someone cheered.

Tom dropped two twenties on the table to cover the bill. Then he took a swig from the bottle of Tyrconell before swinging the bottle towards Grant's face, faking out at the last possible second. The bottle hurtled towards the television set, shattering the screen and becoming imbedded in the body of the set. "Tell someone who cares," he said.

Grant spit on the floor. "Crazy fuck. Just like your old man."

Tom dropped his throwing hand to his side. Everyone in Jo-Jo's waited for him to make the next move. Nothing could happen here unless he willed it. His father had possessed the same knack when needed — the ability to make a room full of people balance on a knife's edge while they waited to see where he'd make the blade land.

"Nice place," Jason said to Jo-Jo. "Too bad I can't stay." Then he crunched through the broken glass on the floor, and past the cardboard waitress, now lying flat on her back. Before stepping out the door, he paused, expecting heckling, but getting silence instead.

Tom slogged along the road to the small community of trailers on the outskirts of Everlasting that had once housed the employees of the Helpert Mine. The night sky, a cosmic gymnast, performed its routine with ribbons of green and white. Bright stars shone through the colors, stars he could no longer name. Too many years had passed since he had sat on his father's broad shoulders and followed a finger tracing the constellations. Tom had wasted his life, keeping his nose to the ground, afraid of what he'd see if he looked up. And then he'd stayed in Whitehorse, waiting for the call that didn't come, until it was too late.

If no one lived in the trailer now, he would sleep one night on his father's couch, then blow this town once and for all. He didn't need these people, never had. They were the ones who'd turned their backs on him when the shit went down. The adults turned frosty first, then the teachers in his school, and finally the other kids. In the months before good old Grant Burch stove in his dad's head, Tom had become a social outcast. Only Elizabeth Fang had stuck around, but Tom had tried to chase her off. What she hadn't understood was that Tom couldn't share his father with her — there wasn't enough of Henry to go around after the fire.

The aurora borealis grew riotous by the time he reached home where drifts clogged the drive. Sucking on a cigarette to soothe his nerves, Tom rapped on the door. It bounced open beneath his fist. Inside the trailer, instead of the world's greatest father, he found the lonely gleam of light reflected off snow.

The driveway leading to Henry's old trailer was blocked with drifts, so So-Wah parked on the road. She told Henry to stay put, then followed Tom's footsteps through the snow and up the steps.

When she called his name, he answered, "The one and only."

She expected a slim youth, but saw a man with Henry's bulk instead. Tom sat with his back slumped against a living room wall. Enough light shone through the windows to allow her to see the puddle of melting snow that radiated out from his body. One arm rested on a knee. "Well, I can't say you didn't warn me."

"Jo-Jo told me what happened at the Bar & Grill. Don't take Grant's insults personally — the man's a jerk."

"He was right."

"About what?"

Tom's voice cracked as he forced out the truth. "Henry wasn't home the night that woman died — he wasn't ever home back then." He turned his face away from So-Wah's view. "But he didn't ask me to lie. I made it all up — the movies we watched, the snacks we ate, everything. I told the police what I wanted to be true."

"Oh, sweetheart!"

"He was pissed off when he found out what I'd said. He claimed the only thing he was guilty of was fucking stupidity."

"That would make a fine quote for his funeral."

"Yea. Too bad I missed it."

So-Wah grinned. "Who the hell said you did?"

For the time being, Tom felt like walking. His belly was full of BLT sandwiches and chocolate birthday cake thanks to So-Wah and Elizabeth, with whom he was staying. The sun peeked over the horizon, giving the day the illusion of warmth, though not the reality. Later, once his body cooled to an uncomfortable temperature, he'd hitch a ride with one of the families heading out of town. With any luck, someone would have space for him in a truck or car stuffed full of furniture, cardboard boxes, six-toed cats, and displaced people.

If the fire started by Agnes Everlasting hadn't proved fatal to the village, Tom might have stayed on a while. But in a series of spiraling incidents the all-volunteer fire crew had managed to stall the village's only pump-engine truck, and melt the hose that joined it to a hydrant, before escaping with their lives. Most of Everlasting's business section and six houses succumbed to the blaze.

The village had already lost critical mass with the closing of the Helpert Mine a few years before, and now the only people considering staying were First Nations. Sometime in the near future Elizabeth would head with her dogs and Henry to Whitehorse where a bed in a nursing home waited for him and a new log mansion for her. So-Wah had booked a flight to China, claiming homesickness.

Before leaving town, however, Tom stopped outside the Everlasting Garden of Eternal Rest. He had intended to visit his mother's gravesite, but a funeral was in progress. A loud Indian kid with waist-long braids bawled her eyes out beside a child-sized casket. A white woman, probably the dead kid's mother, crouched with her head down and her arms wrapped around her legs. She rocked her body as though the action could turn time back.

No use trying, Tom wanted to tell her. You can stay still, but you can't ever go back.

Still, the woman looked like she'd loved her kid. Not like Sherri who hadn't even phoned to see what he'd decided to do with her boys. She'd left him to make the hard decision to get them placed in foster care. She was crazy if she thought he'd keep them — men like him didn't suddenly turn into daddy material just because someone dumped a couple of needy kids on their doorstep.

If he waited a few days, Elizabeth would drive him to Whitehorse, but then he'd miss his monthly visit with Corrie and Billy. He didn't want them to develop a false dependency on him, so he didn't do any *bonding* shit with the boys during their two-hour visits, just fed them Kentucky Fried crap and let them skate for a bit at the local outdoor rink. It wasn't much, but the thought of their disappointed faces if he was a no-show spurred him on.

Besides, something had happened that freed Tom to leave right away. During lunch, Henry had sat motionless, except for the motion of hand to mouth and the sawing of his jaw. Cake crumbs had fallen from his mouth onto his chin and chest. He chewed on, seemingly unaware of the childish mess he'd made.

"Saving some for later?" Tom said. It was an old joke, one Henry had liked to make after meals before cleaning young Tom's face and hands with a kitchen towel. One, too, that got a laugh from Sherri's boys.

Henry looked at Tom then, really looked. And he'd spoken, just one phrase with the first letters transposed, "Sy mon,"

"My son", wasn't much, but it was more than some people ever got in their entire fucking lives. Tom said the words aloud, and they hung around instead of dissipating into the air like cheap perfume. "My son."

At the cemetery, the weeping mother struggled to her feet. Something about the woman seemed familiar, but Tom didn't have the time to figure out what. He had a future to meet up with and a past to leave behind, like the trail of his boot prints in the ash-dirtied snow.

As Gentle as a Snowflake

The funeral service of Mattie Alan Barker-Yarddog took place on a snowy Wednesday afternoon. Like Saint Agreta's, Mound Mansion had succumbed to the fire, and so the boy's mourners crowded into the elder Yarddog's prefabricated home to hear Reverend Sebastian's eulogy.

After the service they made their way to the cemetery for the interment. People dressed in black suits and dresses beneath heavy outer wear huddled together under a somber sky. Ashes to ashes, dust to dust. Four Yarddog men lowered an oak coffin into the hole. The straps that cradled it were removed.

Cam, with his burnt hands wrapped in gauze and a stunned look on his face, supported his overwrought brother. Charity choked on her thumb as she sobbed with it lodged in her mouth. Jovan held his daughter tight to his chest as though he'd never let her go.

Beneath her coat, River wore a dressing gown with poppies on a blue background. With her face turned towards the sky, she closed her eyes. Her arms embraced a book, *The Wish List*, in which was tucked a letter. The return addressee was KWSB Fan Club. A handwritten note had let Mattie down with mercy. "You'll be mad at your mom," a kindly soul had written, "just don't stay that way. Sometimes people make mistakes for good reasons."

Snowflakes landed on River's cheek. She doubted the goodness of her reasons, but the snowflake, as gentle as a young boy's lips, delivered a kiss. The kiss forgave her everything.

Dear Reader,

I know — I'm heart-broken about Mattie too.
Maybe, if there's a heaven for fictional characters, Penelope Dryden's rowdy siblings, old Dulcey, or brave Judith Fellman will find the little tyke and take him under their wing.

But there is good news — with each new reader of *Fierce*, Mattie is reborn. Pour out your loving heart in a review somewhere good like on your blog, Instagram feed, Facebook page, or Twitter thingy. Hug *Fierce* close to your heart at your book club's next meeting and say, "Let's read this next." And pass *Fierce* on to a loved one.

♥,

Hannah Olivia

And Now For Something Completely Different

Remember at the beginning of the book, when that reviewer from the Coast Reporter compared Fierce to Monty Python? Not only was that a great compliment, but it also gave me a legitimate excuse to adapt a Monty Python and the Flying Circuss catchphrase.
What's completely different? My new book Move-In Ready is. This contemporary novel has all of the love and friendship of Fierce, but none of the seals or swearing. It's written under my newish middle name, Olivia, which my man had tattooed on his arm as advertising—every tax break helps.
Is Move-In Ready by Olivia Holborn a book that will give you a well-deserved mental break and make bath time fun? Don't ask me, I'm biased. Instead, consult the following unbiased description:

QUINN GOODLANDER, a 19-year-old Chunky Chicken employee, dreams of having more than a bathroom shared with ten unsanitary men. So she applies when a young heiress with terminal brain cancer holds a contest to give away her island estate. Applicants must explain why they deserve to breed Abyssinian cats, collect salt and pepper shakers, and run a nature reserve for the rest of their lives. Even though Quinn's crazy mother often asked, "What makes you think you deserve anything, baby?" Quinn puts red ink to Chunky Chicken paper, writes from the heart—and is accidentally named runner up.
The winner, a narcissistic biologist, plays dirty tricks on Quinn whose kind-hearted quirkiness wins her island-wide affection, including that of the heiress and a sexy farmer. But the greatest threat to Quinn comes from within. Unless she believes herself worthy of happiness, then a self-protecting habit from childhood—that of ending relationships first by making unforgivable mistakes—might cost her everything.

"A rich, warm, imaginative and very human story about a young woman with a troubled past who finally gets an opportunity to fulfill her dreams ... if only she could get out of her own way. Move-In

Ready is utterly engaging, endlessly charming and beautifully written."
-Ellen Meister, author of Farewell, Dorothy Parker

If you're running the bath water, prepping for a long read 'n soak session, and it's any time before May of 2019, I'm sorry. Move-In Ready isn't available just yet.

But you CAN read the first two chapters—enough for a quick dip—and get Move-In Ready news by signing up to the Honeywell Island Newsletter at www.oliviaholborn.com

Reader's Guide for *Fierce*

1. On the day her daughter receives a diagnosis of Angelman's syndrome, Alice says, "If we let her, [Gloria] would be happy." To what extent do the 'normal' characters in *Fierce* allow the disabled characters be happy? Apply the question to society.

2. Resilient people adapt positively when faced with adversity or trauma. Compare the degree of adversity faced and resilience shown by Penny in *We Were Scenes of Grief*, and by Judith in *If the World was Flat*. Do you see yourself as resilient? Why or why not?

3. Penny has an epiphany in *We Were Scenes of Grief* when she says of the unnamed officer, "I touched her hand. It felt hot and firm like a rock on the beach. She smelled of seaweed and I realized that if she was the beach, then I must be the sea."

What does this scene say about the importance of human connection? Do you think intimacy with others is necessary to happiness, or that people can thrive despite loneliness?

4. In *The Fierce with the Fierce*, when Dulcey asks Treeny, "Are you gone too?" Treeny answers, "I'm whatever you want me to be."

Treeny provides comfort, but she is also a figment of Dulcey's imagination. What does this self-deception say about Dulcey? Give other examples where characters use self-deception as a coping strategy. Have you ever used this strategy in your own life? Was it effective? Why or why not?

5. In *River Rising* Tom recalls how, "Getting to Everlasting, Yukon, all the way from Surrey, B.C., had not been easy. He had tried twice before, when he was twelve and fourteen, but both times the police had caught him before he got too far and delivered him back to whichever foster home he was living in. This time, however, he was the legal age to hit the road and run out of money without anyone caring."

Do you see the experiences of Liam in *The Indian Act*, and Tom in *River Rising* as an indictment against the foster care system? How does a childhood of constant dislocation affect schooling, peer interaction, and social bonding? Should at-risk children be made available for adoption early in the process? Why or why not?

6. In *The Indian Act*, Caucasian Liam says to Franky, "Maybe I could learn the old ways too." Does he achieve this goal, and, if so, in what way? How does the idyllic First Nations family in *The Indian Act* differ from the mythological old ananaksaq in *Sedna*, and the flawed but loving Yarddog family in *River Rising*? Do their encounters with First Nations culture change Clio or River? If so, in what ways?

7. *Fierce* starts with a quote from a Robert Service poem: "There's a land where the mountains are nameless, and the rivers all run God knows where." Water in the form of rivers, oceans, rain, tears and even the overflow from a bathtub plays important practical and symbolic roles in most of the stories. Give examples and discuss the symbolism.

8. A classic theme in literature is human vs. nature. Discuss instances of stories in *Fierce* where nature is portrayed as a) an enemy, and b) a divine force.

9. The title *We Were Scenes of Grief* applies to each story in *Fierce* to some degree. How does psychologist John Bowlby's idea that grief is the ebb and flow of processes such as shock and numbness, yearning and searching, disorganization and despair relate to the characters in *Fierce*?

10. Which definition of 'fierce' best applies to the protagonists in the collection — "violently hostile" or "furiously determined"? How does experience necessitate fierceness in Penny, Dulcey, Cally, and Cricket? Does their fierceness resonate with you or repel you? Do you consider yourself to be fierce, and, if so, in what ways and why?

11. "He's already defaced everything else," Wanda says of her son — a teenager who was born without a mouth or nose — when he sketches an accusation against her drunkenness on the family's new Maytag with an indelible felt pen. "Why not this too?"

How are puns, satire, black humor, and absurdity used in *Ugly Cruising* and to what effect? How are they used in the other stories? Does black humor serve to hide or to reveal the truth?

12. "Henry looked at Tom then, really looked. And he'd spoken, just one phrase with the first letters transposed, "Sy mon." "My son", wasn't much, but it was more than some people ever got in their entire fucking lives."

13. When Henry claims Tom as his son in this moment of recognition, the pain of decades-old abandonment seems to fall away. How is the theme of parental acceptance/rejection explored in *Seaweed, The Indian Act, Like Utah's Bingham Canyon Mine*, and *We Danced Without Strings*? What is the importance of parental acceptance in your own life?

13. In *Like Utah's Bingham Canyon Mine,* suicidal Cindy Gourlie is granted absolution by Gwen, a target of her childhood bullying.

What role does forgiveness play in the other stories? In your life?

14. Who is River referring to when she says, "Some things are so ugly they're beautiful." What do you think she means, and do you agree with her? Can this also be said of the book as a whole?

Acknowledgments

I am grateful beyond measure to:

Carolyn Swayze for her encouragement from the beginning, the late, great Ellen Seligman for choosing my book – I still can't believe it – and wonderful editors Jennifer Lambert and Lara Hinchberger for their painstaking care and gentle guidance. Also Kris Rothstein for rescuing me from the slush.

My fellow writers who offered feedback and friendship over the years: Rachael King, Susan Henderson, John Slavens, Roger Norman Morris (whose *A Writer's Life* videos prove that caffeine and the company of cuddly domestic animals are crucial to the writing process), Richard Lewis, T.J. Forrester, Joan Wilking, Jai Clare, Dr. Terri Brown-Davidson, John Beevers, Anna Sidak, Ania Vesenny, Paul Cunningham, Gant Jarrett, Brian Howell, Elisa Washuta, Girija Tropp, Joseph Faria, Thea Atkinson, Luis V. Nunex, Xujun Eberlein, Danielle LaVaque-Manty, Louis Catron, Andrew Tibbetts, Alicia Gifford, Pasha Malla, Tricia Dower, Victor Zorman, Liesl Jobson, my work buddy Steve Middleton, and unnamed but vastly appreciated others.

Francis Coppola for Zoetrope Virtual Studio.

The Canada Council for the Arts for their faith and generosity.

The print and on-line journals who published excerpts and stories.

My beloved husband and sons who refrained from sticking a "Kick Me" sign on my back while I wrote.

And finally, the readers without whom River, Liam, Penny and the rest would have a slim existence. We are very glad to meet you.

About the Author

The influence of Hannah Holborn's various parents – foster and otherwise – has lent her fiction a unique blend of British humor, Slavic melancholy, naturalism, and First Nations sensibility. She has taught life skills to aboriginal women, inner-city youth, the mentally ill, and brain-injured adults. Her prize-winning stories have appeared in numerous journals. She writes quirky, heart-warming fiction and psychological suspense in her office at beautiful Lark Rise Horse House in Mission, British Columbia, where she lives with her husband, Ian.